THE
Goddess
GETS
HER GUY

ASHLYN CHASE

sourcebooks
casablanca

To the Ashlyn Chase Champions—readers who follow me, encourage me, and share my book news with the world. Well, okay...maybe not the whole world. They might have missed a few remote corners, but I know they spread my bookmarks, links, and other promotional goodies everywhere they go. Hang in there, Antarctica... You'll get some book-related goodies soon too.

———⁓⁓⁓———

Copyright © 2019 by Ashlyn Chase
Cover and internal design © 2019 by Sourcebooks
Cover design by Caroline T. Johnson
Cover image © bondarchik/Adobe Stock, Anne Kitzman/Adobe Stock

Sourcebooks and the colophon are registered trademarks of Sourcebooks.

Published by Sourcebooks Casablanca, an imprint of Sourcebooks
P.O. Box 4410, Naperville, Illinois 60567-4410
(630) 961-3900
sourcebooks.com

Printed and bound in Canada.
MBP 10 9 8 7 6 5 4 3 2 1

Author's Note

A reader, who has read *all* my books, finally asked me what the ether was. Oh, crap. I wasn't expecting that question. Hey, *I* knew what I meant, so I figured everyone else would get it from context! Apparently not.

Without blowing your minds, let me say that the concept of a fifth element has been bandied about for centuries. Here it is in a nutshell.

According to Merriam-Webster:

The ancient Greeks believed that the Earth was composed of earth, air, fire, and water, but that the heavens and its denizens were made of a purer, less tangible substance known as either "ether" or "quintessence."

Okay, so that's where the ancient idea originated. Want my explanation? Of course you do, because where there are facts, myths, or traditions, there are writers willing to bend them a bit to make the story more interesting. So keeping in mind that I'm kind of a spiritual gal, here's what I mean by "the ether." There is, or may be, a realm that houses the stuff we can't touch or see, but on some level, we open-minded (some would say gullible) folks intuit its presence.

Enough people have had near-death experiences and described a similar tale of soul travel, a bright light, etc., to make me think the afterlife is more than wishful thinking. Where do souls go? Is that the ether? Did you know about 60 percent of the population claims to have had visitations from the spirits of loved ones?

We artsy types speak of a muse being with us when things are going well or deserting us when our creative wells go dry. And what about those "coincidences" that seem like anything but? Perhaps "they" can see our needs from *the ether* and pull a few strings. Or not. You decide.

Chapter 1

POWERFUL GAIA, ALSO KNOWN AS MOTHER NATURE, entered the courtroom in a whirlwind, and everyone rose.

Her makeshift court was fashioned out of a giant cloud, so standing would have been impossibly dangerous for some of the accused. Even though shapeshifting birds and dragons could have hovered, she didn't believe in death sentences for those without wings—especially before the trial. So she'd had her gods create a temporary solution. A small section of Fenway Park's bleachers was missing, but oh well, it was off-season, and they served the purpose. When she had taken her gilded throne, everyone sat on the floating benches.

Gaia surveyed the gallery. In attendance were werewolves, dragons, a vampiress, and a whole flock of phoenixes.

"Welcome to my tribunal. Some might call it a kangaroo court, but you *will* have representation. As you're aware, there are several cases to be heard, but all of them are for the same crime."

One of the younger phoenix boys glanced at a nearby dragon and whispered, "What's a kangaroo court?"

His friend answered, "I think it's an Aussie version of *Judge Judy*."

Gaia folded her arms and glared. "You will be silent until asked to speak. *All* of you. Is that clear?"

Several voices answered, "Yes."

She huffed. "All right. Now, even though you will be represented, it is *my* tribunal, because I'm the superior commander of everything and everyone. I'm the *goddess of all*. See this throne? Mine. See this ether? Mine again. You will treat me with the utmost respect—as is my due. Got it?"

"Yes, ma'am," someone said.

She shot to her feet. "Who said that?"

No one fessed up.

"I hate being called ma'am. It makes me feel old. Even though I'm *literally* older than dirt. I'm vain. Deal with it."

"Sister, shouldn't we get on with the trial?" Fate asked from the front row. The delicate brunette goddess seemed nonplussed.

Gaia sighed. "Yes. You're right. I should begin with introductions." She pointed to the sister who had just spoken. "My sister Fate will be the voice of the defense."

"They couldn't help it!" Fate shouted and jumped to her feet. She wore a light-blue toga that matched her eyes.

"Not yet, you idiot!"

"Oh. I thought you said... Never mind." She sank back down on the front bench. "Carry on."

Gaia rolled her eyes. "And for the prosecution, my sister Karma." She swept her hand to the other side of the aisle, where a red-haired beauty with catlike green eyes and a slightly evil smile rose and waved. She wore a smart black suit with a sparkly shoulder pin.

Barely audible groans met Mother Nature's ears. *Ha! Fearing Karma is a sure sign of guilt!*

"And now I will read the list of defendants. Please rise when your name is called. Werewolf Nicolas

Wolfensen, dragons Drake Cameron, Rory Arish, and Shannon Arish, Vampire Ruxandra…" Gaia glanced up from her list. Locating the youthful-looking vampiress in the red dress, she asked, "What's your last name?"

"LeBlanc," she said. "But I haven't used it since I—"

"Yes. Since you fake-married a *human*. I know. That's why you're here, dumbass."

The blonde bombshell clenched her fists and leaned forward, looking like she was about to object, until Nick, the werewolf, clapped his hand over her mouth. Drake, the dragon, grasped her arms so she couldn't land the punch she was aiming at Nick's head. She struggled against their powerful grips, her loud protests muffled.

"Thank you, Wolfensen, Cameron. Your cooperation has been noted. Another outburst like that, Ms. LeBlanc, will land you in my ethereal jail—indefinitely. Understood?"

When Ruxandra finally calmed down, Nick tentatively removed his hand. As he wiped the blood from two puncture holes in his palm onto his suit pants, she whispered, "Ass kissers."

Mother Nature cleared her throat. "I will now continue reading the list of the accused. Phoenixes Antonio Fierro, Miguel Fierro, Gabriel Fierro, Dante Fierro, Noah Fierro, and Luca Fierro."

"What did we do?" Luca, the youngest, asked.

"I'm getting to that part. As I said, you're all accused of violating the same law. My number one edict. Does anyone remember what that is?" she said with syrupy sweetness.

"Revealing our paranormal powers to a human," Antonio, the elder of the phoenixes, supplied.

Mother Nature tapped her nose. "Since you're the patriarch of the large phoenix brood in front of me and you know the law, I wonder why so many of your offspring violated it? Did you keep the law to yourself? Did you forget to teach it to them?"

"No, Goddess. I did teach them the law. But when young men reach a certain age, they need a mate. Since no paranormal is allowed to expose their special status, finding a compatible being who isn't human becomes very complicated."

She crossed her arms. "And yet some managed. Two of your sons aren't here."

"Ryan and Jayce. They were fortunate—sort of. Ryan died and reincarnated in phoenix form during a fire. His mate, Chloe, wouldn't leave him. She was able to survive because she shifted into dragon form. They witnessed each other's paranormal powers during a life-and-death situation.

"My other son, Jayce, has paranormal hearing that afforded him the ability to eavesdrop on a telephone conversation that identified his potential mate as a dragon. In both cases, they revealed themselves to a fellow paranormal being accidentally. Some would say they were lucky."

"Yeah. Dragons and phoenixes. And now they can't have children. Half a dragon and half a phoenix do not a creature make," Gaia said.

Phoenix Gabe groaned.

"Ha! Your middle son knows what I mean. Don't you? How many of you remember that he became a dragnix for a few harrowing moments?"

All the Fierros raised their hands.

"And how did that work out for you, middle child?"

"Not very well. The top half of me was a huge dragon trying to balance on the bottom half, consisting of my phoenix bird legs and tail. I tipped over a lot, and when I tried to fly, I couldn't control my direction."

Antonio cleared his throat. "May I point out that his situation wasn't the result of interspecies mating. I believe that was your mis—"

"Be quiet!" Gaia roared. "Did I ask you to speak?"

Antonio shook his head.

She rose and began to pace. "Yes. Mistakes were made. And that happened because I was trying to be nice! I should have known better. I don't usually listen to my children griping and moaning. It seems like that's all they do. Well, no more Ms. Nice Guy."

She took a deep, fortifying breath. "And some of you have found out the hard way how serious I am about mating with poor unsuspecting humans. For instance, Werewolf Nick, what did I say I would do if you revealed yourself to a human?"

"You said you'd send me to an island the size of a postage stamp."

"And what did you do?"

"My animal instincts took over, and I marked my mate before telling her what I was. Then I had to tell her everything."

"And what happened?"

"I found myself balancing on the ball of one foot on an island the size of a postage stamp."

"Correct. Be warned, everyone. I have many more creative punishments up my floppy white sleeves, so you should remember that."

Fate rose. "May I speak, Sister?"

Mother Nature stared at her a moment, then shrugged and returned to her throne. "Since I've named the defendants and mentioned the crime they're accused of, I suppose you can. But please state the crime they're accused of again. I'm afraid their little pea brains might not have retained the information."

Fate bowed slightly. "Even though the paranormal entities present are accused of revealing their supernatural powers to humans—"

"*Unsuspecting* humans. Don't forget that part."

"Yes. Regardless, I do not believe they had any choice in the matter."

Mother Nature leaned her elbow on the armrest, supported her cheek on her fist, and tried to look bored—but she was listening. The problem had grown to epic proportions, and Gaia didn't want a repeat of the last time a group of humans realized the city of Boston harbored several paranormal creatures.

Fate implored her with outstretched hands. "They are healthy para-humans with healthy sexual appetites. You created them that way, Sister."

Gaia waved away the logic in front of her face, saying, "Yet many manage to do without mates."

Fate jammed her fists on her hips. "Forgive me, but if I were able to put you on the stand…"

"Which you are *NOT*."

"Yes. I know that. I just said *if I could*, I would have to ask why you gave them this catch-22?"

"I made them catch what?"

"No. It's an expression that came from a book. You must have seen the movie…"

"The only movies I watch are what's happening right outside my ether. I just wish there weren't so many horror movies."

"Yes, well…you made them want to mate. You even set up mating rules. For instance, dragons are only fertile for one month every five years. Then you make them rare as fuck and scatter them around so it's hard for them to find each other. Do you know how difficult you made *my* job as a result?"

Gaia smirked. "What *is* your job, by the way? I don't see you doing much at all."

Fate narrowed her eyes. "You create beings with souls. I find them mates. Therefore, I create soul mates. Many of your children are happy because of my work."

"And who told you to make their soul mates human? Maybe I should put *you* on trial?"

Fate stopped her oration and appeared to be thinking. Good. She needed to think about what the hell she was doing.

Fate lifted her chin. "Might I remind you how you were complaining about how useless your ancient muses were? How you wished you had some modern muses who could help the others to navigate these changeable times? And now, you have those modern muses— because they were once humans and are now mated to a paranormal." Fate raised her voice. "I call Amber Arish, the muse of air travel, to the ether."

A pretty young woman with green eyes and honey-colored hair appeared and stood next to Rory Arish. The dragon wrapped an arm around her and returned her warm smile.

"I call Bliss Russo-Cameron, the muse of email."

A confident brunette appeared next to Drake Cameron and took his hand.

"Brandee Wolfensen, the muse of photography and videography."

A feisty redhead slid in next to Nick Wolfensen, offering him an unapologetic grin.

"Misty Carlisle Fierro, the muse of modern parenting."

A petite brunette with big blue eyes appeared next to Gabe and tucked her arm around his waist, fitting perfectly under his arm.

Gaia gave a brief nod to her minor goddesses. Each young woman, previously human in every way, answered with a respectful bow.

Gaia sighed. "And your point is?"

"Without the mating of these women with one of your accused, you'd still be drowning in a sea of email, trying to sort through pictures of kittens and videos of dumbasses trying things at home that they were specifically told not to do, all the while watching for planes, helicopters, and drones about to crash. And if that weren't enough, you'd be dealing with frustrated, overworked, or immature parents who forgot to tell their kids not to play with matches or lighters and stuff going up in smoke!"

Karma spoke up. "Don't forget trying to use those little rectangles people put in their pockets."

Gaia frowned. "Handkerchiefs?"

Strawberry-blonde dragon Kristine—the muse of mobile communication devices and wife of Jayce Fierro—appeared on her own. "Um, I think she means cell phones, Goddess."

"You see how out of touch you are?" Karma cried. "These modern muses are saving our butts."

"And we wouldn't even have them if not for your rule breakers here." Fate gestured toward the bleachers of the accused with a sweep of her arm.

"Wait a minute. Karma, you're on their side?"

"What goes around comes around isn't just for the bad stuff, Sister. You did them a favor by granting them minor goddess status, and they do you many favors every day. I don't see the problem here."

"But...their mates broke my law! I had to do something to keep the humans quiet. And how many times can I go around musing people? The last human I offered the honor of becoming a muse turned it down! I have just about had it with my children not listening to me!" She jumped down and stomped around her throne.

Misty stepped forward. "If I may be so bold, Goddess..."

"You may not! Just because you're the muse of modern parenting doesn't mean you can tell *this* Mother what to do. I just need to be obeyed. Can you make that happen?"

"With your gift of free will, I'm afraid not. However, I have found a good explanation delivered in a calm, nonthreatening way, with respectful two-way communication, helps a great deal."

Gaia took a deep breath, letting it out in a whoosh and slumping. "Fine. I'll try it your way." She climbed back up and perched on the edge of her throne, leaning forward. "Children, I made the law for a good reason. If humans learn of paranormals in their midst, they'll feel threatened and try to kill you...or worse. They'll want to capture, experiment on, and try to use your powers for themselves. In fact, we've already had that happen, and naturally, I had to straighten out that mess." She pointed. "You remember that, Wolfensen. Right?"

"Indeed," Nick said respectfully.

"Cameron?"

"Yes, I do."

"And Ruxandra—wait, what *is* your last name now?"

"Morgan. My husband's last name. He's still human, by the way. You didn't have to 'muse' him."

Luca leaned forward and whispered in her ear. "Isn't your husband Kurt, the wizard?"

"Yeah," she whispered over her shoulder.

"The human wizard." Gaia laughed. "What some people lack in imagination they make up for in foolishness."

"Hey!" Ruxandra didn't have a chance to defend her choice. Luca reached over and clapped his hand over her mouth.

"What I was going to say, Mrs. Morgan, is that during the whole lab-rat debacle, you were also instrumental in stuffing that cat back into the bag."

"What cat? What rat? We had werewolves, shifter bunny rabbits, and a merman."

Gaia let out a long-suffering sigh.

"Perhaps I can help after all," Karma said.

Gaia glanced over, hoping Karma could get this trial back on the rails. "Speak, Sister! And please say something useful."

With an unrepentant smirk, Karma launched into her speech. "Goddesses, shifters, and vampires of this kangaroo court, I see, as perhaps no one else does, the joy and misery people bring to one another's lives. In some cases, these lives are very long. And what is life without love? Even a short life is worth living, especially if there is love.

"Love is the best part of life. You, my dear sister, knew this and capitalized on it. To continue the species, you created the mating instinct and tricked people with love to trigger it."

Mother Nature smiled and leaned back in her throne. "Yes, that was a brilliant trap I set, wasn't it?"

"Of course!"

Karma was stroking her ego. Ordinarily, this would be a welcome change, but the sly expression on her face said she had something else up her Chanel sleeve.

"The thing is, dear Gaia, you made sure almost no one was unaffected, and you even created some unpleasant emotions, if sexually healthy people weren't gettin' any."

"Yes, yes. I know all this. Your point is?"

"My point is…" Karma whirled on her and rudely pointed right at Gaia's face. "You've fallen into your own trap! You, my dear, bitchy sister and goddess of all, need to get laid!"

The entire court gasped, followed by a few barely suppressed snorts and giggles.

Gaia sprang to her feet and clenched her fists. Her face heated with fury. In the next split second, she could strike her sister down with a lightning bolt. Or she could wrestle herself under control and model the behavior she wanted from her children.

Fuck. That. Shit.

She disappeared. Popped herself right out of the court and onto her planet Earth to think. She had a lovely view of Lake Louise in western Canada. If she wanted to, she could stay here all day.

Unfortunately, she had to be mature. Damn it. And she suspected her sister might be right. She'd never thought to make herself or her deities immune to the sex drive she'd given every other species. In fact, the gods would have been *really* bummed out if she'd done that—they were such a randy bunch. Especially Zeus! What a man whore!

She took a few deep breaths, remembering the few times she'd experienced sex. Yeah, it was awesome… kind of. The actual loving was wonderful. It was the best part. Birth, however, sucked. If she hadn't made it painful, overpopulation would have become a huge problem much sooner.

She had given birth to some of the gods and Titans. The Giants nearly killed her, and that was when she'd sworn off sex. How many centuries ago was that? Or was it millennia? Oh, wow. She hadn't had sex in several thousands of years!

Maybe Karma was right. She needed to get laid. But how? She was related to most of the gods. She couldn't just pick some random human and risk falling in love— then revealing her big secret. That was what the paranormals were on trial for right now! Mother Nature knew she could be a bitch, but she refused to be a hypocrite.

"Fuck. I'm screwed, and not in the good way."

———

Dr. Aaron Samuels was just finishing a heart transplant when the fingers of his right hand began to shake. He immediately pulled his hands away, took a deep breath, and tried again. When the shaking reoccurred, he looked up at his colleagues, another less experienced but very competent surgeon and two OR nurses.

"Can you take over for me, Erik?"

"Of course," the surgeon said. He jumped right in and finished attaching the final artery.

Aaron surreptitiously glanced at the nurses' eyes. Facial expressions could be hard to read in the OR since everyone wore masks. However, after years of working together, these nurses were like reading a book. Their eyes spoke of concern for him and possibly fear for the patient. When they glanced at each other, he saw an unspoken agreement. Without words, they managed to communicate something like "Did you see that?" and "I sure did."

As soon as the other surgeon had finished closing the patient's chest, Aaron strode off, hastily removing his bloody gloves. Without a word to anyone, he went straight to the hospital administrator's office.

The woman's door was closed, but he smiled at the secretary and asked if he could go in. "It's important."

She buzzed her boss.

"Dr. Samuels is here and would like to see you. He says it's important."

When the secretary gave her okay, Aaron hurried into the inner office and closed the door behind him.

"I'm sorry to interrupt, Marge. This will only take a moment."

"Of course, Aaron. What can I do for you?"

"I will be speaking to my director as well, but I'll need a leave of absence immediately. My hands began shaking in the OR. Erik took over for me, and everything

is fine with the patient, but obviously, I'm not fine. I
need to speak to a neurologist."

"Has this happened before?"

"Once. I chalked it up to fatigue. Tom finished for me
that time. I don't want to push my luck."

"No. You shouldn't. I'm glad you spoke up, and I'm
glad you're going to get someone to look into the problem. I'll place you on leave of absence immediately."

"Thank you." As Aaron shook the woman's hand, the
look on her face spoke of pity. He hoped to hell there
was nothing happening to him that would elicit that look
again.

─⁓─

Someone joined Gaia, but she didn't look up.

"Sister…"

"Go away, Fate."

The quiet deity chuckled. "If I had a nickel for every
time someone made that wish…" She gracefully moved
next to Gaia and rested a hand on her shoulder. "I'm not
going anywhere."

"Then what do you want?"

"It's what *you* want, Sister—and how I can help."

Gaia glared at her for a moment, then realized Fate
was sincere. Her posture sagged. "Fine. Sit down. But
I'm not sure you can help."

"That's a start."

"What is?"

"Just letting someone in. You need to talk. I imagine
you feel the weight of the universe on your shoulders
every single day."

The powerful goddess of all snorted. "You think?"

When Fate remained quiet, Gaia decided talking it out might not be a bad thing. "You promise to keep everything I say private, just between the two of us?"

Fate smiled. "I promise."

"Good." Taking a deep breath, she was about to launch into her usual diatribe but stopped herself. This was different. She wasn't scolding stupid paranormals. She and her sister were just talking. With a snap of her fingers, two lounge chairs appeared.

"Thank you," Fate said. As soon as the two were comfortably seated, Fate snapped her fingers and produced a tray with two coconuts with straws and tiny colorful umbrellas sticking out of them.

"What's that?"

"Refreshment."

Mother Nature took the coconut and sniffed the contents. "This isn't my coconut milk."

"No, darling. It's something humans invented, but give it a chance. It's yummy."

Gaia shrugged. She had to admit humans occasionally had brilliant ideas. Perhaps this was one of them.

She took a sip. She tasted the sweet tang of citrus fruit and something else... It had a certain *zing* to it. "Mmm, you're right. I hate to admit when my children have improved upon my original creations, but this is delicious."

"I'm glad you like it. Go ahead and take a long, slow sip. It can really warm and relax you on its way down."

Mother Nature did as suggested. "Mmm." Gazing out over her lake, she noted the beautiful snowcapped peaks in the background and the sparkles the sun created as it played upon the surface of the blue water. It almost looked like another of her creations that man had improved upon...diamonds.

She sighed. "Yeah, I guess humans aren't that bad. I'm just so used to their screwing up everything I've done for them. But not all are like that. I understand there are even some who are trying to protect my beauty, even though most of it is cordoned off in national parks."

"Yes, Sister. There are groups of people committed to keeping your gifts, your beauty, and the very balance that sustains them, knowing your forgiveness and resources have limits."

"Ha! It's my patience that's limited." Her straw made a gurgling sound as she reached the bottom of her drink.

Fate handed her another coconut filled with the same liquid, then settled back in her lounge chair and tucked her hands behind her head. "You have outdone yourself in places like this."

"Thank you. I know."

"Wouldn't it be nice to have someone special to share this with?" Fate asked.

Gaia turned away from the scenery and scrutinized her sister's face. "What are you getting at?"

Fate stretched and adjusted her hands behind her neck, closing her eyes. "Nothing. I'm just saying it must be lovely for the humans you and I have brought together. You created them to want love, and I'm the one who makes that love happen—when they let me. You should see the bliss on their faces as they stare into the eyes of their beloved."

Mother Nature nodded. "Yes. I had the best of intentions...once."

"How's your beverage?"

Mother Nature took another sip. "It's delightful. What is it called?"

"Its name is Bahama Mama."

"Oh, how nice—named after another mother. Well, it's lovely. Thank you for bringing it. And talking to you seems to be helping. I feel much more relaxed now."

"Good. Now, I was wondering if I could offer you something…"

Gaia glanced over at her, skeptically. "Offer me something? What is it? A clone of me? Someone to hold the tectonic shelves together during the next earthquake?"

Fate chuckled. "If only I had that ability, Sister. But no, I was hoping you would allow me to find you a partner."

Gaia sat up straight. "A partner?"

"Yes. More than just a quick lay. Someone to appreciate a sunset with. Someone to walk next to as you stroll along one of the beautiful beaches you made. Or just someone to listen when you've had a tough day. You seem *much* more relaxed now, and we've just been talking a few minutes."

"Hmm, you might be onto something."

Fate sat up, her eyes bright. "You'll let me, then?"

Gaia took another long sip of her drink. "Okay. Whatever." She wasn't sure what exactly she was agreeing to, and she'd probably regret it. But for some reason, she was open to anything now.

"And while we're at it, maybe you can be a little less harsh on the shifters and vampires for revealing their true nature to their human mates. I understand they wait until they can trust the person completely."

Flapping her hand, Gaia slurred, "Zure, why not?"

"So can we go back and adjourn the court? Let the paranormals go with a stern warning?"

"You go. I'm gonna zit here and zulk."

Chapter 2

FATE HAD ADJOURNED THE COURT AND WAITED FOR THE muses and paranormals to leave. Summoning the oldest goddesses, she quickly filled them in. "Goddesses! She agreed to it!"

Gasps all around were followed by a burst of laughter from Karma. "I don't know how you managed it, Fate, but I can't wait to see what happens."

Fate pointed a long finger at her sister Karma. "*You*, stay out of it."

"Why? I think it sounds like fun."

"No, your job could easily get in the way. You know how you can be…"

"Oh, so you think I'll be ironically vengeful just because our sister is bossy, arrogant, and rude?"

"Yes."

Karma smirked. "I admit it's tempting."

"How about if we just run the candidates by you first? Then you can weigh in on the state of *their* karma—good or bad."

Karma tipped her head this way and that as she considered her limited involvement. "Okay. I guess that makes sense. No need to make her regret her decision…" She mumbled under her breath, "…right away."

"So, goddesses," Fate said, "How do you propose we begin finding a suitable mate for the goddess of all?"

"Isn't that your job?" Artemis asked. "I mean,

I'm goddess of the hunt, but that's for wild animals. The only thing I can contribute is the caveat that this person should be her equal. Someone she cannot bully. Someone she must come to respect."

"Perhaps we should hear from Aphrodite," Minerva suggested wisely.

"Excellent idea!" The remaining goddesses murmured their agreement and looked to the goddess of love.

"Oh dear," Aphrodite began. "Some have had luck with blind dates. It's not perfect, but at least she would have a chance to spend some time, one-on-one, with the god you choose for her."

"I hear she likes Apollo," Fate said.

Minerva crossed her arms. "I've also heard her call him a brownnoser. Think, everyone. If it's one of the gods, then it isn't very blind, is it? She knows them all."

Fate nodded. "That's true. But how do we get around that and still find someone who even comes close to being her equal?"

Karma giggled. "Who says only a god can stand up to her? I think it would be an interesting twist to set her up with a paranormal."

Fate grimaced. "Is this about karma again, Karma?"

"Busted. But wouldn't it be perfect justice?"

Fate jammed her hands on her hips. "We're not looking for justice. We're looking for a mate who will make her happy. I think that will benefit us all. Not just you and your twisted sense of humor, Sister."

Karma shrugged. "Oh well. You can't blame me for trying. It's what I do."

"Maybe you can sit this one out," Minerva suggested.

"The rest of us can come up with a plan, and you can weigh in on the possibilities. Is that fair?"

"Fine. I've got things to do, people to punish and reward. I don't just look for bad behavior, you know."

"We know, Sister. Toodles," Fate said and wiggled her fingers at Karma.

Karma disappeared, and everyone breathed a sigh of relief.

"All right, now that she's out of the way, what other ideas can we come up with? I'm willing to listen to any and all possibilities."

"How about online dating?" Aphrodite said. "That way, she can pick from any number of men. I think the more control you give her, the more likely she'll be to follow through."

Fate scratched her head. "I hadn't thought of that. That's actually brilliant. However, I'll have to set up her profile myself. You know how she feels about technology."

The goddesses groaned.

Minerva smiled. "That makes sense. Let's not bog her down with the details. We want to get this off the ground before she has a chance to rethink her decision."

"Yes," Fate agreed. "I'll look at the questionnaire and ask her to write the answers with her favorite quill, but I won't tell her what it's for. I'll just say I'd like to get an idea of what she would like in a man."

"Perfect," Aphrodite said. "I have a list of questions from some of the human dating sites." She snapped her fingers and produced a sheet of paper with all the pertinent questions and room to write Gaia's answers.

"Thank you, Aphrodite. Thank you all. I appreciate your ideas and feedback. I think this is going to go so well."

From somewhere in the ether, Karma cackled.

Sitting in a trendy tavern in the middle of the day was so out of character for Aaron, he couldn't remember doing it—ever. But here he was, nursing an imported Dutch beer and his ego.

Aaron had gone to Boston's best neurologist and had been handed the provisional diagnosis of ET. Essential tremors. It used to be called familial tremors because it was an inherited condition. Fortunately, it was fairly benign. He remembered his great-aunt shaking when she tried to do something that required fine motor skills.

To say he had mixed feelings was an understatement. He had hoped his condition wasn't something degenerative, like a form of Parkinson's disease with initial symptoms that behaved a little differently. Ruling that out was a great relief. But with no cure for ET, his career as a surgeon was over.

His leave of absence was not only a blessing but also a form of torture. Now he had nothing but time to ruminate over his life. His choices. His career. He'd never wanted to be anything but a doctor.

There were other things he could do with his MD, but did he want to? He had been thinking about retirement at some point anyway. Whether forced on him or not, this was that point. He was trying to look at it in a positive light. The whole world and all its possibilities were opening to him. This was an opportunity. Right?

Sure, his inner sarcasm answered. He had to wrestle his attitude back into something positive.

He needed to make the necessary calls to arrange everything, like drawing on his savings until he could use his 401K, looking at whatever liquid assets he had, possibly talking to a Realtor about selling the large family home in Brookline… That brought up having a conversation with his daughters. He nearly groaned aloud.

The bartender must have noticed. "Everything all right?"

"Yeah. I'm just thinking about my options now that I'm an empty-nester. I hate the thought of downsizing, but living with just my cat in a big house doesn't make sense."

"Ah. Yeah, I hate to move. All that packing, and of course nobody is willing to help. Unless—you said you had kids?"

"Yes. Two daughters. Both of them are out of the house and living on their own, but they'll certainly have feelings about selling the place where they grew up." It was also a physical tie to their mother, who had died when they were children. "However, I raised two smart, practical young women, and I'm sure they'll understand."

"You'll figure it out," the bartender said and left to check on his other customers.

All of this roamed unchecked through Aaron's head over and over until he finally picked up the phone and texted his daughters, asking for a conference call that evening. It sounded so clinical. But trying to keep his own emotions under control right now would help them all.

—∿—

Fate met Gaia at her Boston location. Gaia had the entire top floor of a tall building on State Street, which was enclosed by a great glass bubble, making the space invisible to humans. She gazed out over the setting sun, which bathed the city in her orange and yellow hues.

Fate scanned the questions before handing them to her sister. *Oh boy, this is going to be a challenge.* Still, it was the only idea she had at the moment.

"What's this?" Gaia asked. She snapped her fingers, and suddenly it was daylight again inside the bubble.

"I'd love your input, considering you're the one who will be choosing your mate. I usually do the choosing for others, but you're different. I need to know exactly what you're looking for, and answering these questions will help me find someone who's looking for the same things."

"Different? Well, you're not wrong, Sister. I appreciate your consulting me first. Yes, I will fill out your questionnaire."

Out of thin air, Gaia produced a stick of charcoal and quickly filled in all the spaces. She handed it back to Fate, who snatched it and said, "Thanks, darling. Toodles," then disappeared quickly.

Fate hung out in the ether, reading the answers to Gaia's questionnaire before she shared it with the other goddesses.

"Oh boy. Big mistake."

Reading the scribble to herself, she groaned aloud several times.

Name: Gaia.
Age: My exact millennia don't matter. Age is just a very long number.

Location: Wherever I want to be at the moment. Most of the time in Boston, where I can observe my seasons and some of my least stupid people.

Relationship status: Single. Never married. It's complicated.

Kids: Billions.

Want kids? Gods, no! I'm not crazy about the ones I have.

Body type: Whatever I want it to be.

Ethnicity: Same answer.

Height: Depends on my mood. I can tower over anyone if I want to.

Religion: Me.

Politics: Ugh. I would never participate in that travesty.

Are you a smoker? Only with the occasional volcanic eruption.

Do you drink? Not until recently. I think I will take it up as a regular hobby.

Do you have pets? Only the entire animal kingdom.

Education: Live and learn.

Employment: Ruler of all.

Income? None. And I get no thanks either!

Fate sighed deeply. "I guess it's back to the drawing board."

—◊—

"I called you all here because I need your help." Fate gazed at the puzzled faces of the modern muses. She had chosen a beautiful garden setting, hoping the pastel colors and floral scents would put everyone in a cheerful mood.

Brandee, the muse of photography and videography, raised her hand. "May I ask why Gaia isn't here?"

"Well, er—yes. I am Mother Nature's sister and acting in her stead. I know you're used to taking your orders directly from her, but this must stay between us and the other goddesses. Trust me when I say it's for her own good."

Bliss, the muse of online communication, narrowed her eyes suspiciously. "And what does that mean? I know she can be a pill, but she's the boss. Going behind the boss's back is usually a bad sign."

Fate nodded. "I understand, but let me explain the situation." She took a deep breath, knowing this could go either way. Best to flatter them first... "Because you're her trusted, talented, *modern* muses and this is a modern problem, I really can't do this without you."

"Ha, I'm not only a muse—I'm a dragon queen. I know when me arse is bein' kissed," Chloe Arish, the muse of fire safety, said in her Irish lilt. "Get to the point, woman."

Fate marshaled her frustration and forced a smile. "Quite right. I need to find a mate for Gaia. She has already given me permission to find suitable candidates. As you can imagine, finding someone she can learn to love and respect is a tall order. I thought you might have some ideas."

The muses gazed at each other. Their wide eyes seemed to indicate surprise—or disbelief. Fate hoped it was the former.

Misty, muse of modern parenting, raised her hand. "Don't you still put soul mates in each other's paths regularly?"

"Well, yes, but this is different. Gaia has no soul mate. She has no equal. I can certainly arrange a meeting, but I was hoping you'd tell me where to find quality single men."

Kristine snorted, and a curl of smoke escaped from her nostrils. "Well, don't look in bars."

Fate, remembering how Gaia took to alcohol, realized it might be the *perfect* place to arrange a meeting. She would be more relaxed and unable to use her supernatural talents in public—hopefully.

"I think most of us would agree that firefighters are some of the nicest guys around," Kristine offered.

"Yes! They're selfless heroes," Bliss agreed.

"O' course you'd be thinkin' that. We're all married to firefighters," Chloe said. "However, I *was* a firefighter, and let me enlighten you. Not all are 'nice guys.' One was downright disrespectful to me because I was a woman and he thought I couldn't do the job properly."

"Until you proved yourself. I'm a firefighter too," Kristine said. "In fact, I'm a captain. I know several of these brave men and women better than most."

Fate perked up. "And do you know of any who Gaia might be interested in? Someone without faults? Someone able to stand up to a supernatural mate who will always think she's superior?"

Kristine's posture deflated. "Ah, no. I'm afraid not. All humans have faults."

"All paranormals have faults too," Misty added.

"Some more than others," Kristine said and elbowed her.

Misty rolled her eyes. "Yes, Gabe was a challenge,

but totally worth it in the end. He's the best husband and father anyone could ask for."

Fate wasn't sure she was getting what she needed, but at least she had allies. "Thank you for coming. I know you're all busy. Please keep our meeting in the back of your minds. If you think of someone who might be a good match for the goddess of all, I'm just a shout away."

Chloe snorted a curl of smoke, just as her fellow dragon Kristine had. "Sure, we'll think on it, but don't expect any shouts soon."

Fate drummed her fingers on her antique desk. She'd learned one valuable lesson from the meeting with the modern muses. Her biggest challenge wasn't to find someone without faults. It was to find someone whose faults didn't clash with Gaia's faults. What she usually did with soul mates was to find someone with strengths to fill in their partner's weaknesses and hope they fit like a jigsaw puzzle.

So all she had to do was list Gaia's weaknesses and find someone with the opposite strengths. Right? Easy!

A pencil and paper appeared on her desk. Taking a deep breath, she began to list her sister's many faults.

1. Impatience
2. Knee-jerk reactions
3. Sarcasm
4. Disrespect
5. Intimidation
6. Empty threats

"Oh my. Where am I going to find someone with an unlimited supply of patience, logic, ability to think things through, and a careful tongue, who respects and listens to others and acts with kindness?"

She leaned over and pounded her head on the desk three times.

"Hi there. Looking for me?"

Her posture snapped to attention. A five-foot-tall, half man, half goat satyr had materialized beside her.

"Who are you? Wait. Let me guess…"

"Pan."

"That's what I was about to say!"

"And what I was about to say is you're doing this all wrong."

Fate crossed her arms. "Doing *what* all wrong?"

"Finding a mate for Gaia."

"How do you know about that?"

He shrugged. "Word travels. Now, let me point out the obvious. You're only thinking of Gaia's faults. What about her strengths? Hobbies? Activities she enjoys? She and someone else will have more fun if they have common interests."

"Oh." Fate scratched her head. "I guess you're right. Having fun with a mate is important. I hadn't thought of that."

Pan tipped his horned head. "I think I'd be a good match. I'd like to volunteer."

"You?" Fate covered her mouth and tried not to laugh. "Didn't you trick some poor girl into falling in love with a donkey?"

He rolled his eyes. "That was centuries ago, and Mr. Shakespeare exaggerated. But"—he held up one finger—"that's something Mother Nature and I have in common. We love a good practical joke."

"Oh, puleeease. The two of you would wreak havoc!"

Pan chuckled. "I daresay our dates would be a lot of fun."

Fate vehemently shook her head. "Get lost, Pan. You're not the one."

He smirked. "Fine, I'll go, but when you run out of other gods for her to decimate, call me."

"In a pig's eye. Wait—don't take that literally!"

He winked and was gone.

—⁓—

Karma lifted her sunglasses. "How goes the challenge of the century, Sister?" She stretched her long legs over a lounge chair next to her private pool.

"More like the challenge of the millennia." Fate plopped herself on the lounge chair beside her.

"I referred someone to you."

Fate's eyes widened. "Pan? *You* sent Pan?"

"No. Why? Did someone else send him?"

"I doubt it. He said he heard rumors and wanted to volunteer."

Karma laughed. "What did you say?"

Fate sighed. "A resounding 'Thanks, but no thanks.'"

"Good. I'm not sure he has ever made up for that horrible practical joke he pulled in the sixteenth century."

"I confronted him on that. He seemed to think the whole thing was wildly exaggerated, and it may have been. You know writers…if the truth isn't quite dramatic enough, they'll embellish it. But he did give me something to think about. Instead of trying to find someone with opposite faults, I should be looking for someone with common interests. Faults can be overlooked if you're happy and living a better life because of your mate."

"Exactly true. Is that what you were doing? Looking for someone who is basically a saint?"

"No. Why would you say that?"

"Hon, our sister is so riddled with faults, I can't think of anyone with opposing assets."

Fate let out a huge sigh.

"Here." Karma produced a pitcher of ice water and two tall glasses.

"Is that all you got?"

"I'm in need of hydration. If you want something else, get it yourself."

Fate snapped her fingers and held a sparkling orange mimosa. "Some hostess you are."

"I'm not hosting a party, Sister, and if I were, you'd be crashing it. I was just lying here, enjoying the sun. Alone."

Fate rose. "Well, pardon me. I didn't realize I needed an engraved invitation to come to you for support."

Karma waved away her remark. "Sit back down. Of course I'm here for you if you need a shoulder to cry on."

Fate shook her head. "Unbelievable. I'm not in tears. I just thought two heads would be better than one."

"So you're rethinking my offer to help. Hey, if you want me to come up with a list of assholes to punish by setting them up with her, I can help you and myself both."

Fate laughed. "Yeah, right. Like any of our gods wouldn't see that coming."

"Who said it has to be a god?"

"What are you suggesting? A human who knows nothing of the paranormal world? That's exactly what she doesn't want."

Karma shrugged. "Well, it's either that or a paranormal. Flip a coin."

Fate was about to laugh until she realized Karma might be onto something. There were plenty of men, both human and paranormal, who could give Gaia a run for her money—so to speak. And some knew about gods and goddesses, even worshipped them.

"Most men would cower from her, but there are a few with the self-confidence to stand up to her and not crumble when faced with her abilities," Karma was saying.

"Perhaps…" Fate tapped her lip as she mentally ran through a list of men she'd destined for greatness but whom she hadn't found mates for. There weren't many. "Is there any world leader without a mate?" Fate asked.

"None who actually deserve one at the moment."

"How about someone smart and selfless? Do you know of any heroes with very high IQs?"

"Aren't those two things antithetical? How smart is it to run into a burning building or sacrifice yourself in another way?" Karma asked. "We'd be back to square one."

Fate snorted. "Well, there goes the only suggestion the modern muses came up with."

Karma gave a slight shrug. "Gaia isn't all bad, you know. In fact, deep down, she has some very positive traits."

Fate snickered. "Must be deeper than I've ever looked."

Aaron wandered aimlessly around his large living room. He had immediately retired from the Boston hospital where he'd worked for thirty years as a cardiac surgeon. Kind of necessary since he'd been diagnosed with essential tremors. At last, he dropped into his favorite chair, and as soon as he did, his black-and-white cat jumped onto his lap.

"Hi, Cat. I'm sorry we never gave you a more imaginative name, but you came when Ruthie called, so in a way, it's your fault." He scratched behind the cat's furry ear, and the feline began to purr. On the housekeeper's day off like this, he had *no one* to talk to but his cat—not that he talked to Mrs. Rivera very much. He had to keep his family's magical witch power a secret, and it was easier to do if he didn't communicate much with people who had no knowledge of magic and the paranormal.

"Can I confide in you, Cat? Of course I can. You won't tell anyone, will you, boy?" He sighed deeply. "My hand trembled during a transplant. I can't afford to nick an artery if even one finger trembles."

He ran his currently steady hand over the cat's soft back. "I have a beautiful million-dollar home in Brookline, but what's a home without a family in it? No offense. You're part of the family, but you don't take up much room. What are we doing here?"

He answered, "I'm talking to myself. That's what I'm doing."

He let out a huge groan. Despite feeling odd about it, he continued his musing aloud. "My wife died two decades ago. You weren't around then. I've raised my daughters, and they're both living their own lives in their own homes, starting families. My nest is empty. Again, no offense. We'll call it empty-ish.

"I miss my daughters, who I could talk to frankly about our Wiccan roots. I have one useless power. The power of invisibility." He chuckled bitterly. "I might as well be invisible right now. Couldn't have gotten a useful power, like my girls' power to save one life a day with supernatural intervention."

Cheek resting against his fist, he thought about how pathetic he seemed. He couldn't stand being this way. He hadn't told anyone about his diagnosis. "Maybe it's a good thing they're not here. The girls would worry, and I don't want to burden them. They just think my early retirement is a well-earned vacation. In a way, it is. I've been itching to do something new, but a pigeonhole is hard to break out of. And I'm getting too old to learn a new specialty.

"What can I do? There has to be more to my life than waiting for grandchildren to be born. I need to do *something* to make myself feel *useful* again." He reflected back on his undergrad days. "I took a course in botany once. I really enjoyed it. Maybe I could take up gardening…"

He thought about a friend of his who'd discovered a rare plant in the rain forest—it became one of the wonder drugs of the century. Aaron had recently been on a trip to the Brazilian rain forest, but it was brief and with a totally different purpose. His family's nemesis had to be dealt with, and he was only there to supervise. His son-in-law's family had actually taken the bad guys down. He couldn't even participate in his own coup.

He scratched his head. "If I were to cultivate some kind

of wonder drug, what would it be? Hmm… Well, what's the number one cause of death? Heart disease, right? I'm in the cardiology field. Who better to research a cure for weak or damaged hearts? An undiscovered medicinal plant won't be easy to find, analyze, test, patent, and get approved, but I'm done feeling sorry for myself!"

His daughter Kizzy had recently moved to Puerto Rico with her husband, Noah Fierro. When learning about the island his daughter was moving to, he had stumbled across a fact that surprised him, namely that Puerto Rico contained the only tropical rain forest in the United States.

The couple was still in that honeymoon stage, so he wouldn't intrude by staying with them, but he could book his own hotel room nearby, then offer to take them out to dinner and make it seem as if he was taking a long-awaited tropical holiday. No one needed to know he was exploring the idea of switching to research.

Feeling more excited about this than anything else in recent weeks, he placed Cat on the floor, popped out of his chair, and strode to his office where he kept his computer. Nothing said he had to act on the idea, but it wouldn't hurt to poke around online and check out areas besides San Juan, which was the spot he had learned about before she moved. He was concerned mainly about hurricanes after his daughter told him she and Noah were moving there to aid in the aftermath of Hurricane Maria.

Scanning specifically for information about Puerto Rico's rain forest, he first learned its name, El Yunque, and thank goodness its pronunciation was included in the article…El Yu-ke. The fact that it rained year-round was no surprise. Twenty feet per year, though? He'd definitely have to pack his rain gear.

Then he saw facts that interested him as a doctor. Since rain forests have also been called the world's pharmacy and he hoped to discover something no one else had, Puerto Rico was a good place to start. There were species of flora and fauna only known to exist in El Yunque.

The more he read, the more he needed to know. It would be easy to get lost, poisoned, or eaten in any rain forest, but he would learn how to be safe.

He admired his daughter and son-in-law for their selflessness. They were doing everything they could to help those on the island who were still in need, she as a doctor, he as a firefighter and EMT. Plus almost the entire Fierro family had moved there and were volunteering with Habitat for Humanity, actually rebuilding neighborhoods which the hurricane had destroyed.

Aaron, pragmatic man that he was, realized money made the world go round, but without it, all the island had was its hardworking people and natural resources. For years, he'd put plenty of money aside for a rainy day. Now he realized how ironic it was.

He dug his cell phone out of his pocket, brought up his contacts, and smiled as he clicked on Kizzy's number.

"Hi, Dad!"

"Hi, honey. It's good to hear your voice. I've missed you."

"I've missed you too."

"How would you feel about my coming for a short visit sometime soon?"

"Really? I'd love that!" she answered. "When?"

"As soon as I can arrange a pet sitter for Cat."

Chapter 3

DAWN FOREST HAPPILY HUMMED TO HERSELF AS SHE weeded her garden. She and Luca were lucky enough to have found a cute little house just outside San Juan. It was made of cinder blocks, surrounded by a cinder-block wall, and in the front, an iron gate was the only opening. Not the most attractive look, but practical…especially during hurricanes. She sensed someone coming toward her and looked up. When she saw her beloved Luca, she broke into a grin. "Hi, hon!"

"Hi, babe. How's it going?"

"It's getting there. The garden was neglected for a long time, and I'm not sure I have a green enough thumb for this. Did you come out to tell me about a new job for us?"

"No new business today. I thought I'd just come out and gaze at my beautiful fiancée."

Dawn laid down her gardening tools, rose, and slipped her arms around Luca's waist. "How did I get so lucky?"

"I don't know. Good karma, I guess." He grinned.

Before they could kiss, a whirlwind spiraled up right next to them, and Mother Nature appeared.

"Gaia!" Luca instinctively stood between the powerful goddess and Dawn. "What do you want? Are you here to punish me for telling my future wife about my paranormal abilities?"

Dawn put her hands on Luca's shoulders and peeked around him. "I'd never tell anyone about paranormal abilities. I have my own freaky secrets."

"Words. Just words," Gaia said as she crossed her arms. "How do I know you mean them?"

"I know how people react to my psychic abilities," Dawn said. "I'd never want anyone I love to be feared or mocked for being different."

Mother Nature nodded. "Good. But that's not why I'm here. Are you two going to give me a chance to talk?"

"Yes, of course. I'm sorry for babbling," Luca said.

"I'm here to speak to your wife."

"Me?" Dawn said.

"You are his wife, right?"

"I will be. We're getting married in a few weeks."

"Oh. Time is fairly fluid for me. Congratulations. Now I'd like to speak to you alone."

Luca kept a protective arm around her. "I don't want to leave. How do I know she'll be safe?"

Mother Nature's jaw dropped. "Of course she'll be safe! All I do is look out for my children. How could you even ask that?"

"I'm sorry. I've just heard rumors you can be...um... tough."

She waved away the comment. "You shouldn't listen to rumors. I don't have to carry out my threats very often."

"Threats?" Dawn's eyes widened.

"Nothing to worry about. I'm not threatening either of you. Actually, I have a job offer for you, Dawn."

"Seriously?"

"No, I came all this way and exposed myself to a human because I'm kidding."

Luca mumbled under his breath, "I guess the rumors of her sarcasm are true."

"I heard that, Fierro. Now run along so I can talk to your soon-to-be wife."

Luca nodded, then kissed Dawn's cheek and whispered, "Yell if you need me," subsequently withdrawing into the house.

"Goddess, I'd offer you a place to sit and a cool drink, but I'm afraid I don't have a bench yet. We were going to build one... A swing, actually."

Mother Nature snapped her fingers, and a white bench swing appeared beside the flower bed. "Something like this?"

Dawn's eyes rounded. "Exactly like that."

Mother Nature smiled, sat on it, and patted the spot next to her. "Consider it a wedding gift."

Dawn cautiously sat next to the powerful goddess. "Thank you. That's very generous of you."

Gaia nodded once. "My pleasure—and not just because you're named after my favorite time of day. Now, let me get to the heart of the matter. You may have heard I hired a few modern muses. They've all been humans, or I should say former humans, since they must become minor goddesses to carry out their duties. Most are married to paranormals."

"Oh? No, I hadn't heard."

Mother Nature smiled. "Good. That means your future sisters-in-law are keeping their mouths shut."

"My future sisters-in-law? They're working for you?"

"Some of them, yes. And I've hired a couple of

women from other families you probably don't know. There are only six in all. I can't stress enough how useless my original nine muses are in this modern day and age. That's why I need new ones."

Dawn didn't know if she should say something or just wait and hope Gaia explained what she was getting at. She opted for respectful silence.

"So, getting to the point, I'm here to offer you a job. I know about your psychic ability, and I hear you're technically adept?"

Dawn considered her answer carefully, wanting to be as honest as possible. "I'd say I'm adept at some technical things but not others. No human being can be good at everything."

Gaia tipped her head. "I was told you had a technical job back in Boston. Is that not true?"

Dawn sensed she was treading on shaky ground. "Well, yes, I worked on a help desk for ScholarTech. So I guess you could say I know a little about technology and a lot about teaching software."

Mother Nature looked at the sky and smiled. "Finally. I've been looking for someone who can help unravel the mystery of modern technology and actually teach my original muses how they can be more useful to me."

"And you think I'd be a good teacher?"

Gaia shrugged. "I have no idea, but beggars can't be choosers. I need someone who's already aware of the paranormal world, someone who would welcome a little goddess power while using it responsibly, and someone who's trustworthy and won't spill the beans about any of this."

"I—I guess I fit the criteria, but I'm not sure that's what *I* want. I'm already very busy."

Gaia folded her arms and leaned away from her. "Busy gardening? That's what you call busy?" She waved her arm, and the garden instantly came to life with vibrant color and sweet scents.

"Wow! Thanks. But no, not at all. I have a job, plus Luca and I are setting up a private detective agency, and then I'll have two jobs. With my psychic powers and Luca's criminal justice degree and former job as a cop, together we can solve any number of cases. We're very excited about it, and I wouldn't want to lose my focus. I'm not sure I could handle three jobs without doing one or more poorly."

"My modern muses are given a very generous bonus."

"But I'm already getting a generous bonus from Karma Cleaners."

Gaia's brow wrinkled. "Karma Cleaners? What's that?"

Dawn straightened. "You don't know? I thought with all the goddesses working there, you'd be well aware of the business."

Gaia smiled, but Dawn sensed something simmering beneath her calm exterior.

"Tell me about this business."

"Well, I guess I can. I'm not allowed to tell any human unless they want to have their karma cleaned."

"Oh? Please continue."

Dawn knew she had made a mistake but didn't know how to get out of it. *If Gaia doesn't know about Karma Cleaners, then Karma must not have wanted her to. But now that she knows this much, how can I weasel out of*

telling her more? She worried her lip and thought about
her words carefully.

"Tell me the truth. You won't get in trouble unless
you lie to me...and that includes lying by omission.
Don't try to weasel out of it."

She must be able to read minds.

"Yes, I can. Now don't make me search your mind
for the information I want. It can be a little painful for
you and disgusting for me. A person's gray matter is
slimy and jiggly."

"Ewww... Okay, I'll tell you what I know. I don't
know everything, of course. Just what I've been taught
and experienced firsthand."

"I understand. Please go on."

Dawn pushed the swing with her foot before thinking
to ask the goddess. "Oh, do you mind if we sway a bit?"

Gaia chuckled. "I'd enjoy it. Go ahead."

Dawn pushed off with both feet and enjoyed the
breeze while moving through the air. "Okay. Here's
what I know. One day, I was desperate to get out of the
circumstances I was in. I'd been involved with the local
gang in my old neighborhood. I didn't know how to get
out. I was doing everything I could to straighten out my
life, but it just wasn't working. I'd stayed in school and
was going to college. As many times as I tried to sepa-
rate myself from the gang, they kept dragging me back
in. They said I was their 'early warning system' because
of my psychic ability. They used me to alert them to the
cops as they made their drug and gun deals.

"I desperately wanted help to get out but had no one
to turn to. I tried to get my grandmother to move, but
she wouldn't hear of it. She was raised in that house,

and when my mother went to jail, she raised me there. I couldn't break her heart by telling her I could be following in my mother's footsteps, so I protected her by pretending that everything was fine. But it wasn't fine. I hated being used by the gang, but I was powerless to stop them.

"One day, I was really wishing my circumstances were different, out loud. I said something like, 'Fuck my life. I wish I could start over and pretend to be useless to the gang.' I began to cry and hug my pillow. Nothing happened right away, but about six months later, I was approached by an old woman. We chatted for a bit, and then she twirled and became a beautiful young woman. She told me they had been watching me since that honest plea for help. It took them a bit of time to respond, because they had to research my past."

"Who is 'they'?" Gaia asked.

"Oh. The Karma Cleaners. It's a group of goddesses and former graduates who are based over an actual dry cleaner." She chuckled. "My supervisor, Lynda, said their motto is 'We can get the stains out of your clothes *and* your soul.'"

"That's very interesting. Tell me more," Gaia said.

Dawn bit her lip and hesitated. Gaia just lifted one eyebrow. "Okay. Here's the rest. I'm a graduate of the program. I worked in a community youth center and helped kids avoid getting into gangs, quitting school, dealing drugs, and all the other dangers kids living in the inner city face."

Gaia gave her a slight smile, then schooled her features. "That's good. It seems like you managed to turn your life around. Did Karma Cleaners do that for you?"

"They just guided me so I could change my own karma. My actions after that naturally improved my karma, and good things began to happen." She gazed at the back door of her rented home. "One of the best things to happen to me was Luca. I went from avoiding the cops to working with them. I helped find and rescue a missing four-year-old girl. It was dangerous, but I didn't hesitate. My karma was officially clean after that. As a graduate, they offered me a position like Lynda's. Finding people with rotten karma who really, really want to change."

"And what do you do when you find them?"

"Well, nothing at first. I spot people I think might be candidates and recommend them to the main office. Then they do the watching and researching and get back to me if they feel I should intervene."

"I see. How do you spot them?"

"Oh, that's easy now that I'm a psychic detective. We get people looking for help all the time. I can see out of their mind's eye, get flashes of their future, and read their aura. I know if they genuinely want help or have other agendas."

"Interesting. Well, thank you so much for your time, Dawn. I'll let you think about my offer. I could really use your help—even temporarily."

Dawn smiled her relief, thanked Gaia again for the swing, and was ready to bid the powerful goddess a warm and sincere farewell when a question only the goddess could answer occurred to her.

"Mother Nature, may I ask you a question?"

"Sure."

"Why did you let a hurricane devastate Puerto Rico?"

"Oh. That. Yeah… Did you hear about the giant earthquake that dropped half of California into the Pacific Ocean at the same time?"

Dawn's jaw dropped. "No! How could I not have heard about that?"

Gaia smirked. "Precisely. I was a little busy holding together tectonic plates that day. As soon as I was free, I grabbed hold of the tail of that hurricane and unwound it. You and the rest of the western Caribbean are welcome."

"Karma?" Gaia bellowed into the ether.

Karma appeared out of the mist and strolled up to her sister. "No need to holler. Are you looking for me?"

"Damn right I am. Sit your ass down and tell me all about this Karma Cleaners agency of yours."

Karma shrugged. "Okay, but why don't we find a nice spot in the French countryside and have a couple glasses of champagne?"

"That sounds good. Wait! Are you just trying to relax me so I won't be mad at you?"

"I figured it couldn't hurt."

"I've heard of this champagne, but isn't it used for celebrations? We are definitely not celebrating!"

"Do you mean to tell me you've never had champagne?"

"No, I haven't."

"Well, we must remedy this situation immediately." Karma snapped her fingers, and they were sitting at a sidewalk café in Paris. A waiter appeared. "Garçon, we'd like two glasses of your best champagne, please."

"*Oui*, madam." He walked briskly into the restaurant.

"Nice one, Karma. You said French countryside. Now here we are in a densely populated city where I can't shout at you without causing a scene."

"Oh, is that what I did?" Karma smirked, and Gaia's eyes narrowed as she stared down her sister.

At last, Karma sighed and snapped her fingers again, and they sat in a field of lavender. She opened a picnic basket and withdrew a bottle of champagne and one crystal flute, which she handed to Gaia.

"Nice try again, Sister. You and I both know that lavender has a relaxing effect. Why do you think I invented it?"

"Because people need to relax." A loud pop exploded as she released the cork from the bottle and Gaia jumped. "And so do you, especially if we're going to have any kind of polite discussion."

"Polite? Was it polite to completely shut me out of this little business of yours? And which goddesses are you employing? And how many humans know about this?"

Karma filled Gaia's crystal glass to the rim.

The powerful goddess took a tentative sip. Then another. "Mmm... This is an interesting beverage. I like the little bubbles tickling my nose."

Karma smiled. "I knew you'd like it."

"Aren't you having any?"

"I will. You enjoy yours first."

"I think I will." Mother Nature took a big gulp the next time the goblet met her lips and the next. She giggled.

"Yummy, isn't it?"

"It really is. There's a touch of sweetness but not too much." After another big gulp, Gaia drained the glass.

"Have another. This time, I'll join you." Karma watched her sister place one hand on the ground behind her and recline slightly, holding out her glass for more of the potent wine. As soon as she'd refilled Gaia's glass, she began her sales pitch.

"I didn't think you'd want to be bothered with my little enterprise, dear Sister. After all, you have enough to do."

"Ain't that the truth."

"I know, right? So when the goddesses were complaining they were bored just sitting around playing harps all day, I thought 'What would Gaia do?' Then it occurred to me that I'd seen good parents deal with this. The most effective strategy was to put them to work! The kids either welcomed the task or complained but did it anyway. The chores got done, and they didn't complain about being bored anymore."

Gaia sipped her champagne quietly. Some of what Karma said made sense. She hadn't seen her goddesses for quite a while, and that was just fine with her. She had enough on her hands trying to keep track of her modern muses. Former humans with minor goddess status required frequent monitoring. And the gods! Holy moly, they were always trouble.

"I'm still miffed you didn't share this with me. A human had to tell me about this enterprise. *A human!*"

"Ah. So you were discussing the paranormal world with a human?"

"I was offering her a job as a modern muse. She wouldn't have been human much longer."

"Wouldn't have been? Do you mean she didn't accept the job?"

"She will. She's just too busy at the moment, she said. Too busy setting up her new psychic detective business with her paranormal husband—and too busy working for you!"

"Ah. You must mean Dawn. She's one of our stellar graduates. Imagine if we hadn't helped her get out of that gang? She would have wound up in jail, just like her mother. And she never would have found that little girl."

"Granted, it sounds like a worthy cause, but really, what if the human fails? What if they tell every degenerate they know about you and your enterprise?"

"First, they know we're watching their progress. We'll know if they're backsliding. Plus they have regular check-ins with their karma officer."

"Karma officer? What are they? The karma police?"

"More like probation officers."

"Hmm… And this works?"

Karma smiled in earnest. "It works beautifully."

"Well, stop it!"

"Excuse me?"

"You heard me. I never sanctioned this. Any new activity by my gods, goddesses, and muses needs to go through me."

"That's insane."

"It is not. I'm setting boundaries."

"Even when those boundaries are stupid?"

"Who are you calling stupid?" Gaia snapped.

"I didn't call *you* stupid. I called your *decision* stupid. That isn't personal." Karma rose and placed her hands on her hips. "Now, if you want to get personal, Sister, you are not only a bitch but an impulsive control freak who lacks trust in anyone else. You even expect failure! What kind of mother is that?"

Gaia was taken aback. Tipping her nose in the air, she rose several feet in the air. "Well, thank you for your input. I need to go somewhere to be alone." She disappeared in a whirlwind, and a sudden rainstorm bombarded the field of lavender.

———

"I'm sorry, Karma. Did I get you in trouble?" Dawn asked. The two of them sat at her small kitchen table, sipping coffee.

"No more than usual. Don't worry. I can handle her. I've been doing this job ever since the first caveman screwed up."

Dawn grinned. "Really? How did—you know what? Never mind. I have a more important question to ask you."

Karma tipped her head. "Please, go ahead."

"Mother Nature wanted me to do something for her. I said I was too busy. Should I have said yes? Do you think that's why she got so mad?"

Karma took a deep breath and let it out slowly before she spoke. "It's hard to say why she does anything. But if you're truly too busy, you were right to say no."

Dawn's brow wrinkled, and she remained quiet.

"You're not the first one to turn her down, you know."

"I'm not?"

"Nope. In fact, I could introduce you to the brave woman if you like."

"Yes. I'd really like that."

"Now, you should know she eventually changed her mind…but you don't have to."

"You mean she became a modern muse after all? Why? What changed her mind?"

"I'll let her answer that." Karma tipped her face up to the ceiling. "Bliss? Karma to Bliss. Can you pop in for a moment?"

A pretty brunette appeared. She glanced at the table and snapped her fingers. Suddenly, the kitchen table expanded, and an extra chair appeared. "Hi, Karma. And who might this lovely young woman be?"

"Bliss Cameron, meet Dawn Forest, soon to be Dawn Fierro."

Bliss's eyes rounded. "Of the legendary Boston fire-fighting Fierros?"

Dawn smiled. "Well, yes and no. My future husband, Luca, became a cop."

Bliss chuckled. "Oh yeah. I heard about that. It must have caused quite the stir in a family of firefighters."

Dawn rolled her eyes. "You could say that. They called him the blue sheep. He's a PI now though."

"Nice. My husband, Drake, is a firefighter. He worked with Jayce Fierro for a while. But that's not why you called me, is it?"

"No. Karma said you had originally turned down Mother Nature when she wanted you to become one of her modern muses. Did she retaliate?"

"Who, Gaia? Not at all. She would never do that. She needs us too much."

"But if she needs me and I said no…"

"Don't worry about it." Bliss snapped her fingers, and a cup of coffee materialized in front of her. "I said

THE GODDESS GETS HER GUY

no for a very good reason. She wanted me to become the muse of the internet."

Dawn's jaw dropped. "The whole internet?"

Bliss chuckled. "Yeah. I'd have lost my mind. We eventually compromised. I'm the muse of email. It's fairly easy. I just lean over a potential dum-dum's shoulder and whisper, 'You might not want to send that.' Or 'Just save it in your drafts folder and think about it for a while.' If Gaia's asking you to do something that's too much, say no and stick to your guns."

Dawn scratched her head. "It's not unreasonable. It's just that I already have a job, and my fiancé and I are trying to grow his PI business, and now Gaia wants me to teach the original nine muses how to use technology."

Bliss groaned. "Good luck with that. They're not known for their left-brain skills. They handle the arts, mostly—all right-brain stuff. That's why Gaia's hiring."

Dawn turned to Karma. "What do you think? Is it worth it to try? I also have my job with...well, you know."

Karma shrugged. "It sounds temporary. I can give you a leave of absence until you're ready to come back."

Dawn glanced between Karma and Bliss.

"It's okay. Bliss knows," Karma said.

"Whew! I didn't want to spill the beans again." Dawn wiped invisible perspiration off her forehead.

Karma chuckled. "And I appreciate that."

Bliss rose. "I think I've given you all the guidance I can. If you don't need me for anything else, I sense an idiot about to commit career suicide with a scathing email. You can call me if you need me."

"Thank you. It was nice meeting you." Dawn shook her hand.

"Likewise." Bliss grabbed her coffee mug, returned the table to normal size, and disappeared.

"Well, you have a lot to think about. I need to leave too," Karma said.

Dawn nodded. "I'm grateful for your help. I'll think about that leave of absence."

"Anytime." And with that, Karma vanished.

Chapter 4

Pouting on a log in the El Yunque rain forest, Gaia picked up a coqui. Placing him gently on her open palm, she brought the tiny tree frog level with her face.

"Why can't my sisters, paranormals, and humans be more like you, coqui? All you want to do is climb leaves, eat bugs, and chirp your cute little song. Although, granted, when a bunch of you get together, you can make quite a loud racket."

The coqui just stared at her. At least he seemed to be paying attention.

"You see? You're a wonderful listener. That's all I want…just someone to listen. If my sister thinks I'm a bitch, maybe it's because no one listens to me."

"I'll listen to you," a low male voice said.

Gaia bolted upright without turning around. "Was that you, coqui?"

A chuckle sounded from behind her. "No, I'm not your frog, but maybe I'm your prince."

She whirled around, and the little tree frog jumped off her hand into the bushes. Standing behind her was a handsome gentleman of about fifty or sixty years. Silver strands lightened his sideburns, but the rest of his hair was dark. His eyes were a deep, soft blue and sparkled with delight.

Gaia's hand touched her décolletage as she took a

deep breath and then laughed. "I thought it was strange that my little frog used a human voice."

The gentleman smiled. "That's all right. I talk to myself too sometimes."

She reared back. "I wasn't talking to myself. I was talking to my coqui."

"Ah, yes. Well, I'm afraid I don't have a coqui to talk to. My daughters are all grown up, and I retired a bit early, so now if I stay home too long, I wind up talking to myself or my cat. I'm told it's okay, and I guess it is, but sometimes I'd really like another opinion."

"You want my opinion?"

"Sure. Do you mind if I sit with you?"

She smirked. "You might not want to after you hear what I have to say."

"I'll take my chances." He winked and sat on the log.

He winked at me? No one has ever winked at me before. Mother Nature lowered herself slowly to sit beside this odd stranger.

"So what opinion do you think will scare me away?" he asked.

She hesitated. She didn't really want to scare him away. But she was used to speaking her mind, and most people didn't seem to like it. Maybe she could try softening her words.

"Well, I was going to say you talk to yourself because you're lonely. Maybe. I could be wrong."

"No, you're quite right."

She blinked. "I am?"

"Yes, you are."

They just sat there, staring at each other for a long moment. Eventually, he held out his hand to her.

"I'm Aaron Samuels."

"Oh." She shook his hand. *Now what?* She couldn't tell this human she was Mother Nature. "Um, you can call me Gaia."

"Lovely to meet you, Gaia."

"Really? It's lovely to meet me?" She tipped her head back and studied his handsome face. There was nothing but sincerity in his eyes. "I thought you'd be defensive. Humans—I mean *people* don't like being told they're lonely."

He shrugged. "If it's the truth, getting upset won't help."

Gaia had never encountered a human like this. "You're so…forthright." *And right right.*

He smiled. "It's probably a holdover from my former career as a doctor. I had to give people the facts. Sometimes, their reality was difficult to hear and the news was unwelcome, but they had to hear it for their own health and safety. Lying wouldn't do them any good."

Mother Nature nodded sagely. "I've always felt that way too. So why do people get angry when they've been told the truth?"

"You mean if someone tells them they're lonely?"

"Yes."

"Why do you think?" Aaron asked.

"Maybe they think it means they have no friends."

"Ah. That's a pretty typical misunderstanding," he said. "People can have loads of casual friends and acquaintances, but that's different from having real or *close* friends."

She tapped her chin as she mulled it over. "What exactly is a real friend?"

"Real friends are the people who you can trust and tell your secrets to." He picked up a pebble. "Although I wouldn't call this rock my friend."

"No. You probably wouldn't call my tree frog a friend either."

He smiled but didn't say anything.

She let out a long sigh. "I have sisters. Could they be my friends?"

"Sure. Can you tell them anything? Can *they* tell *you* anything?"

Not without causing a tsunami or avalanche… Mother Nature suddenly realized what the problem had been. Sure, she could tell just about anyone the truth, but could she handle it when the situation was turned around?

"You know what, Aaron? You've given me something to think about." She was glad she had talked to *and* listened to him.

"Good. Getting us to think is one of the major advantages a real friend can offer."

"Oh. So does this mean you're my friend?"

"I can be. Would you like us to be friends?"

"Yes." She didn't even have to think about it.

He rose and offered his hand to help her up. "Do you have a cell phone number you can give me?"

"No. I don't need a phone. When I want to talk, I'll just come and find you. How's that?"

"But what if *I* want to talk? How will you know?"

She was tempted to say she'd just keep her frequency open, but that would alert him to the existence of a paranormal world. She couldn't tell him who she was. And because she couldn't tell him who she was, that meant she wasn't telling him the truth—that she couldn't tell him her secrets. Damn. He couldn't be her real friend after all.

"I—I guess it won't work out after all. I'm sorry." She ran down the hill, around a thick copse of bushes, and disappeared.

"Wait! I'll buy you a phone!"

Like I need someone to buy me a phone when I hired a muse whose whole job is keeping track of those damn things. Peeking at him from the ether, she noticed he hadn't moved. He stared in the direction she'd run off to but hadn't chased after her. Disappointment warred with relief.

"Don't do it, Pan."

"Why not?"

Karma reclined on her opulent blue-velvet fainting couch. "Because she'll eat you alive."

Not to be discouraged, Pan laughed. "She'll never get past my horns or my hooves. They're very hard to digest."

Fate, who was looking on from Karma's matching armchair, rolled her eyes. "It's an expression, you goof."

"I'm not a goof. She doesn't make mistakes."

Both Fate and Karma burst out laughing.

Pan could see he wasn't going to get anywhere with these two. He would simply have to go around them and approach Gaia directly. She seemed to appreciate the direct approach anyway.

"Well, thanks for your input. I'll be going now."

"Wait," Karma said.

But before she could try to talk him out of it, he popped into the ether. If he went to the GAIA office building in Boston, he'd have to make an appointment and wait around for her. Goddess knew how long that would take. She could let him sit there forever. Some of the gods hung out and played cards all day, but that wasn't for him. He wanted to have some fun, and if he could get her to have a little fun with him, he'd be a shoo-in. If anyone needed fun…

Now where was she? "If I were Gaia, where would I be?" Somehow he realized an Eastern European brothel might not be the right answer. That's where he'd be, if he could be anywhere. *Would she come if I call her?*

There was only one way to find out. "Gaia? Gaia, I need to speak with you—in private."

The white-haired goddess appeared but not in front of him or beside him. She hovered a few feet above him.

"What is it, Pan?"

"Ah! Delightful to see you, Goddess. Can we go somewhere pretty and talk?"

She gave him the side-eye but eventually said, "Sure."

The two of them materialized in a forest. It didn't take long for him to realize the forest was in the tropics. Warm, heavy mist covered most of the early morning landscape, and a parrot cawed in the palm tree over their heads.

"Have a seat," she said, pointing to a wet log.

"Uh, this isn't exactly what I had in mind."

"No? You don't like my rain forest?"

"Well, it's not that I dislike it. It's just a little damp. Tropical is fine, but how about a sunny beach? Or better yet, a boat at sunset?"

She folded her arms, but they didn't change location.

"You wanted to speak to me privately. You can do it here better than on a crowded beach or boat."

He sighed and sat his hairy bottom on the damp log. "Okay."

She sat beside him but not close enough to touch.

Oh well. I'd better get to the point. He knew she wasn't the most patient goddess. "The reason I was hoping for a more romantic spot is that I wanted to ask you out." He smiled, and a bouquet of mixed tropical blooms appeared in his hand. He extended it to her, but she just looked at it.

"You cut down my flowers."

"Only a few of them…"

"A few here. A few there. Before you know it, fields of flowers disappear."

"Fine. I'll put them back." The bouquet disappeared, and so did his smile. This wasn't going well at all.

"Look, Pan. It's nice of you to want to…um…take me out, not that I know what that means, but I hear a relationship needs to include physical attraction."

"But I *am* physically attracted to you! Who wouldn't be? You're gorgeous. Long white flowing hair, the wind rippling your gauzy gown, revealing your gorgeous figure—although you could stand to do a few sit-ups…"

Gaia's eyes widened, and her lips thinned. "Get out, Pan. It's nice that you're attracted to me, but I am not attracted to you! You don't keep your long hair clean, and you stink. Do you understand? Not attractive."

He lowered his head, aiming his goat horns at her ample breasts. Steam exited his nostrils. Fortunately, before he could do something he'd regret, she disappeared.

"Damn." Not one to be easily discouraged, Pan took a moment to ponder her criticism. If her only objection to him was his hygiene, he could take a bath, get a nymph to cut his hair and groom him, and try again.

———

The Fierro family had decided to maintain their tradition of a big Sunday dinner, even in Puerto Rico. They'd been doing it in Boston for years—even after their sons moved out of the house. Each was expected to be there, except in an emergency. Why should Puerto Rico be any different?

Fortunately, the faraway family members could be transported by their wives, both of whom were modern muses. A minor goddess could hold onto a human or paranormal being and pull them into the ether. From there, it was a small matter to materialize wherever they wanted to be.

Chloe and Ryan were particularly glad about the family moving far away. Ryan had been caught in a backdraft during his time with the Boston fire service, and a very public funeral had been held for him. He didn't dare show his face around Boston, so he and his wife, Chloe, had moved to her castle in Ireland.

Because Chloe had also been a firefighter in Boston, Gaia had talked her into becoming the modern muse of fire safety, in charge of things like stoves, matches, and gas fireplaces…all the things invented since the ancient Greek muses grew up.

The only son staying in Boston was Jayce. He and his wife, Kristine, were both firehouse captains. If they moved away and wanted to continue their jobs as firefighters, they'd have to start all over…going through training, probation, and then working their way up to lieutenant. It would be a long, long time before they achieved the rank of captain again.

But Gaia needed a muse to handle mobile communication devices—cell phones, two-way radios, and anything else that popped up in the future meant to connect people. So Kristine took the job. She and Jayce were able to get on the same schedule because they worked in different houses, and they made it to almost every family dinner together.

In Puerto Rico, along with the youngest son, Luca, were the rest of the second-generation Fierros: Miguel and Sandra, Gabe and Misty, Dante and Mallory, and finally Kizzy and Noah. Soon Dawn would be part of the family too.

The patriarch and matriarch of this whole phoenix brood, Antonio and Gabriella Fierro, had finally fulfilled their dream of retiring in a tropical climate. No more Boston winters! Antonio said he wanted a bumper sticker to that effect. If he ever became ungrateful for twenty minutes in San Juan traffic, he'd be reminded he no longer had to put up with two hours in Boston traffic and then shoveling out his parking space!

Basically, life was good. The family brought their strength with them and tried to help other islanders regain the stability they had known before Hurricane Maria devastated their infrastructure.

Dawn's grandmother Annette had become fast friends with Gabriella, who'd convinced her to move there too. The two of them worked together, shopping and cooking these huge feasts, and the rest pitched in

where needed. This time, it was Annette's turn to plan
the menu and coordinate their efforts.

"Dawnie, did you bring butter for the rolls?"

"Yes, Grams. I know how these guys love to slather
it on."

"Oh good. And Sandra, did you bring a salad?"

"I sure did," the willowy blonde nurse said cheerfully.

"Dante and Noah, could you please set the tables?"
Annette asked.

"Sure, Mom." Noah elbowed Kizzy and winked. The
dark-haired doctor snapped her fingers, and three picnic
tables, pushed together end to end, set themselves with
eighteen plates, bowls, and sets of silverware, like a
Disney cartoon.

"Not fair, Kizzy," Mallory kidded.

"Hey, if you were a witch or a muse, you'd do it too."

"Yeah, well, Gaia didn't need my specialty in the
arts. She's got plenty of original muses for that. My only
job is keeping my mouth shut about the rest of you."

"Wait a minute. I count eighteen places. We only
need seventeen," Annette said.

Kizzy slapped her own head. "Oh, I forgot to tell you.
I invited my father. He's vacationing here this week. I'm
sorry. I should have asked you first."

"No, don't be silly. Of course he's welcome. It
even makes the spots at the table nice and equal. Hey,
Antonio!" Annette called out. "How's my jerk chicken
doing?"

"Fine. Same as your dumbass burgers."

Annette and everybody within earshot—which
included almost everyone—burst out laughing. "That's
what paranormal hearing gets you."

Gabriella came out of the house carrying a big bowl of fresh fruit salad. "What did I miss?"

"Oh, just your husband being his usual comical self," Annette said.

Their special guest rounded the corner of the home to meet everyone in the backyard.

"Dad!" Kizzy rushed over and threw her arms around her father.

"Dr. Samuels, I presume!" Antonio met him with a smile and handshake. "Welcome to our little gathering."

Aaron laughed. "Little? Thank you for having me. Are you sure you can squeeze in another person?"

"The more the merrier," Gabriella said.

Everyone took a place at the table and started serving themselves family-style, passing bowls and platters around. Antonio came over with a pile of grilled chicken and went back for a mound of hamburgers.

Chloe jumped up. "Oh! I forgot the potato salad." She disappeared into thin air and returned quickly with a large bowl in her hands. Then her jaw dropped. "I'm sorry. Does Aaron know about everyone here?"

Aaron smiled. "I know many of you are phoenixes. Some are witches. A few are even dragons, I believe."

Chloe slapped a hand over her heart. "Whew. I wasn't sure if I was going to have to wipe your mind of my little disappearing act."

"Well, I didn't know you could do that, but watch this…" Suddenly, Aaron disappeared and reappeared a few feet away.

Kizzy chuckled. "Nice one, Dad." She glanced around the table at the others. Nobody batted an eyelash. "My dad is a witch, like the rest of my family."

Aaron smiled. "Not exactly like the rest. Each person in the family has their own special power. Ruthie, my youngest, is very psychic. Kizzy here is a natural healer. I just have this one little trick of invisibility." He shrugged. "Not that useful, since I don't like to eavesdrop."

"Don't feel bad," Gabriella said. "The only power I have is the hairy eyeball."

Most of her sons laughed.

"Yeah, we all know that look," Luca said. "The one our mother gives us that means 'don't even think about it.' She perfected that before I was born."

Gabriella smirked. "And that's why you all turned out so well."

The rest of the dinner went as expected. Lively chatter around the picnic tables, different conversations in different areas. Passing salt, passing butter, passing gas and the occasional burp.

When it was fairly quiet, between dinner and dessert, Dawn spoke up. "I need some opinions on something."

"Go ahead, dear." Annette riveted her attention on her granddaughter.

"Gaia offered me a position, and I was told she wouldn't be mad if I turned it down. So I did. I'm really worried she won't be happy with me now."

"Wow," Kristine said. "What job did she offer you?"

"She offered to make me the muse of technology." Dawn grimaced. "I'm afraid I can't do it. I only have an associate's degree in computer science."

Annette leaned back. "What did I tell you about saying *only* when you're talking about your associate's degree?"

Dawn rose and flung her arm out as she announced loudly and proudly, "I have an associate's degree!"

Luca chuckled. "Don't be a smart-ass, honey."

Dawn sat her butt down on her spot at the bench. "Sorry."

"What exactly are you worried about?" Gabriella asked. "Gaia's reaction to your saying no? Or the idea that if you said yes, you wouldn't be able to do it?"

Dawn sighed. "Both, I guess."

Luca rubbed her shoulder. "You have enough to do right now, sweetheart. You're working for Karma Cleaners, you're helping me start my PI business, and you're setting up our household."

"I know. It's just that, well, she's the goddess of all. Mother Nature herself! How do you ignore her requests?"

"A lot of people do," Aaron said. "Think about climate change."

A whirlwind suddenly blew in from the corner of the yard and stopped beside where Dawn was sitting. As the wind died down, Mother Nature appeared with her hands on her hips. "Is someone talking about me? It didn't sound like I was being summoned, so I assume I'm being discussed behind my back."

Most of the table didn't react unusually. Dawn may have sunk down a couple of inches, but Aaron sat up straight, his eyes wide.

Gaia glanced over at him and did a double take. "You!"

"I'm sorry," Gabriella said. "I thought you knew everyone and everyone knew you. Let me introduce you to Dr. Samuels, Gaia."

He cleared his throat. "We are…acquainted."

Gaia smiled shyly. "Yes, we are. Now you know my big secret."

"Is that why you ran away?"

"We can talk about that later, but first I need to reassure this young lady," she said, patting Dawn on the head. "I'm not the least bit mad at you. I hope you'll change your mind later, of course. However, if you don't, I understand. You're doing things that will benefit others. *All* of you young people are. I'm quite proud."

"That's very kind of you, Gaia," Antonio said. "Dawn should have the right to make her own choices."

"And what do you have to do with it?" Gaia tipped her head.

"I'm the patriarch of this family…or most of it," he said, nodding at Aaron. "What happens to my future daughter-in-law concerns me."

"Relax, Mr. Patriarch. I won't force anyone to be one of my treasured minor goddesses, like Chloe here, and Kristine, and Misty…"

"Um…that reminds me. I've been meaning to speak to you, Goddess," Misty said.

"Oh? About what?"

Misty chewed her lip, and Gabe took her hand. "Tell her," he said.

"I—I'm not comfortable with my job as the muse of modern parenting."

Gaia stumbled backward. "You're not? But you're doing so well."

Misty gave her a sad smile. "Thank you, but it's really taking a toll on me. I have my own little one, and soon I'll have two." She patted her round abdomen.

"Watching other people messing up their children, especially when they're so young, well…sometimes I want to shake those parents and scream at them."

Mother Nature rolled her eyes. "Welcome to my world." After a quick glance at Aaron, she continued, "But I understand. You're right to tell me if you can no longer handle the pressure. But who will I get to help the parents who are trying to do a good job but are simply overwhelmed? There are so many responsibilities and so little support for many of them."

"You know who would be perfect for that position?" Gabe said. "If I may be so bold as to make a suggestion?"

"Go ahead, middle Fierro son."

"A mother who has raised seven sons, worried about several firefighters in the family, including her husband, but remains supportive and has never lost her sense of humor or kindness."

"Who could that be?"

Gabriella stared at her son. "Gabe? Are you talking about me? Don't you think you should've mentioned that to me first?"

He shrugged. "It's just a suggestion."

Gaia smiled. "And a darn good one! I haven't watched you as carefully as perhaps I should have, Gabriella. As soon as I knew you were loyal to your family beyond all else and that you could be trusted completely with their paranormal secret, I didn't give you much thought."

"That's probably a good thing," Antonio whispered to his wife.

"Hush," she whispered back.

Gaia tipped her head and studied her. "I accept your offer. Misty can train you."

"But I never offered," Gabriella said.

"You would have. If for no other reason than to help your daughter-in-law."

Antonio laughed. "She's got you pegged, dear."

Gabriella turned to Misty. "Do *you* think I can do it?"

"I can't think of anyone better suited to the job," Misty answered. She smiled for the first time since Gaia appeared. Then Misty's gaze dropped to the ground. "Would I have to give up my muse powers and the cure for MS you gave me as a reward for taking the job?"

"Not if we can find another way for you to help me."

"And would I become a minor goddess?" Gabriella asked.

"Of course. That's what a muse is."

"Then I accept!" Gabriella hugged Misty. "How wonderful to be able to visit my children wherever they are, whenever I like!"

Several groans were heard around the table.

Hands on her hips, Gabriella scowled at the group of them. "I won't just pop in unannounced! I know you have love lives."

Group giggles and titters helped ease the tension.

"Can she try it for a while, then the two of you talk about how it's going?" Antonio asked. "That's what I did as a captain with my FOPs."

"Fops?" Gaia raised her unplucked eyebrows.

"It stands for *firefighter on probation*. All firefighters go through a trial period."

Gaia tried to hide her amusement. "I guess she'll have to be a GOP. Goddess on probation."

More laughter resounded around the table. Aaron and Gaia exchanged a secret smile.

"Would you care to join us?" Gabriella offered. "We have plenty."

"Thank you, but I can't stay. I have an avalanche to prevent."

"Oh! By all means. Another time then."

Mother Nature nodded once and disappeared.

Chapter 5

"THANK YOU FOR COMING," AARON SAID AS HE MET GAIA in a deserted area of the island.

"Of course I came. You called me. So what do you want me for?"

Aaron smiled. "I know you're a pretty busy woman... or should I say you're a pretty woman who is busy. That's the way I see you."

Mother Nature's posture relaxed, and a glowing blush colored her cheeks.

"Anyway, I was hoping to talk to you, because we didn't get a chance to discuss our accidental meeting yesterday at the Fierros' household."

"Yes. I was surprised to see you. But not displeased. I ran a quick energy scan and found that everyone was either supernatural or knew about the paranormal world."

Not displeased. Well, that's a start. "I was wondering if you knew about me before the party."

"Knew about you?"

"That I'm a witch."

Gaia stumbled backward. "You're a witch? You mean you wear a black robe and hood and do all those crazy rituals at night under the full moon?"

Aaron sat on a rock and snickered. "No, I'm not that kind of witch. I seem to have been born with certain powers and beliefs that have been passed down for generations. We were a matriarchal society, with you, Gaia, as our supreme deity. I can't tell you what an honor it is to meet you."

Gaia sat on the lawn next to him. "Okay, that's kind of cool. I'm sorry I didn't talk to you more yesterday. I had a crisis to handle." She shook her head. "Always with the crises."

"I'm sure, Goddess, you must have a lot going on. I'm sorry to give you any more to do. If you're busy and you'd rather talk some other time…"

"No, no. I'm here, and I like your company. I would rather be talking to you than trying to undo some idiot's mistakes."

Aaron smiled. *She likes my company?* He couldn't help but feel incredibly pleased. "Actually, I was thinking I might be moving here. Do you come here often?" He mentally rolled his eyes at his cheesy-sounding line.

"No more than any other place that needs my help. Where would you be moving from? And why?"

"Brookline, Massachusetts. I'm getting tired of the winters there. My daughter loves it here, and as you know, my home has been feeling rather empty. I might become what's known as a snowbird. I have two daughters. Ruth is in Boston with her fiancé, and they're expecting their first child. Kizzy is down here with her new family. They all seem like delightful people, and I enjoy the good-natured teasing and lively energy."

"Yes. They are good people, I think."

"You're not sure?"

"I've thought others were wonderful and then they did something stupid, but everybody makes mistakes, even me."

"Really?" Aaron exclaimed. "I didn't think you made any mistakes at all."

"Oh, that's kind of you. But no. I misjudge people sometimes. I think giving humans and paranormals free will might have been one of my biggest errors. They seem to abuse it regularly."

Aaron chuckled. "Indeed. As a cardiac surgeon, I gave patients important advice following their surgery, which some of them ignored completely. It can get discouraging."

"What is a cardiac surgeon? I know you cut people open, but why?"

"Oh. It's a doctor who specializes in heart problems. I wouldn't cut anyone open if their lives didn't depend on it."

"Ah. Problems of the heart. Now, that wasn't my mistake. It just came about on its own."

"I imagine many things have evolved that you hadn't anticipated."

"Oh my, yes. So if you move here, are you going to be a cardiac surgeon in Puerto Rico?"

"Not exactly. I'm ready for a change, but I want to use my knowledge and experience. I was thinking I might like to study some of the plants in your beautiful tropical rain forest. There are many cures we have yet to discover. I would be extremely gratified to discover a new treatment or cure for diseases of the heart."

"Dis-ease of the heart…" They were suddenly transported to a mountainside in the rain forest. "You mean this?" Gaia reached down and plucked a short stalk with two leaves growing together in the shape of a green heart.

Aaron's mouth fell open. *Did she just hand me a cure?* "What is it? What does it do?"

"You said you wanted a plant to ease problems of the heart. Here it is." She shrugged. "I don't name my creations. You can name it if you think it needs a name."

Aaron couldn't believe his luck. Not only had he been handed some kind of cardiac remedy, but he would be allowed to name it! Perhaps it would be named after him. *Ah, but I'm getting ahead of myself.* Perhaps this little plant was well known to the medical community already.

"No. I don't think anyone knows about it," Gaia said.

"Are you reading my mind?"

She smirked. "Li'l bit. Don't worry. If you don't want me to listen in, either ask me not to or don't think so loud." She held her hand out to him. "The herb only grows here, on this very steep slope."

Taking her hand, he walked over to the edge of the cliff and gazed down. The mountainside was covered with these double-leaved plants.

"Oh my Goddess! There are millions of them. But you say they only grow here? And no one else has discovered them?"

"No one. Not even the tribes that once populated the island. People settle near water sources. The nearest river is miles away."

"Amazing…"

"So what now?" Gaia asked.

"I will have to test it first. I need to see what it's made of—break it down to its chemical formula. And then I'll compare it to other items in the pharmaceutical formularies. If indeed it's something new, I'll find the

best delivery system for it. And then I must find test
subjects—"

Mother Nature threw her hands in the air. "Oh, for
heaven's sake, no wonder it takes you humans so long
to do anything."

"Excuse me? You know how I do things?"

"Oh, not you. Just people in general."

"Ah. I understand. There are things that need to be
checked and double-checked and triple-checked just to
make sure they're safe for human consumption. Don't
you agree that what people put in their mouths and
bodies should be safe?"

Mother Nature sighed. "All I know is I handed you
something that does what you wanted it to do, and yet
you're going to change it, then double-check, triple-
check, and go through all kinds of chemical rigmarole.
Why question Mother Nature?"

"It's nothing personal, Gaia. I'm positive you would
not have given me something that would hurt humans.
But it's bureaucracy. All of these things have to be
recorded, tested, proven, and presented to the powers
that be—oh, not you, of course. You're the ultimate
power..." *Stop it, Aaron. You're babbling!* "I'm sorry
for any confusion. Let's just say it would not go on the
market without a lot of scientific examination and analy-
sis, and if it's going to do anybody any good, it has to
go on the market."

"I understand what you're saying, and I'll try not to
take it personally."

"Good. It's not meant to be personal. It's strictly
the way things are. And we already talked about being
honest..."

She scratched her head. "So many things seem absolutely ridiculous to me. I wish people could just trust me. I knew what I was doing when I invented *most* of this stuff."

Most of it?

"Some of what I created morphed into its own thing, but had my beautiful world just been left alone, I wouldn't hurt anyone."

Aaron thought about it and couldn't agree. Sharks? Killer bees? Scorpions? Rattlesnakes?

"Not if you leave them alone, like humans are supposed to."

I can't get used to you reading my mind.

"I know. I'll try not to."

"Well, Gaia, I thank you for your help. I'm very excited about the possibilities."

"You're welcome. You might want to get started on this right away. I imagine you'd like to see it come to fruition during your lifetime."

"Ha ha." He smiled and was relieved when she smiled back. "I wish I could take some back to Brookline with me, but I'm sure it won't be allowed."

"Let me guess...bureaucracy?"

Aaron nodded. "Yes, quite so."

"Well, you have to do what you have to do. Oh, speaking of that, I have a tsunami to stop."

"Oh dear. You better get to—"

Gaia disappeared, and Aaron was left holding a heart-shaped leaf. It would take years to go from this form to a usable pill or liquid and then to human trials. But first, he had to do what he could here on the island. "There must be a university with a good botany or chemistry department that survived the hurricane," he said.

—∿∿—

"Are you sure about this?" Karma asked.

"Not really, but do you have a better idea?"

Karma paced across Fate's lush garden with her hands behind her back. "It's risky."

"Of course it is. Nothing worthwhile is without risks."

"Did you get that off a T-shirt?"

"Coffee mug."

"Same thing."

"Come here and sit down, Karma. You're making me nervous," Fate said.

Karma slipped into the small chair opposite her sister at a wrought-iron bistro table.

"Tea?" Fate snapped her fingers, and two bone china cups plus a steaming porcelain teapot appeared on the table.

"I hope there's ginseng in there. It's supposed to stimulate brain cells. We need all the help we can get."

Fate tittered and poured a cup of tea for Karma and another for herself. "You can fix it however you like."

Karma snapped her fingers and took a sip of her ginseng tea with honey. "Delicious. Thank you, Sister."

"You're welcome. Now, how do we introduce two people who already know each other for a blind date?"

"It shouldn't be hard. Just summon them both here, and tell them what we have in mind."

"Then stand back and wait for the inevitable fallout?" Fate asked.

"Oh, ye of little faith." Karma took another sip of tea. "Look, Gaia already knows what we're doing. She won't be surprised. In fact, I think she'll be pleased we chose someone she already likes."

"I'm not so sure."

"Well, we won't know unless we try." Karma shrugged.

"True." Both goddesses finished their tea in silence. Karma was hoping some kind of plan B would occur to her as they sat there, but nothing came to mind.

Fate snapped her fingers, and all the items on the table disappeared. "All right. Here goes nothing."

"Wait a minute," Karma said. "The way to a man's heart is through his stomach, right?"

"What are you thinking?"

Karma snapped her fingers, and the table was set for lunch. A small rose in a bud vase graced the center.

"Perfect! Okay, now, before we chicken out, let's do this." Fate rose and looked at the sky. "Apollo! I beseech you. Come here!"

The handsome sun god floated to earth in a gleam of light.

"Fate! Karma! What a pleasant surprise."

"Here's hoping," Karma muttered under her breath.

Fate gave her sister a quick headshake. "Apollo, dear. We hoped you'd join us for lunch."

"Sure. That sounds great." Apollo produced a third chair, but before he sat down, Fate created another one.

"Is someone else joining us?"

"As a matter of fact, yes. But first, what would you like to eat?"

"Oh, whatever you have is fine with me. A roast pig? A side of beef? You decide."

The goddesses hesitated. At last, Karma spoke. "Of

course. Let's have both." She snapped her fingers, and both legs of lamb and generous slices of pork roast appeared on three plates. The fourth held a vegetarian meal.

"Now, we must invite our other guest." Fate took a deep breath.

Here goes nothin', Karma thought.

Fate ignored her and called out, loud and clear, "Gaia! I beseech you. Come and join us for lunch."

As soon as Gaia appeared, Apollo rose. "Great-Grandma! How nice to see you!"

Gaia's eyes nearly bugged out of her head. Facing her sisters, she screeched, "Are you insane?"

"Of course not," Fate answered. "We just thought, you know, a handsome young god, a beautiful goddess... He's not really your grandson, is he? I can't keep track of them all."

"And he is your favorite god..." Karma added.

Gaia dropped her face into her hands and mumbled, "Gawds, no." Then she raised her head and shouted, "No gods! They're almost all related to my grandson, Zeus. Maybe some gods and goddesses don't care, but I do."

"Okay, okay. We didn't know how you'd feel about it, but we had to try."

Gaia folded her arms. "Perhaps you shouldn't try anymore."

"What do you mean? Don't tell me you're giving up," Fate whined.

Apollo's gaze traveled from one goddess to the next. "Wait. Was I supposed to be my great-grandmother's date?" He burst out laughing.

"Geniuses," Gaia mumbled sarcastically, and then she disappeared.

Fate sank down onto her chair. "Oh dear. That did not go well."

Karma rolled her eyes. "You think?"

"Great-aunties, I appreciate your invitation to lunch. I can't wait to devour this appetizer and visit with you a bit."

"You can take it to go," Fate groused. All the food was wrapped and in a sturdy bag a moment later.

He shrugged. "Fine. Well, thanks for the snack and a good laugh—even if it was at my expense."

As soon as he was gone, Fate let out a deep breath. "Thank goodness he thinks it was a joke."

Karma rolled her eyes. "Probably because it was—however unintentional."

—❦—

Gaia wished she had someone to commiserate with, but who would believe what her stupid sisters just tried to pull?

Suddenly, Aaron popped into her mind. He'd been a supportive friend. She liked how he didn't tell her what to do or how to think. He just listened and initiated reasonable discussions. Even if she didn't know what he was talking about half the time, he didn't treat her like a moron. When she didn't understand much about his job, he simply explained what his noble cardiac surgery profession was like. He also shared his hopes and dreams with her. Could she make herself as vulnerable?

Maybe I could try…

Now, where was he? She closed her eyes and homed in on his energy. *Ah! He's visiting one of the Habitat for Humanity sites where his son-in-law is building something*. She was curious about that too. Sometimes, her humans reminded her of her ants. Industrious. Never giving up. Never leaving a fallen friend behind. When humans came together like this, she had to like them.

She materialized behind the concrete blocks that were already stacked and reinforced. These walls would stand up to the next hurricane she couldn't stop because she was busy elsewhere. Gosh, she still felt bad about that.

Striding around the corner of the building, she spotted Aaron talking to tall, dark-haired Noah Fierro and admiring the work that had already been done.

"Only part of the island has had electricity restored, and a lot of temporary generators are still being used," Noah said.

Aaron shook his head. "I can't imagine living here without air-conditioning." He wiped the sweat from his brow. "Look at me. I'm sweating, and I'm not even doing the hard work you and your brothers are doing. How do you stand it?"

Noah winked. "If it gets to be too much, we shift into bird form and fly up into the mountains for a bit of a cooldown."

When the two of them spotted Mother Nature, Noah gasped. "Oh no! Please don't get mad at me, Goddess. I haven't let humans see me shift. Unless they already know what I am."

"Relax, phoenix. You're not in trouble."

Noah let out a deep breath. "Thank goodness."

"I was actually coming to see you, Aaron. Do you have a few minutes to talk?"

"Of course."

She smiled. "Want to go where it's cooler?"

"Oh yes, please."

Instead of the mountains, she transported Aaron to his home in Brookline and snapped her fingers. His air conditioner roared to life.

"How did you know where I live?"

"I simply followed your heart. They say home is where the heart is."

"My heart is in my body." Aaron smiled teasingly.

Mother Nature chuckled. "I was talking about your energy, silly. I followed your mind's eye to see where you were in Puerto Rico. But then I saw your heart split between there and your home in Brookline, Massachusetts."

"And where is your home?" Aaron asked.

"Wherever I want it to be. Mostly, I stay in my garden penthouse in Boston."

"Boston?" Aaron said.

"Yes. Why are you surprised? I like to see my seasons come to fruition each year. I see many different people coexisting there. I get to witness all kinds of progress as well as tradition and history. It's an interesting place and keeps me entertained."

Aaron grinned. "That it is. I never thought of my city next door as entertaining, but you're right. There's a lot to be said for Boston if you're observant."

"I was hoping we could just talk. Not about anything in particular," Gaia said. "I just need to be with a friend."

Aaron scooted his chair forward and leaned in. "Feel free. I'd be happy to listen."

"I knew you would. That's why I like…um…being with you."

Aaron leaned back, looking pleased.

Suddenly, the phone rang. Aaron fished it out of his pocket and checked the number. "It's my other daughter, Ruth, Goddess. Do you mind if I take this?"

"Of course not. I like that you care about your daughters."

Aaron answered, "Hello, Ruthie."

"Oh, Daddy…" *Sniff, sniff.*

Aaron leapt out of his chair and strode to the next room. It wouldn't do him any good, since Mother Nature could hear both sides of the conversation anyway. But she let him have the illusion of privacy.

"What's the matter, pumpkin?"

"Daddy, can I come home?" Ruth sniffled some more.

"Why? Did something happen with you and Gordon?"

"Yes. He said he doesn't want children. And he walked out on me."

"Are you kidding? And he didn't tell you until now?"

"Yes. I'm eight months pregnant, and now he tells me he doesn't want a family. So he finally decided he was not going to stay with me and be forced into having one."

"Oh, honey. It would've been nice of him to tell you this sooner."

"Yeah, no kidding. But there's something else. I finally told him I'm a witch. He laughed and called me delusional."

"Oh dear. Was he going to leave before or after you told him?"

"Before. I've been trying to tell him for months. He called me deceitful—about the baby—so I thought I'd better come clean about the one secret I'd been hiding, in case we got back together. But if he can't accept the real me, we shouldn't be together anyway."

"Do you think a memory-loss spell is in order?"

"I already did it. I didn't want to take any chances."

"Good girl."

"But now I don't know what to do. I'm just panicking at the thought of being a single mother and losing the man I loved at the same time."

Gaia heard Aaron grinding his teeth.

"I'm so sorry. Of course you can come home. I want you to."

"Thank you, Daddy."

"You don't have to call me Daddy. I know when you're feeling vulnerable and need my help. But you're a strong woman. You'll get through this."

"I know. I guess I just feel like a scared little girl suddenly and need to be taken care of for a short while. Soon enough, I'll be taking care of my own child."

"I understand. When do you think you'll get here?"

"To Puerto Rico?"

"I mean to our home in Brookline."

"I've already started packing. I can pick up most of it later, but I can get there with a small suitcase in about an hour."

"Okay. You have your key, right?"

"Yes. I'll let myself in. When are you coming home?"

"As soon as possible."

"Do you need me to pick up anything on my way? Some extra food maybe?"

"Just get whatever you need and want. Mrs. Rivera is on vacation, so the refrigerator is pretty empty. I'll shop later."

They said their goodbyes, and Aaron rejoined Gaia in the kitchen.

"I hate to impose upon you…"

"You need me to take you back to Puerto Rico, pack your things, and get back here as soon as possible?"

"Well, almost as soon as possible." Aaron smiled. "As quickly as the airline can get me here, so only as quickly as *humanly* possible."

"Are you sure? I can get everything taken care of in the blink of an eye," Mother Nature said.

Aaron shook his head. "I know, but I can't think of a way to explain the accelerated timeline. Ruth thinks I'm in Puerto Rico. I need you to take me back now. Then I will pack, say my goodbyes to Kizzy and the Fierros, and get myself home in a matter of hours. It's no big deal."

"It sounds like a big deal to your daughter."

Aaron gave her the hairy eyeball.

She threw her hands in the air and said, "Okay. I understand. I'll get you there immediately, and you can get yourself back the slow way." She gave him a smirk. "Thank you for not alerting curious humans."

Aaron chuckled.

She rose and put her hand on his shoulder, and the two of them reappeared in Aaron's hotel room in Puerto Rico.

"Thank you, Gaia. Are you sure there was nothing specific you wanted to talk about?"

"Positive."

"All right. Will I see you later?"

Gaia nodded. "Of course. When the mood strikes, give me a call."

"Or you can call me." Aaron shot her a quick grin.

Mother Nature left him throwing his things in a back-pack and suitcase as quickly as he could.

———

Gaia wanted to talk to Kristine, her muse of cell phones, radios, and all the communication devices that go mobile. He had said to call him. Well, that was something she would have to learn how to do like a human so he didn't have to stand in the middle of Boston Common and shout.

Kristine was at work when Gaia popped in. The young redhead turned around and shrieked. She was in her office with the door closed; otherwise, Gaia would have changed into street clothes and knocked on the door.

"Goddess! I didn't hear you come in."

"Yes, I suppose I startled you."

"You really did. In the future, would you mind knocking?"

Mother Nature looked at the ceiling, and a *knock, knock, knock* sound came from above.

Kristine tipped her head as she looked at Gaia. "Was that you?"

"Unless there's someone upstairs who knocks on their floor."

The muse sighed, walked over to her door, opened it a crack, and didn't see anyone around. She closed it again and locked it. "What can I do for you, Gaia?"

"I want to learn how to use one of those little black phones that you carry around—correction—that *every-one* carries around."

Kristine's eyebrows tented. "Seriously? What kind would you like?"

"How would I know what I need? I put you in charge of all that stuff so I wouldn't have to know anything about it."

Kristine slapped herself upside the head. "I forget how much you don't know about modern technology. Let's go to the nearest store as soon as I finish my shift. We're going to have to use my address, and your bill will come to me, and I'll pay it."

Mother Nature rolled her eyes. "Don't be silly. I'm not going to pay for this thing. Neither are you. Just get one and show me how to use it. I'll *borrow* the airwaves." She said "borrow" as if putting air quotes around it.

"Okay. I have an old one in my drawer at home. Give me a second to go get it." It took about two seconds, but she popped out and back in with the item.

Kristine held out a black rectangle with one glass side, and on the other side was some kind of purple plastic coating. Plastic was something Mother Nature had never intended man to invent, but it was here now, and people seemed to think they couldn't live without it.

"Okay this is the On button here." Kristine pointed to a thin bar at the top. "But it has to be charged in order for it to work. This one is completely out of juice—I mean battery charge. Juice is an expression. Let me just plug it in for a couple of hours."

Gaia said, "I don't have that kind of time. You want it charged with electricity?"

"Yes, that's the idea."

Gaia grabbed the phone from her and shot a little

lightning bolt into the box. Then she handed it back to Kristine.

She took it gingerly and inspected it. She touched the On button and said, "I'll be darned. How did you know how much… Never mind. That did the trick."

Kristine showed her where to put her contacts, how to take pictures, and imported a few apps she deemed necessary. She even taught her how to play solitaire if she had to wait for long periods of time. Everyone knew Gaia was not good at waiting.

"Thank you, Kristine. You're very good at your job. I'm glad I made you a muse."

"That's the nicest thing you've ever said to me."

"Yes, I'm trying to be a little nicer these days," Gaia said softly.

"For what it's worth, I like the new you."

Chapter 6

RUTH DRAGGED HER SUITCASE UP THE WALKWAY OF HER old home in Brookline. She sighed as she looked up at the top step and the front door. *I never thought I'd be moving back here again.* Using her key, Ruth let herself in. Since the housekeeper and her father were both on vacation, she'd try to numb her mind in a constructive way by taking over some of the housekeeping duties. If she lived here long enough, of course, childcare duties would come first.

Boy, she wished Kizzy were here. Her sister and best friend would make everything so much more palatable. But Kizzy had moved out when she got married to Noah Fierro. Now she and her husband had relocated to Puerto Rico, and seeing her would be very difficult. Ruth would not be able to travel in her eighth month. Still, she really wanted her sister nearby for the birth in case something went wrong. She had been told she had very narrow hips, and as a maternity nurse, she'd seen more than a few emergency C-sections. The moms and babies usually came through them just fine, but Ruth knew there were always risks.

Kizzy's witch power could save a life supernaturally. Just one life per day, but if it came down to a choice, Ruth would make it easy for her. The baby's life should be saved, of course.

Her room was on the second floor, so she dragged

her suitcase up the stairs one riser at a time, trying not to strain too much. *I can't believe that asshole Gordon let me do this by myself. Sure, he had surgery this morning. So what? I could have used some help moving out tomorrow, but he wanted me gone before he got home. Coward.*

I guess that's just the kind of thing I would've put up with for the rest of my life if we went through with our marriage. In a singsong voice, she spoke aloud to no one in particular. "The heck with what Ruth needs. The heck with what the baby needs. It's all about what Gordon needs." She shook her head.

Once she got everything to her room and heaved the suitcase onto her bed, she looked over at her little pink dresser. It was as empty as she felt. Fortunately, her father hadn't done anything with her childhood room, like turning it into a gym. She burst into tears, falling on her bed. She clutched the pillow and cried hard.

A knock at her bedroom door startled her.

"No one is supposed to be here," she whispered to herself.

A female voice from the other side called, "I'm a friend of your dad's. Can I come in?"

"Oh!" Maybe her father had asked a neighbor to look in on her. Yes, of course he did. "Come in!" she called out.

A woman with long white hair entered the room. She wore a classic-looking powder-blue suit and a pillbox hat, like something Jackie Kennedy might have worn.

"Hello, dear. My name is Gaia. As I said, I'm a friend of your father's, and I know Kizzy too. This is my first time meeting you though."

Ruth managed to stand and shake the woman's hand. "Then you probably already know I'm Ruth. Ruth Samuels." Her lower lip quivered a bit, realizing she'd continue to be Ruth Samuels. Not Dr. and Mrs. Gordon Draper.

"Yes, your father called me. I'm sorry your fiancé is such a doofus."

At first, Ruth was shocked, and then she burst out laughing. "That's a good word for it. He's being a doofus, and I feel duped."

Gaia wrapped her arms around her and said, "Don't be sad. You're not alone. Your father cares about you very much, and you don't know it yet, but so do I."

Ruth stepped back and looked at this woman. She had intelligent eyes and soft, unlined skin. It was very difficult to pinpoint her age. Certainly, she was at least in her thirties, but the white hair really surprised her.

"So I guess you heard all about it," Ruth said.

Gaia nodded. "Why don't we go to the kitchen and have some tea? I think I know what you need."

Ruth sighed. "Yes, tea would be lovely."

She followed the woman down the stairs and into the kitchen. She filled the kettle while Gaia took an actual plant out of a satchel that Ruth hadn't noticed before.

The plant was made up of a couple of leaves that looked like hearts. They were about two inches long and the same across. The pretty leaves were stuck together at the bottom, making the point of a heart shape, and about halfway up, they divided and made the rounded tops of the heart.

"I've never seen leaves like this." Ruth picked one up, turned it over in her hand, and admired it. "It's pretty. Kind of like one quarter of a large shamrock. Is it part of the clover family?"

"I know what you mean, but no. It's a lovely plant that's in a class of its own. I think you'll be surprised how wonderful you'll feel after having tea made with it."

"Oh. This is a tea leaf?"

Gaia nodded. "It can be used in any number of ways. Tea is certainly one of them." She dunked the leaves in two cups of hot water that seemed to have boiled much faster than Ruth would've expected.

"So this is your home now?" Gaia asked, looking around the room.

"I guess so." Ruth took a sip of the brew and was surprised by the sweetness of the taste. She hadn't even put any sugar in it. "This is delicious. What's the name of this tea?"

Gaia shrugged. "I don't know. It's something your father found. He'll have to tell you more about it—if he wants to."

Ruth cocked her head and wondered at this strange woman. Well, whatever the plant was called, she was right. It made her feel better. In fact, she hadn't felt this good in a long, long time. After another sip, she felt as if she could stand up and take on the world. This was definitely unusual!

"You say my father knows about this?"

"Oh yes. He wants to create some sort of medicine from it. He's very excited about the discovery."

"I'll bet," Ruth said. With each sip, she felt stronger and happier. It was hard to believe she had been in tears only a few minutes ago. "I should call my dad," Ruth said.

"He might be in the air as we speak."

"I know he was in Puerto Rico this morning, but I doubt he would be able to board a plane this fast."

She fished her phone out of a pocket in her maternity top, then called his number. The number just rang and rang. Finally, she got his voicemail. "Hi, Dad. It's Ruth. I'm in your kitchen—" She cleared her throat. "I mean, *our* kitchen, having a cup of tea with your lovely friend, Gaia. I feel a lot better now. I'll see you when you get home. Thank you again for letting me move back in. I love you."

Ruth hung up and tucked the phone back into her pocket. "Well, if you were supposed to check in on me and make sure I'm okay, you have done your job admirably. I can't explain it, but I feel wonderful. I know my child and I will be all right. Thank you. If you have things to get to, I totally understand."

Gaia smiled. "Yes I do have things I need to get to. And you're right. You are going to be fine."

Ruth shrugged. "I've never felt better in my life." Then she beamed and escorted Gaia to the front door. "Thank you for coming and checking on me. I can take it from here."

"I'm glad to hear that. I'm sure your father will be too." She lifted the satchel and put it gently into Ruth's hand. "I'll just leave a few of these seeds with you. If your father can't get the seeds to grow, tell him I'll help. I have quite the green thumb. I can plant a whole greenhouse full of them."

And with that, the strange woman walked down the stairs and around the corner of the house as if she were cutting through the backyard. Perhaps she was. Ruth knew their next-door neighbors but not the ones behind them. That must be where she lived.

———~~~———

The following day, Aaron entered his home in Brookline and dropped his suitcases. "Ruthie?"

Ruth strode out from the kitchen and over to her father. "Hi, Dad!"

"Sweetheart." He spread his arms open wide. "I'm sorry it took me so long. I got rerouted and delayed even though I grabbed the first flight out."

She hugged him as if she'd just come for a visit. Aaron had expected his daughter to throw her arms around him and burst into tears, but she seemed almost cheerful.

"I'm so sorry about what happened, honey, but it'll be all right. You're home now."

"I know, Dad. I feel fine. Really. I know we're going to be perfectly all right."

Aaron was having a hard time believing what he was hearing. Why wasn't she reacting as expected for a jilted, eight-months-pregnant woman? "Have you heard from Gordon?"

Ruth shrugged one shoulder. "Not a peep. And that's fine with me. Would you like something to eat? I have some sandwich makings in the kitchen. I had to restock the shelves for myself, and I only got small amounts, mostly because I wasn't hungry at the time. But I did get a gigantic amount of comfort food to share. How about some chocolate chip cookies and vanilla ice cream?" She winked and flounced off to the kitchen.

What the heck was going on? She was fine? She

didn't seem to even miss Gordon. She'd thought he was the love of her life. Aaron never cared for the guy. He was one of those surgeons with a God complex, not that he was judging doctors in general. Gordon was a selfish prick. He was still a selfish prick.

He followed Ruth into the kitchen and said, "I'm not really hungry, but I could certainly use a cold drink."

"Of course." Ruth opened the fridge and said, "What would you like? We have your usual Heineken, or some Arnold Palmers…you know, the half lemonade, half iced tea drink. There's no liquor in it. That's what I've been drinking."

"That sounds delicious. Let's both have a glass of that."

He couldn't very well tell her how to feel. If this was just some kind of temporary upswing, he'd certainly let her have it. Grief and loss could bring on all kinds of mood swings. Perhaps she'd just listened to Gloria Gaynor's song "I Will Survive". Who knew?

The two of them sat at the kitchen table with their Arnold Palmers. "So, how are Kizzy and Noah?" Ruth asked.

"Kizzy and the whole extended Fierro family are doing great. You should see Noah's fantastic building skills. I swear that boy can do anything…and all without breaking a sweat."

Ruth chuckled. "Yes, she got a good one. And to think you didn't like him at first."

Aaron shook his head at himself. "It wasn't that I disliked him. I'm afraid I just saw things…well…less clearly in the past. I'll admit to being overly money-driven. And of course, no one was going to be good enough for my girls. But I've had my eyes opened in a few significant ways. Especially lately."

He wasn't about to say how he had not changed his mind about Gordon though. Instead, he let her steer the conversation.

"Boy, we really dodged a bullet with Gordon backing out," she said.

"Oh?" At last, she was going to talk about the reason she was here.

"Well, yeah. He didn't want kids. I have one on the way, and if he's not into it, he'd probably be a terrible father. And husband."

Aaron's eyebrows rose.

"Of course I was devastated. At first," Ruth said. "But then a visit from your friend and neighbor, Gaia, really helped me."

Shocked, all Aaron could do was repeat himself. "Oh?"

"Yeah," Ruth said. "She came over yesterday. Right after I got here in fact, and we had a delicious cup of tea together. I never knew she was our neighbor. She seemed familiar, but I don't recall meeting her."

"No, I don't suppose you have."

"She's beautiful but in a truly unique way. I have no idea how old she is... You must admit she's gorgeous. That long white hair is amazing, but she has a completely unlined face. And the way she dressed!" Ruth chuckled.

Oh no. Did she show up in her toga? "How did she dress?" Aaron asked as innocently as he could.

"She looked like Jackie O. She wore a beautiful powder-blue suit and a pillbox hat, of all things."

"Oh, right. These days, that's unique, I guess."

"So anyway, I was blubbering my head off when she got here, and after one cup of tea, I was fine. I should show you the interesting tea leaves she brought."

Aaron cleared his throat. "Yes, I'd like to see that."

Ruth retrieved the satchel and pulled out one of the leaves he had been introduced to in Puerto Rico. Gaia had obviously brought his cure to Ruth. But to experiment on her without any kind of prior clinical trials? Unthinkable! He hadn't even broken it down to its components yet. *Nobody knows what's in it! How could she?* And his daughter being pregnant… He rose suddenly, almost tipping the table. Ruth grasped her drink before it sloshed.

"What's the matter, Dad?"

Aaron gritted his teeth, then took a deep breath and tried to calm himself. "It's nothing, baby. I'm just tired. I need to grab a nap."

"Oh, I hadn't even thought about how tired you must be after your travel. Why don't you go ahead and nap? I'll run out to the store to pick up more food. Now that you're home, I should get two of everything. I was just getting portions for one, not knowing how long I was going to be here by myself. You didn't need to rush home. I'm really sorry if I cut your vacation short. You can go back if you want…"

Aaron raised a hand. "No, sweetheart. I'm perfectly content to stay home now. I had a nice visit with your sister, but I'd like to keep an eye on you, even though you seem okay."

"I'm *really* okay, Dad. I can't explain it. But I seem to have recovered from a broken heart in record time."

A broken heart... Suddenly, he realized the mis-communication or misunderstanding he'd had with Gaia. He was talking about damaged hearts. She must have taken that to include the sadness that feels like a broken heart. But still, testing this tea on his daughter without his knowledge or hers? Gaia had some explaining to do.

"Okay, honey. Going shopping for two of everything sounds like a good idea. Why don't you do that while I take a nap?"

"Okay, Dad. Is there anything special you want?"

"No. Whatever you select will be fine."

"I'll see you whenever you wake up." She kissed his cheek, grabbed her purse, and sashayed out the back door.

As soon as she had pulled out of the driveway, he stood in the middle of the kitchen and yelled, "Gaia!"

—∿∿—

Gaia was tending a shepherd's flock while the lazy boy was sleeping. She thought he could use the rest in a war-torn land, but with a shout like that, Aaron must be in huge trouble and had a greater need of her help.

What could have happened to Aaron? Did he change his mind about leaving Puerto Rico? There were all kinds of dangers for those unfamiliar with her tropical island. Had he fallen into quicksand? Was he being chased by a shark? Was he battling one of her caimans? Perhaps he fell off a cliff. Perhaps he was adrift at sea or lost in the mountains. Maybe he was even swallowed up by a sinkhole! That could happen, as Puerto Rico had the largest subterranean river in the world, and the caves were gradually wearing the surface thin. All this worry took place in a nanosecond.

She kicked the kid's ankle to wake him and disappeared into the ether before he opened his eyes.

She quickly located Aaron's energy back in Brookline, Massachusetts, and appeared in his kitchen.

"You bellowed?"

Aaron jabbed his hands on his hips. "Yes, I bellowed." He took a deep breath and said through gritted teeth, "Gaia, you may be a goddess, but I can't believe you tried a medicinal cure that had never been analyzed or tested on my daughter. My *pregnant* daughter!"

Suddenly alarmed, she gasped. "Is she all right? Did something happen to her?"

"No. Not yet. But I won't be allowing her to have any more of your 'tea' in case something shows up later."

Mother Nature crossed her arms. "You screamed for me because nothing is wrong with your daughter?"

"Of course not. It was your audacity that made me scream. Do you know what could have happened?"

"No. What?"

"Side effects, that's what! Have you never heard a TV commercial for any medication, ever?"

"No. I pay no attention to commercials or TV. Why? What are side effects?"

"Nausea, vomiting, diarrhea, blindness, shortness of breath, cardiac arrest, liver damage, kidney damage, brain damage! There are many possible side effects, and almost all medications have them. So tell me, why? Why would you do that?"

Gaia threw her hands in the air. "She needed it. If anyone was suffering from a broken heart, it was her.

I simply gave her the cure that you wanted. And it worked. She was calm and downright happy when I left. Did that not last?"

"Oh, it lasted, all right. But it's unnatural."

Gaia bristled but was trying so hard to change her behavior that she took three deep breaths before answering. "You're telling me she's fine. It worked. And something *I* invented is unnatural? I'm Mother friggin' Nature, for frig's sake!"

Aaron folded his arms and stood with his feet apart. "I didn't mean the substance was unnatural. I meant her reaction is unnatural."

"You'd rather she be crying her eyes out, emotionally devastated, blaming herself, perhaps becoming suicidal or homicidal with all the hormonal changes on top of her already upsetting situation?"

"No! I would not, but…" Aaron pulled out a kitchen chair and slumped into it. After a long pause, he said, "I think we had a miscommunication back in Puerto Rico."

Gaia took the seat opposite him. "We did? What would that be?" She was really trying to imitate his reasonable communication style. She liked how he *usually* spoke to her in a respectful tone and hoped it would return soon. Perhaps if she tried using the same type of voice, it would calm him the way his gentle tone calmed her.

"I just didn't realize you were talking about the heart as an emotion. I was talking about the heart as anatomy." Aaron scratched his head. "Did you think I was talking about a sad heart rather than a blocked blood vessel?"

Gaia shrugged. "I really didn't understand half of what you were talking about. I just know you were concerned about people's damaged hearts. To me, that meant you needed something to fix desperately sad or broken hearts. Was your daughter not heartbroken?"

"Yes. She was. And I'm glad she isn't wallowing in it." Aaron let out a deep breath. He looked her in the eye for the first time since they had begun this conversation, and she could tell his mood was changing, mellowing. At last, he smiled. "I have to admit it's rather exciting that we…no, *you* discovered something new. It could potentially be a huge discovery."

"I want to give you credit. I wouldn't have even thought of it except that you suggested it to me. A lot of what I've created has been forgotten or overlooked. In the beginning, I just did what I did and thought 'Well, that's nice' and kept moving on.

"What humans did with my inventions didn't concern me until they began to hurt my precious planet and everything I placed upon it. There are so many of those instances now, and that's what steals my focus. Pollution is rampant. I can barely counteract it anymore. Cities have what people call smog, and they don't put a stop to it! They just wear masks and keep polluting! My oceans, once completely self-cleaning and full of food, are now full of garbage, plastic, and oil spills! Plus destroying the fresh drinking water by poisoning it with chemicals…" She shook her head. A tear shimmered just thinking about those things.

Aaron reached across the table and took her hand. Surprised, she straightened her posture but let him hold onto it. His hand was warm and soft, not the hand of a laborer but the hand of an academic.

"I'm sorry I bellowed," Aaron said.

"I understand. You were afraid for your daughter. I'm sorry I caused you concern."

"So what do we do now? Is there an antidote?"

Mother Nature dropped his hand and leaned back in the chair, aghast. "You wish your daughter to go through the pain and suffering she was experiencing before I gave her the cure? What are you, some kind of sadist?"

Aaron's jaw dropped. "How dare you! Of course not. I love my daughter."

"How can you say that and wish pain upon her?"

Aaron's lips thinned. He took a few moments before speaking his next sentence. "I think you should leave before this escalates into a larger argument."

Gaia rose. "Fine. By the way, you're welcome!"

She left in a whirlwind and stayed in the ether for a few moments while she composed herself. *How could he be so ungrateful?* And worse, a possible sadist! What a total surprise this man turned out to be. She'd treated him as a friend and thought he was a good human being, but he must be terrible. The man was cruel! He wished heartache on his own daughter. What a horrible, horrible person!

"How did I not see this before?" She shook her head. Perhaps it was time to visit her sister. Not Fate. She was too kind. Something should be done about this, and Fate would just give her some namby-pamby philosophical shit, like "if it's meant to be, it will be." But she was sure Karma would know *exactly* what to do.

"Karma!"

Gaia's redheaded sister showed up in black stilettos

covered with spikes. Her short red leather skirt and vest contrasted with the white T-shirt she wore. The message imprinted on the shirt just said *I'm watching you*.

"Yeah? What do you want? I'm busy."

Gaia took in her sister's outfit and looked her over from head to toe. "You look like you're ready to do some serious damage."

"You would too if you had just heard what I just heard."

"Are you watching the news again? I told you not to do that."

"No. I was simply doing what I always do. Waiting for someone to say my name and checking out what's happening from the ether. Do you know how many calls I get from high schools every day?"

"More than India, where people still believe in you?"

"A lot of people believe in me. They just think I'm an idea, not a deity."

"I can imagine. So high school, eh? Are kids saying 'what goes around comes around' and wishing you would pound the daylights out of their nemeses?"

"Exactly. Don't people realize other individuals have their own points of view? Usually, no one is all right or all wrong. A combination is more likely. Or sometimes they want the same thing, but they just want to go about it in different ways. It's hard to determine whether or not somebody is truly in the right and someone else is truly in the wrong."

"Is that what you have to do?"

Karma laughed. "Gaia, what did you think I did…just made this shit up on the fly?"

Gaia shrugged. "Pretty much."

Karma shook her head, then took her sister by the hands. "Why don't you come with me and see what you think."

Gaia was going to tell her Aaron needed a good swift kick, but what her sister had said about high-schoolers made her stop and think. Was she being immature? Was she expecting someone else to feel the same way she did about everything? That would really suck.

"Okay, I'll go with you. But I'll hang back in the ether. No matter what happens."

"That's exactly what I want you to do. And try to keep a lid on your temper. You may see some crazy stuff."

Gaia bristled. "My temper? What's wrong with my temper? I'm usually in a very good mood."

Karma burst out laughing. Finally, when she could compose herself, she waved away the last of the giggles. "Sorry, Sister. I just…well, you… *Have you met yourself?* Who are you trying to kid? You've been in a pissy mood for a long, long time."

"I have not. I was in a very good mood until just recently. I was going to tell you about it, except it seems like… Well, never mind. Let's go see whatever you want to show me."

Karma nodded. "Okay. Let's go."

Chapter 7

GAIA FOLLOWED KARMA'S ENERGY TO WHAT LOOKED LIKE an old brick building in a city. The building was four stories high, and the brick wall around it was covered in graffiti. Small windows looked like they only partially opened. Over a doorway with wide steps to the outside were the words *Woodrow Wilson High School* and the numbers 1926. Okay. It was old but not falling down, so there were probably still students in there. "Why are we here?"

Karma pointed out a young girl sitting on the steps crying. "See her? She was just bullied."

"Bullied? How?" Gaia really didn't like bullying, especially when someone accused her of being the bully. That just wasn't true. She was a parent after all.

"The girl's mother isn't well-off, and the other kids know it. They live on social security and have to budget every penny to go to rent and food, so the girl goes without new clothes and niceties the others have. She hasn't been to a stylist in over a year, and one of the mean girls just decided to give her a haircut—not a good one."

"Well, that seems pretty mean to me. What are you going to do to those girls?"

Karma's eyebrows rose. "The girls? I'm not going to do anything to them, and I'm not going to do anything to the mother. This girl is the one who needs to learn the lesson."

Gaia crossed her arms. "Are you nuts? Hasn't she suffered enough?"

Rolling her eyes, Karma said, "You really don't know anything about my job, do you?"

Gaia jammed her hands on her hips. "What do you mean *I* don't know anything? Anyone can see you're blaming the victim. What are *you* talking about?"

"I'm going to help this girl learn what she needs to do to take care of herself. It's the only way. Her mother is not going to get a well-paying job, and the kids are not going to stop being mean. The only way this girl is going to make it in life is if she toughens up and takes care of her own needs."

"Seriously?"

"Well, yeah, but that's not all up to her. I'm also going to give her some help."

"Oh! I didn't know that. You didn't say…"

"Look, I don't have to tell you everything. Do you tell me everything?"

"Probably not. You take care of your thing. I take care of my thing. Fate takes care of her thing—whatever the hell *that* is. Anyway, it all seems to work together, and it's better if we don't meddle or get in one another's way."

"I agree. So stay here and watch this."

Gaia waited in the ether as her sister appeared down the street and strode up to the school, pausing on the step below where the girl was crying.

"Hey."

The girl looked up, recoiled, sniffed, wiped her tears, and said, "What?"

"Are you sick of being pushed around, taunted, and made fun of?"

The girl leaned back and eyed her suspiciously. "How did you know?"

"The clues are obvious, but I didn't really *know*. You just told me."

The girl heaved a heavy sigh. "Okay, yeah. I'm a loser. So what?"

Karma crossed her arms and looked at the girl carefully. After a few seconds of sizing her up, she asked, "How old are you, sixteen? Seventeen?"

"Sixteen. I'll be seventeen in a couple of months," the girl said.

"Perfect. You can get a job. You can help your mom, you can get new clothes, and you can put these girls out of your head, because you'll be too busy doing other things. They don't deserve your peace of mind. I don't want you to toss and turn all night and then come back tomorrow feeling even worse."

"Where am I going to get a job?"

"What is it you need?"

"Huh?"

"What do you need that your mother can't afford to give you?"

"Oh. Just some new clothes. Maybe some haircare stuff."

"Has it ever occurred to you to work at a store that sells clothes? Or sweep up hair from a salon floor? If that's what you really need and it will give the girls less ammunition, you should go after it like a lifeboat in the ocean."

The girl looked down at herself. "Nobody's going to hire me."

"Stand up. Let me help the hair situation a bit, and

then for goodness' sake, march into someplace with your chin up and show them why they should hire you."

"Okay…" She rose and brushed the chopped strands of hair off her old skirt, which was plaid and pleated and looked like it had been somebody's school uniform at one time.

Karma reached into a long pocket inside her leather vest and withdrew a comb and pair of scissors. Before the girl could object, she combed the frazzled hair into a style and cut away the strands that didn't belong. "There. Done."

The girl glanced at the cars parked along the sidewalk and rushed over to look at herself in a side mirror. "It's cute!"

"Of course it's cute. Did you think I'd do to you what those a-holes did?"

"I—I didn't know. I've never seen you before. I just figured you couldn't make it worse. Do you go to this school?"

"No. You might say I went to the school of hard knocks. Now, hold your head up high and get a job."

"But my clothes…"

"Can you beg or borrow one outfit?"

The girl thought hard. "I have an aunt who looks like a million bucks, but we're not the same size."

"Would she loan you money for an outfit?"

"Maybe, but I wouldn't be able to pay her back until I got a paycheck, and how could I show up for work wearing the same thing every day?"

"You're throwing roadblocks in your own way. Stop thinking about why you can't do something, and begin thinking of ways you *can* make it work. Get a couple of separates. One pair of pants and a jersey. One skirt and a blouse. Mix and match to get a different outfit each day for four days. I promise they will pay attention to the kid who really wants the job rather than every other kid who just throws them a resume with a 'whatever' attitude."

The girl looked up at Karma, and her expression began to soften. Eventually, she cocked her head and said, "Wouldn't they get mad at me for trying on something I couldn't afford to buy? Like that girl in the *Pretty Woman* movie."

"Well, don't be an idiot and try on the most expensive thing in the store."

The girl chuckled. "I'll give it a go. Will I see you again? I'd like to tell you how everything comes out."

Karma smiled. "You never know." She strode away and continued walking until she reached the corner, and as soon as she was out of the girl's sight, she popped back into the ether.

"Is that it?" Gaia asked. "You just told her to get a job?"

"Do you want to see what happens when she does?"

Gaia smirked. "No. Why don't you just tell me?"

"Okay, she gets to the store that she likes with her aunt. Roxanne—that's her name, by the way—puts a few outfits together, tries one on, then goes out to the store manager and gives the spiel that I told her to. And she's hired on the spot. Not only that, but their clothes look so cute on her, the woman lets her model them while she works until she earns them, and then she can take them home."

"Seriously? Nobody does that."

"Not without some coaching." Karma winked.

Gaia thought, *Perhaps my sister isn't as mean as I thought she was.* "I guess sometimes you don't go after the same person I would, but look how well that turned out."

"Oh? Who would you have 'gone after'?"

"The a-hole who chopped off her hair."

"Oh, you mean the kid who fell, holding the knife she used, and cut her own hand?"

Gaia laughed. "And did you have anything to do with that fall?"

Karma perched on a bench, swinging her spiky boots back and forth in the ether. "Maybe…but I'll never tell."

All right, maybe I'll just talk to her about my situation and let her tell me what she would do instead of me telling her what I want her to do, Gaia thought. "Do you have a few minutes?"

"Sure. Would you like to go get a drink?"

"Oh yes. That sounds good. Where should we go?"

"Let me take you to this new place I just found," Karma said. She took Gaia's hand, and the two of them appeared in an alley of a busy neighborhood lit up with neon signs. Lots of people, lots of laughter, high heels clicking on the sidewalk, music playing…

This lively atmosphere wasn't what Gaia was hoping for. "I wanted to talk more privately."

"We can talk privately in the restaurant. No one will be paying any attention to us, and besides, it'll be too noisy to make out more than a word or two if anyone did try to listen in. Wait, is that what you're wearing?"

Gaia looked down at her long white tunic. "Do I need to blend in?"

Karma laughed and snapped her fingers, and Gaia

looked down at herself again. She was wearing skinny jeans, high-heeled brown boots, and a clingy blue blouse that crisscrossed in the back.

"Hey, I look pretty good."

"Of course you do. I dressed you."

"Yes, you did. Well, thank you."

"Hang on. I need a second." Karma snapped her fingers and suddenly wore a lighter pair of skinny jeans, the boots without the spikes, and a green clingy top with cutouts on the shoulders. "Okay, I'm ready. Let's go into this bar, and you can tell me all about it."

As soon as they entered, a familiar female stood and waved to them from a table. "Yoo-hoo! Over here!"

Oh crap. Fate's here. What could she want?

"Sister! What are you doing here?" Mother Nature asked in what she hoped was a cheerful tone.

"Karma called me."

"I called her," Karma reiterated.

"Why? I thought we were going to have a private conversation."

"I thought you might like to hear what Fate has to say before you go into a death spiral on someone who hurt your feelings. She may give you another take on things."

Gaia snorted. "Death spiral. So dramatic." She lowered herself into her chair. The waitress came over and asked them what they wanted to drink. Gaia turned to her sisters. "I liked what you recommended before. Is there something else I should try?"

"Cranberry and vodka is nice," Fate said.

"That's a Cape Codder," the waitress said.

"How about a tequila sunrise?" Karma suggested.

Gaia tipped her head this way and that. "I like Cape

THE GODDESS GETS HER GUY

Cod. I've never had tequila though." She looked at the waitress. "What would you like better if you were going to choose between those two?"

The young waitress smiled. "I'd probably get the Cape Codder because, well, I don't like tequila that much." Whispering behind her hand, she added, "You have to ask for the good stuff or you get the cheapest."

Mother Nature nodded once. "A Cape Codder it is."

The other two sisters decided to order Cape Codders as well. "With Stoli," Karma added.

"How are things going?" Fate asked.

Gaia narrowed her eyes and said, "I could ask you the same thing."

Fate cleared her throat. Sitting up straight, she plopped her laptop on the table, then opened it in front of Gaia. "I tried rewriting your online profile. The answers you gave me wouldn't have attracted anyone except possibly some kind of nut. So here's what I said about you." Fate brought up a page with a flattering picture of Gaia and the profile, which read very simply: *I am a young at heart, nurturing, outdoorsy kind of girl. I love nature walks and finding a pretty spot to observe a sunset. If you enjoy those things and can be a good listener, that's all I need. I'm not looking for anything in particular as far as relationships go. I'd rather see how things evolve.*

Gaia leaned back in her chair. "That's it?"

Fate shrugged. "That's it. I don't think I can say much more without raising red flags. Do you?"

"Let me think." *Should I ask her to add that I'm all-powerful? No. She must've thought that would scare men away. Should I ask her to include my desire to make*

the world a better place? No, I don't want a militant
political activist either.

At last, Gaia opened her eyes and sighed loudly. "All
right. I think you have it. Is there anything special you
want me to do? Should I look at other people's profiles
and pick one? I don't know how this works."

Fate smiled. "I haven't posted this yet. I was waiting
for your approval."

Gaia nodded. "Approval given."

"Okay." Fate pushed one button on the computer
keyboard and folded her arms. "Now we wait."

Karma smiled. "You see how much easier it is to just
let go of ugly feelings and move on with your life?"

"Is that what I'm doing?" Gaia asked.

"I think so. I *hope* so. You were about to ask me to
zap someone for you, right?"

Gaia let out a defeated *puh* sound, and her posture
slumped.

The waitress came over with their three drinks and set
them on the table. Gaia was about to guzzle hers when
Fate held up her glass. "What should we toast to?"

"Toast? Oh yeah. I've observed that tradition before.
Seems silly to me."

"How about to moving on?" Karma suggested.

"Perfect!" Fate raised her glass, and Karma clinked
it. Then they both reached across the table and clinked
Gaia's glass as she just sat there holding it. "To moving
on," her sisters said in unison.

"Whatever," Gaia muttered and guzzled a mouthful.

The other two took a sip and set down their glasses.
The tangy sweetness pleased Gaia. Her cranberries were
usually a little bitter, but humans had found a way to

sweeten them with sugar cane and enjoy their unique taste. The thing they called vodka didn't seem to change it much, but it gave it that little kick she noticed other drinks had.

"So, Sister, you were asking what you need to do for this online search," Fate reminded her.

Just then, her computer made a soft *ding* noise.

"Oh! You have a poke."

Gaia's brows rose. "A poke? Someone poked me?"

Karma chuckled. "It's an online term."

Mother Nature shook her head. "I'll never get used to all these crazy modern expressions. Okay, so tell me what a poke really means."

Fate grinned. "It means someone saw your profile and likes it. Already! They would like to talk with you."

"How do I know if I want to talk to them?" Gaia asked.

"Excellent question." Fate turned the computer screen toward Gaia. "Click on his name, and read his profile. If you're interested, you can poke him back."

Gaia chuckled. "Okay. With all this poking, people might wind up with bruises."

"Think of it like a tap on your shoulder," Karma added.

Gaia clicked on his name and read a little bit about him and saw his picture. Something about him seemed familiar. "Why does this guy look familiar to me?"

Fate shrugged. "I suppose everyone might look a little familiar to you. You created them, after all."

"I created infants. Not adults. Their parents raise them. They live their lives. Basically, they create themselves. I simply threw the DNA together. It's kind of like mixing up a cake batter, putting it in the oven, and then turning it over to someone else."

"Got it. In that case, I'm not sure why he looks familiar. Karma, does he look familiar to you?"

Fate turned the monitor toward Karma, who took one look and gasped.

"Oh no. You don't want him. If you ever watched the news, you may have seen his face. Let's just say you're too old for him."

Gaia frowned. "Too old? My age isn't even on here."

Karma raised her brows as if to say *Put it together, Sister.*

He must like them young. "Oh! Oh no, no, no. Definitely not what I want." Gaia jumped up. "Let's go. I'm not sure this online dating is for me."

Fate put her hand on Gaia's arm. "Wait. Don't give up yet. That was just the first one. All you have to do is ignore it. I'm sure there will be others."

The machine dinged again. Gaia was ready to walk out, but curiosity won her over. She settled back in her chair and glanced at Karma. "You'll look at all these guys too, right?"

"If you want me to."

"I most definitely want you to."

The next poke resulted in a nice picture and profile. This one sounded interesting. Karma knew nothing bad about the person, so Gaia was intrigued. "What do I do about it now? Just poke him back?"

"Yes. If you guys want to communicate for a while before you meet, that would be smart. You can text or email or whatever makes you most comfortable."

Gaia laughed. "I'm not comfortable with any of these technical contraptions. Now what?"

"Didn't you talk to your muse of mobile

communications? I thought she gave you something to communicate with people."

Mother Nature reached into her pocket and pulled out the cell phone Kristine had given her. "This? I can talk to him on this? But what if I don't like him, and then he has my phone number and calls and calls and calls?"

"You can communicate with him another way," Karma suggested. "Message him on Facebook. If he gets to be a nuisance, you can block him. We'll show you how."

"Message him? Facebook?" Gaia pinched the bridge of her nose. "I'm so confused!"

Fate sighed. "Tell you what. Just set up a place to meet. You can always shake hands and walk away if you don't hit it off."

"Okay."

"So, shall we poke him back?" Karma asked.

Gaia shrugged. "I guess so."

"You should give him your phone number," Karma said. "If he abuses it, I can take care of him." She winked.

"Yes," Fate said. "He'll need that to text you if he can't make it. Then you won't wind up sitting and waiting and waiting. Very embarrassing."

Karma added, "If you decide you want to talk to each other, he can call the same number and you can talk. If you don't like him, you can always ask him to stop texting and calling. That should do it. You don't really have to worry about blocking someone unless they become a nuisance."

"Or you can just say, 'New phone. Who dis?'" Fate said and chuckled.

"I don't get it," Gaia said.

Fate patted her hand. "Don't worry. We'll be with you every step of the way, Sister. Let's set up something so you can get to know each other, and if you like him, then you can find a place to meet."

"Okay." Gaia sighed. "Let's do that."

Right before they all went their own ways, her sisters kissed both her cheeks, then exchanged some kind of sly look.

Oh crap. What have I gotten myself into?

—∞—

Gaia arrived at the restaurant where Fate had set up her first meeting with the young man she had chosen for her. All Gaia knew was what his picture looked like and that he seemed to be into nature and *the craft*.

It was that second part that intrigued her. He called himself a Wiccan priest, and Fate explained he already believed in the Goddess, so revealing her real identity wouldn't be too difficult. He might not believe her at first, but at least he would believe her eventually. Many of the online profiles she'd read seemed to favor other religions or none at all, which would deny the existence of a goddess altogether.

She spotted him at the back of the restaurant, and he rose immediately. He wasn't bad looking. A little on the short side, so she shrank herself a couple of inches to appear about the same height. He had longish light-brown hair, parted in the middle. He also sported a nice tan, meaning he had probably been outside in the sun. So his claim to like the outdoors and nature seemed valid.

Encouraged, she walked briskly to the table and put

out her hand for a handshake. "Hi, I'm Gaia. I take it you're Bruce?"

He took her hand and kissed her knuckles. "Yes, I'm Bruce. It's lovely to meet you."

Interesting. Kissing my hand and 'lovely to meet you'... Perhaps he was European. No accent though.

"So did you want to eat here? Or take something to go?" he asked.

"I hadn't thought of ordering something to go, but that sounds wonderful. We could take a walk, find a nice spot, and watch the sunset, since both of us like to do that."

"Indeed."

Gaia glanced at the menu to look as if she didn't already know what she wanted, but most restaurants had at least one vegetarian option. She'd just ask for that and be done with it.

The waitress came over and asked, "Are you ready to order?"

"I would like a vegetarian wrap on whole wheat bread," Gaia said.

"That sounds good to me too," Bruce said and closed the menu. "Is there any way we can get that to go?"

"Oh. We don't usually do takeout, but I'll ask the chef to wrap it in plastic."

"No plastic!" Gaia calmed herself. "Can he wrap it in something biodegradable, please? Like plain brown paper?"

"Um, sure." The worried-looking waitress disappeared into the kitchen, and the two of them gazed at each other. One of those uncomfortable silences set in.

"So..." they said at the same time and laughed.

"You first," Bruce said.

"No, you. I insist."

"All right. Your profile didn't say much about you. What do you do for a living?" he asked.

Gaia shrugged. "This and that. Whatever comes my way."

"Interesting. I'm not sure what that means, but if you don't want to tell me yet, that's fine."

"I wouldn't know how to put it any other way. How about you? What do you do?"

"I write books and teach classes in Wicca. I have small groups I train."

"And that pays the bills?"

"Not completely. I also contribute items on consignment to a local store that carries working tools."

"Tools? Like saws and hammers?"

He laughed. "No. Tools of *the craft*. The craft of Wicca."

He obviously thought she had no idea what he was talking about. And truthfully, she didn't. This man puzzled her.

"What kind of tools do you need to be Wiccan?"

"I can see you don't know much about my religion. That's okay. I love to teach, and perhaps you'd like to join one of my classes someday. We worship the Goddess and God as her consort, but you can press pause on that, if it makes you uncomfortable."

It was all Gaia could do not to giggle, though she might have been smirking.

He cleared his throat. "To answer your question, some of the tools I sell are magic wands, crystal balls, stone jewelry with metaphysical properties, capes I embroider, and staffs I whittle myself."

"Wait a minute…magic wands?"

"Oh yes. We use those in our rituals. In the very beginning, we open the circle by casting energy clockwise while surrounding ourselves with protective light. And then at the end of the ritual, we open the circle by casting the energy counterclockwise."

All this was confusing to Gaia. She had dropped in on some of those rituals, since they often called on her specifically, but she just didn't understand all the rigmarole that went with it. "So what else is involved in a ritual?"

"Well, we all write down our intentions in the form of spells, recite and burn them so the energy rises to the heavens, and we bring offerings to the Goddess."

Her back straightened. "Really? What kinds of offerings?"

"Usually wine and some kind of sweets. Small honey cakes or bakery items she might enjoy. But of course, at the end of the ritual, we eat them ourselves."

She laughed. "You have an interesting definition of offering a gift. 'Here's a yummy cake. Oh no, that's not for you. I'll eat it myself, thank you.'"

He smiled. "It's more of a symbolic thing."

After a long pause to mull that over, she said, "So tell me about these other tools. You mentioned capes?"

"Yes. Black capes. For protection."

"Oh, like raincoats?"

"No."

"So they're warm coats to protect you from snow and cold?"

"No. Not that kind of protection. Magical protection from evil spirits."

Her eyebrows shot up. "Protection from a cape?"

"I…uh…the cape is really more of a tradition. Our pagan ancestors had to meet in secret or risk being burned at the stake, so they wore black to blend in with the night."

She laughed. "You realize your ancestors met in their best brown burlap because that was all they had, right?"

His face fell. At last, their waitress arrived with their sandwiches in paper bags inside another paper bag with handles.

"Oh, thank God," he muttered under his breath.

God? Now he's talking to one of my subordinates? This date was not going as expected, but at least they could finally get outside. Maybe he'd make more sense with some fresh air.

They took the food and walked down to the river. There was a lovely winding pathway beside it. "Have you ever been here before?" he asked.

"Yes, as a matter of fact, I have." She smirked. She wasn't taking this very seriously anymore, so she might as well have a little fun while she could. Glancing over at him, she asked, "So what are your books about?"

"Oh, all kinds of things having to do with the craft. I have a number of thoughts on spells, spirit guides, herbs, crystal and candle magic…"

"I'll bet you do. So you must be pretty powerful?"

"My magic is always spot-on, but it's actually the Goddess who has all the power. I just ask her for what I need."

"How do you know what's needed?"

He glanced over at her and frowned. "Well, I know what I *want*. That's usually all any of us know. The Goddess knows what we need."

She nodded. "I think I understand." That seemed like a pretty good answer.

Suddenly, as they were passing a copse of bushes, a familiar figure emerged.

Bruce gasped and froze in place.

Gaia stuck one hand on her hip. "Pan? Really? You're crashing my date?"

Bruce just stayed frozen in one spot, staring directly at the young god with hairy goat legs, hoofs, and horns, who was laughing. His long goatee bobbed with his chin.

"I'll bet he doesn't know who you really are, does he?" Pan asked.

"And I'll bet I wasn't ready to tell him. I might never have, since I don't think it's a good idea anymore."

Bruce finally recovered from his shock and stared at Gaia. "What does he mean 'who you really are'? Wait a minute. Your name is Gaia…"

Mother Nature rolled her eyes. "Yes, it's me. The Goddess." She watched his expression as it changed from incredulous to starstruck.

"But…wait, you…I mean…how…"

Pan laughed again. "What's the matter, priest? Cat got your tongue?" A black cat appeared in Pan's arms, bit him, and ran away. "Fickle feline. So, mortal, did you think she wasn't real? Have you been pretending all this time?"

"I…I…"

Pan crossed arms. "Oh, come on. Spit it out."

The Goddess sighed. "Pan, now that you've ruined everything, I'll have to erase his memory. In fact, get going, and I'll do that right now."

"Sure thing, Sugar." Pan scampered off into the woods, and Bruce's wide-eyed gaze followed him.

When they were alone again, he asked, "Are you really *the* Goddess? Gaia? Mother Nature herself?"

"Yes, I am. And I'm sorry, but I don't want to continue this date. It's all right. Really. It's not you. I mean, not really. You have some odd ideas, but I'm trying hard not to correct people if they're not harming anyone."

"Yes! That's the Witches' Rede. If it harm none, do what ye will…"

She shrugged. "Most people don't even realize the harm they do."

His posture slumped. "I guess when I thought you were too good to be true, I was right."

She smiled. "Why don't you continue to meet up with your cronies and do whatever it is you do? You'll find someone there. But for heaven's sake, you can just talk to me. You don't need all the rituals and tools and… um…offerings." She snorted.

He looked crestfallen. "I—I don't know what to do with my life now. It's—it's all a sham."

She placed a hand on his shoulder. "No, it's not that bad. You're doing what you learned to do, which is nice. But it's for you, not me. You understand, right?"

He nodded but still looked confused.

"Tell you what. It won't matter in a minute." She swiped her hand across his face, and he blinked.

She stuck out her hand. "Well, it was nice to meet you, Bruce. I think I'm going to head home now."

"Would you like a ride? I have my car parked around the corner."

"No, that's okay. I'll just walk. It's a nice evening."

"Okay. Take care." And with that, he jogged across the street, and she strolled off into the sunset.

Chapter 8

"Kizz?"

"Ruthie. How are you? It's so good to hear your voice!" Kizzy exclaimed.

"I'm okay. I'm really sorry to bother you, but it's Dad. He's acting very depressed. Just moping around, and…I don't know. He's just not himself."

"Oh dear. Did something happen?"

"I'm not sure. He seemed to be fine at first, but when he saw that I was doing better—great, in fact—he seemed to get upset. Like it wasn't okay that I snapped right out of it."

"That's strange," Kizzy said. "How's your pregnancy going? Do you feel like you're ready to pop any second?"

Ruth laughed. "Yes. But I was wondering if I could come and visit before that happens? I miss you. And no offense to Dad—he's a doctor and everything—but I don't want him around me in his depressed state. I need some excited support when I go into labor. I think I'd rather have you with me."

"I'd love that! You've got to get down here soon, before it's too late to travel. It might even be too late now."

"I'm sure some doctors will say 'yes, it's too late,' and others will say 'no, it's not. Go ahead.' I think I'd rather make up my own mind."

"You're still seeing your obstetrician, aren't you?" Kizzy asked.

Ruth sat on the sofa and put her feet up. "Yes, and she's wonderful, but she's not you. You know how it is. If anything goes wrong... Well, I'd want you to be my doctor, and early in the day before you save anyone else!"

Kizzy laughed. "Don't be silly. You're not going to need any supernatural help. Emergency or otherwise. You'll be fine."

"I don't know, Kizz. My doctor was concerned about my small hips. Apparently, this baby's got Gordon's big head."

Kizzy was quiet. At last, she said, "In that case, I'd rather have you down here too. How soon can you get here?"

"I don't know. It depends on whether or not Dad will come with me. I don't want to leave him here alone like this."

"Now you've got me concerned. I thought he was just a little down. It sounds like you're really worried for him. What's going on?"

"I don't really know. He's just moping around. It's weird. He mutters to himself. He's up late at night, pacing. And you should see his white whiskers! He's not shaving every morning like he always has."

"Oh dear. That's not like him. He's always groomed to perfection and has a plan for every day. What could've happened?"

"I'm not sure. I think it may have been something with a neighbor."

"A neighbor? I can't think of anyone who would upset him to this point. Can you?"

Ruth adjusted her posture and stuffed a pillow behind her back. "Maybe. Have you met the woman from one street over? I'm not sure which house she lives in, but she's very beautiful. She has long white hair and dresses like Jackie O."

"Huh? I don't think I've seen any neighbors like that. But if she broke his heart, we have to snap him out of it. Do you think they were having a fling?"

"It wouldn't surprise me. He's been alone for twenty years."

"Yeah, ever since Mom died. It's about damn time he got out there. But to get out there and get your heart broken? Oh, I feel so bad for him."

"You know, it's weird, but that neighbor said he called her after I called him crying. And about an hour later when I got here, she came over and we had tea. She made it with an actual leaf from a plant she had in her bag. And after that, I felt incredibly good. I thought it was just the chat and caffeine that perked me up, but that feeling of strength and vitality hasn't gone away. When I offered Dad a cup, he looked like he'd seen a ghost."

"Did he drink it?"

"No. He refused. Then he sent me shopping. He hasn't been the same since."

"This is definitely weird. Yes, come to Puerto Rico, and bring him with you."

Ruth let out a sigh of relief. "Thanks. There's a little something I have to do here, but count on us showing up very soon."

"Just give me a call or text with your flight information. I'll come and get you at the airport. If I can't for some reason, Noah will."

"That sounds good. I miss you, Kizz."

"I miss you too, Ruthie. I'm so glad you're coming. I can't wait to see you!"

"Me too. Maybe Dad will snap out of his depression down there."

"He was perfectly fine when he was here last week. In fact, he seemed to really like it here. I think it will do him good to get away from whatever it is up there that's bothering him."

"I agree. Let's figure out a way to get him to come with me, and if I have to, I'll ask for help to kidnap him."

Kizzy laughed. "Well, you sound great. And soon, I hope all three of you will be here!"

"Your idea was a bust, Fate."

"What idea?"

"The Wiccan priest you fixed me up with. At first, he seemed nice—a little old-fashioned, but not in a bad way. Then he began telling me how he and his friends worship me. Did you know they bring me food and wine, then eat and drink it themselves?"

Fate rolled her eyes. "Talk about old-fashioned. Bringing an offering is a custom from ancient pagan times."

"Well, whatever it was, Pan showed up and ruined everything."

Fate shrugged. "Hey, if it's meant to be…"

"Stop. I don't want to hear it!"

"Look, it's not as bad as all that. It was only your first try. There's a saying, 'You have to kiss a lot of frogs before you find your prince.'"

"Huh?"

"Look, I have to go. There's a wedding that isn't meant to be. I need to get the husband who's still alive to the ceremony before…well, before she commits bigotry."

"You mean bigamy?"

"Oh." Fate giggled. "Yeah, that. Well, toodles!"

Fate disappeared, leaving Gaia more frustrated than ever. Then she decided even though it sounded ridiculous, she was going to try kissing a few frogs. She loved her adorable little coqui in the rain forest, so why not just start there?

Sitting on a damp rock in the middle of some dripping trees and pungent green foliage, she peeked around to be sure she was alone. Before long, one of her cute little coqui hopped up to her.

"Ribbit."

"Hi there," Mother Nature said sweetly. "Would you mind just hopping up onto my hand for a moment?"

The little frog happily jumped up onto her hand and allowed her to bring him up to eye level.

It didn't look like a prince was in there, but oh well. She wouldn't know if she didn't try. She gave the little frog a kiss on the head.

Nothing happened.

I hope I don't have to kiss him on the mouth. I may have invented my beautiful creatures and love every one of them, sort of, but kissing frogs on the nonexistent lips? I just don't know…

"Ribbit."

"Sure. You can go now." She set her hand down next to the rock, and the little frog jumped off. With one more leap, he disappeared into the brush.

She sighed. *What now? Fate did say I had to kiss a lot of frogs, right? Oh dear. This had better work.*

"Come to me, little frogs. It's your Mother who loves you."

Many frogs came hopping over to her, and she rose and scanned the dozen or so that just showed up. Then she saw more and more hopping from a distance. "Oh brother," she mumbled. "I'd better get started if I'm going to do this." She picked up one frog after another, kissing each on its head. Nothing happened. Rinse, repeat. Nothing happened. What the heck? This wasn't the way it was supposed to go, was it? How many is a lot of frogs? At last, she grew weary, and the frogs had all had their turn and hopped off happily.

"I have no idea what that was about." Was Fate trying to be funny? Had she and Karma set up this little joke? It was too embarrassing to ask. She just knew that there was more behind it, but she hated to admit when she didn't understand something. Well, it would have to wait. She had other things to do.

When the last of her stupid frogs departed, she looked around at her beautiful tropical forest. Deciding to take a short break from her usual routine of trying to fix everyone else's problems, she strolled along the hillside, valuing some of her accomplishments.

It was time she took a few moments for herself. She never took an hour or even a few minutes just to witness and appreciate all her hard labor. Gazing over the landscape, she saw the cliff where she and Aaron had stood and admired her beautiful little heart-leaf plants. She strolled over there and gazed down over the mountainside, which was still covered with plants, but some of them looked like they had broken in half.

That was weird. She refused to believe it meant she had a broken heart, but who else could cause all that damage? "Must've been a rainstorm," she mused. "Those are pretty sturdy little leaves, but nothing really does well when it's bombarded with heavy rain."

She couldn't help thinking about Aaron as she gazed out over the plants. She didn't understand why he would continue refusing her help when she could've cut through so many layers of red tape for him. It must be that stupid false pride thing she accidentally injected the male of the species with. She was trying to give them pride in their accomplishments. Instead, she seemed to give them pride to the point of being full of themselves.

This could have been one of Aaron's finest accomplishments. She still wanted it to be, but she didn't dare interfere with the proud American doctor. He would eventually find the things he was looking for if he really wanted to succeed. He said he had to find a place to analyze it, then test it, then document all the side effects he was fearing.

She really didn't think there would be any if it was used in its most raw form. Her leaf could just be swirled in a cup of water, and he'd have exactly the right formula without adding anything to it. She recalled the same situation happening with other plants. Ancient people just chewed the leaf or root or dropped the leaf in their drinking water, but not modern man. They had to powder it and grind it and liquefy it and then do all kinds of things to preserve it. Why did they have to interfere with her expertise all the time?

She really couldn't continue along this line of thinking. She would just get depressed. So she made up her mind to go talk to Fate about the next date, because she could do this. She could find a person or paranormal to enjoy companionship with. Maybe there was nothing else she could have except a partnership or friendship, but she still longed for a loving relationship. She didn't need marriage. She would be hard-pressed to come up with a birth certificate. What would it say, anyway? Place of birth: the universe. Date: more than thirteen billion years ago, give or take a million. *Yeah, that would go over well with a justice of the peace.*

A little froggy leapt up to her feet. "Ribbit."

She folded her arms and looked down at the little coqui. "You didn't get your kiss on the head?"

"Ribbit."

Well, just in case… What's one more? She picked up the frog, kissed it on the head, placed it on the ground, and watched it hop away. "That really was a useless exercise."

She needed an explanation for this. "Fate?" When her sister didn't appear, she opened her mouth wider and bellowed "Fate!"

Fate appeared with her laptop balanced on one arm.

"I'm here. No need to yell."

"What was this nonsense you were telling me about kissing frogs?"

"Haven't you ever heard about the story of a witch placing a curse on a prince, turning him into a frog? The only way to break the curse was to get a princess to kiss the frog, and then he'd turn back into a prince."

"But why didn't you tell me that? I'm not a princess, and all this was for nothing."

Fate looked like she was about to giggle, but she slapped her hand over her mouth. After taking a deep breath and composing herself, she said, "Did you actually try kissing frogs?"

Gaia put her hands on her hips. "What did you expect me to do? You told me I'd have to kiss a lot of frogs before I found my prince. Was that just a practical joke?"

"Not at all. I expected you to understand it was a parable."

"Oh fuck," Gaia muttered under her breath.

Fate cleared her throat. "I have a few more candidates for you to look at. Are you interested? Or would you like to do this another time?"

Gaia let out a deep breath. All the leaves around them fluttered. "Fine, I'll see what you have, but I'd like to sit someplace warm with a sweet umbrella drink while we do this."

"Excellent idea!" Fate said. With the snap of her fingers, the two of them were sitting at a hilltop bar, overlooking the Caribbean islands and beautiful sunny spots where the clouds parted. "Okay, I have three possibles for you to look at." She set the laptop in front of Gaia.

Examining the pictures and profiles, Gaia nixed the politician immediately. She wanted nothing to do with politics and couldn't understand why Fate would recommend someone like that. She hated being lied to. Politicians seemed to do more lying than truth telling.

Next, she looked at the picture of a newscaster. He was handsome but again too much into mankind's failings and foolishness. She imagined his job must be depressing, since she had seen the news a few times and it was always depressing.

Then she saw a basketball player, a star, his profile said. Well, he might be a little full of himself, but she could handle that. She was a little full of herself too, or so she had been told, so who knows…maybe it would work out okay. And if he was used to winning these games, he was apt to be frequently in a good mood. "Okay. This one." She pointed to the tall, good-looking basketball player.

"Excellent choice," Fate said. "I'll set something up and let you know where and when to meet him."

"I thought I was supposed to email or something first."

"I'll check him out with Karma, but I want this to go well for you. If you already like his looks and he makes you happy, that's all that counts."

———

For once, Gaia was encouraged. The date with the basketball player was going well. He picked a lovely restaurant. He was respectful, charming, witty, but kind of dumb. Even so, she wasn't turned off completely. And then…

Pan showed up in all his half-goat glory.

Crap! She'd have to erase everyone's memories, including her date's. "What do you want, Pan?"

"I simply want to help."

"I don't need, nor want, your *help*. Get out."

"Sheesh. Rude! I won't forget this, Gaia." Before he disappeared, he added, "And neither will you."

Since it was such a short visit, Gaia was able to reset the timeline back to before the interruption.

She swirled her red wine. "So, you were saying?"

"Uh… I don't remember, but I have something else to say."

"Sure. What's that?"

"You really need to dye your hair. I don't want to look like I'm dating my grandma. And get those eyebrows tweezed. I hear there are a lot of different ways to have them professionally shaped."

She adjusted her posture, trying not to lose it. "Oh? Where do you hear that?" she asked sweetly.

"Oh, you know…the girls talk outside our locker room. And while you're at it, you might want to find someone to help you pick out clothes—something from this century. The sixteen-year-old groupies dress better than you."

Gaia's mouth gaped open. This wasn't the guy she was sitting with a moment ago. Before, he was full of compliments. Now, nothing but criticism.

"What are sixteen-year-olds doing outside your locker room—besides discussing fashion?"

He grinned. "Oh, they're not all sixteen-year-old girls. There are plenty of juicy women just waiting to take a player home."

"And do you go home with them?"

"If they're willing…why not?"

"Would you continue to do that even if we're dating?"

"Sure. If they're really hot."

"WTF?" That was an expression she'd heard humans and paranormals use when they were baffled.

He leaned forward. "I'm just being honest. You wouldn't want me to lie, would you?"

"I—I guess not."

"Wow. You guess not? You can't even commit to the importance of honesty? That's also a red flag."

"Red flag? What do you mean by that?"

"It means danger. You know. Like at the beach when

people should stay out of the water, the lifeguards fly a red flag. Or maybe you haven't been to the beach lately." He looked her up and down. "You don't exactly have a tan and a bikini-ready body. Do you?"

Gaia stood up so abruptly, the table tipped. As far as she was concerned, it didn't tip quite far enough, so she flipped it, spilling red wine all over his white shirt.

"Fuck!"

"Not with you, that's for sure." She stormed out of the restaurant as people stared at her.

Finding a private spot near Mount Olympus, she cried out, "Pan! Get your hairy ass here, right now!"

He appeared, chewing a mouthful of grass. As soon as he'd swallowed, he said, "Yes, my Goddess?"

"You ruined my date, didn't you?"

"Ruined it? Oh dear. I meant to improve it. Didn't you want to know what your date was really thinking?"

"No. And how did you do it, anyway?"

"Just a tiny truth spell."

"Well, spell this… B-U-C-K-O-F-F!"

His back heels left the grass involuntarily, and before they hit the ground again, he disappeared. She didn't like to manipulate her gods, but this one needed to be reminded who had power over whom. He needed to be punished.

Unfortunately, she heard him laughing from the ether. *Gaaah! Gods are so hard to control!*

―――∿∿∿―――

"Fate, what were you thinking?" Gaia shouted.

Fate entered the ether and sighed. "Why don't we go somewhere, and you can tell me what happened?"

Mother Nature grabbed Fate's hand, and the two of them materialized on the top of a mountain with a beautiful view. It was pretty Mount Lafayette in New Hampshire's White Mountains.

"Okay, so here we are." Fate took up a lotus position on a nearby rock. "What happened?"

"What happened is that you picked a loser for me. A crazy person. I don't know what you were thinking." Gaia clasped her hands behind her back and paced back and forth in front of her sister.

"I didn't pick him, remember? This is why I had *you* pick. I knew you'd try to blame anything that went wrong on me."

Gaia stopped in her tracks and whirled on her. "*I* picked him?"

Fate gaped at her. "I showed you some pictures of possible matches. And you decided which picture you liked."

"I did not."

"Did too."

Karma appeared between them. Her red hair blew in the wind until she grasped it and tied it into a knot. "Don't fight. You sound like children. I think what happened was just a misunderstanding. Now before we move on, try to be clear about how you want these matches to happen. But what I want to know first is what went wrong with each one so far, so the mistakes don't get repeated."

Gaia frowned. "I know it may have seemed like a good idea to match me with a Wiccan. He obviously believes in the Goddess—with a capital G—and a whole host of other gods and goddesses. He was a little star-struck, and I have to admit I enjoyed that a little bit.

"However, he has some weird-ass ideas about me. About all of us. And he's wrong. I don't require people to wear black robes, meet in circles under the full moon, and hold elaborate rituals." She snorted.

Karma shook her head. "So what? If it makes them feel more connected to you, what's the harm?"

"Okay, okay," Fate said. "No one is going to be perfect. And no human knows the real you. You're going to have to deal with that."

"I agree," said Karma. "You are one mysterious mother…"

Gaia folded her arms. "What's that supposed to mean?"

Karma and Fate glanced at each other and giggled. "Look, Sister," Fate said. "We love you. We want you to be happy. We know it's not easy to find a relationship built on friendship and trust in this world. It involves time—and getting to know each other. All your humans have to do that. And your paranormals have an even more difficult time, because they have a secret to protect until they know for sure they can trust the other person completely. Think of the box you've put them in."

Gaia threw her hands in the air. "Is that what it takes? I have to get to know someone and let them get to know me without revealing who I am? That's a really strange set of circumstances. Did you set that up, Fate?"

"Um, no. You did!" Fate lowered her gaze and voice. "I may have contributed to it, however. I never expected it to be this hard. I created soul mates. I thought they would recognize each other. And sometimes, they do. There really are incidents of love at first sight. Unfortunately, these days, a lot of people wind up talking themselves out of the idea. There's only so much I can do for people without interfering."

Gaia sank down on a nearby rock and clasped her hands around her knees. "You're right. It's difficult. I suppose I have a little more compassion for the paranormals, especially when they have to resort to humans, trying to find a partner they can share a life with."

Fate let out a breath she'd been holding. "Finally. She sees it."

"Sees what?" Gaia asked.

Fate and Karma exchanged another glance.

"What? What am I supposed to see?" Gaia rose and jammed her hands on her hips, leaning forward, challenging her sisters.

Karma smirked. "Cancel that thought, Fate. She still doesn't get it."

Gaia whirled on Fate. "So are you going to tell me? What am I missing?"

"Gaia, you've always been a little hard on your people and paranormals," Karma said. "We only wish you would be a little more understanding. It's hard enough that you stick them with this all or nothing rule, never to reveal themselves to humans. Never? What about when they fall in love with one of them? Are they supposed to hide their secret forever?"

"You have seen some of these relationships yourself," Fate added. "They grow and unfold the way any relationship grows and unfolds. They are attracted to each other. They get to know each other. They get to like each other. Eventually, they come to love each other. And then what do you expect them to do? Lie to each other for the rest of their lives?"

Mother Nature shrugged. "Couldn't they just fall in love with their own kind in the first place?"

Fate approached gingerly and put her arm around her sister, probably taking her immortal life in her hands, so to speak. "Love is love, my darling sister. I do create soul mates, and sometimes they're unlikely matches. And sometimes if they're too much alike, that causes problems. I try to find people who complement each other. Just as I was trying to do with you in the beginning of this 'mission implausible.' I was trying to find people whose strengths would help ameliorate your deficiencies and people whose faults would be supplemented by your strengths. I wasn't really impressed with the results of that endeavor."

"Deficiencies? Fate, you know I don't have much in the way of faults to be supplemented by a human or paranormal."

Fate and Karma burst out laughing.

Mother Nature frowned. "What are you... Never mind. I'm not an idiot. I do have faults. I don't like to admit it, since I'm clearly awesome. But you're right, there are things I could do to improve myself. Such as my approach to problems. But you understand how frustrating my problems are, don't you? I'm trying to save this planet while people are determined to destroy it! How would you deal with that? What if all your soul mates just refused to recognize their hunger for each other and went on a rampage against love?"

"I *do* know what that's like, Sister. It's very upsetting. There are those who think romance indicates weakness. They couldn't be more wrong. It takes real strength to put yourself out there and allow someone to know every part of you. The good, the bad, the ugly... Love usually brings out the beautiful and best in people. How crazy is it that some people just turn their backs on it because of their flawed thinking?"

Gaia nodded. "I guess you do understand in a way. But *you* don't have a partner. How do you cope without a companion or partner to share your frustrations with? How do you deal with the exact same thing you're handling for others every day?"

"Who says I am dealing with this alone?" Fate winked.

"Oh? You've been holding out on me?"

Fate smiled and shrugged. "There are a few little things you don't know about me."

"Apparently so!" Karma said. "I didn't even know about this."

"Fate, I really don't think I can handle this whole process," Gaia said.

"Are you saying that humans and paranormals, the very beings you looked down upon, are able to do something you can't?"

Mother Nature clenched her fists, trying to hold in her frustration. She tried and tried until it exploded. "Gaaah!" A huge wind blew up and swirled around the mountain. A glider almost got caught in it and headed for the ground immediately, choosing a safe landing while the pilot still could.

Fate crossed her arms. "I'll leave you to contemplate your possible faults. And I hope you will learn there are some things about the lives of humans and paranormals that require a great deal of bravery. Sometimes, making oneself vulnerable is the hardest thing to do."

Gaia sank down onto her rock and waved her sisters off. "Go now. I need to think."

Chapter 9

WHILE RUTH WAS IN HER ROOM, PACKING FOR HER TRIP TO Puerto Rico, Aaron paced across his own bedroom, ignoring the empty suitcase on his bed. Should he go too? Was he apt to run into a certain overly helpful deity there? Of course he should. His daughter needed him. Or did she? Her sister was also a doctor, and they were best friends.

His mind wandered. He couldn't forget the natural beauty and vulnerability of the goddess, nay, *woman* he now knew was Gaia herself. It was amazing that he'd even met her. The powerful goddess was intimidating without realizing it. He understood why so many were afraid of her and why she was lonely.

He had to admit, he was lonely too.

Since he couldn't stop thinking about her, he had to question whether or not he might need that little heart-shaped plant's cure too. *No.* He was not brokenhearted. And even if he was, he'd never try an untested new medicine. *Not until it's analyzed, compared to similar chemical formulas, and deemed safe.* If the process lasted as long as he figured it would, *time* would take care of the sadness and loss.

Ruth had been hinting she'd like to move to Puerto Rico permanently, to be near Kizzy. She had come right out and asked Aaron, if she did, would he consider moving too?

He was tempted. There wasn't much to hold him to Massachusetts if his dear daughters were both in Puerto Rico. Also, there was the matter of the plants. Regulations wouldn't allow him to take them off the island. That meant if he wanted to continue his work on the discovery of the century, he'd have to do it there.

But with so many scientific requirements, could it be done? Was there a compounding pharmacy down there? Many businesses had been destroyed in the hurricane; he couldn't be sure what was still up and running.

"You haven't started packing yet?"

He jumped. He'd been so preoccupied, he hadn't heard Ruth come in.

"I—I don't know how to pack for a month. I'm not sure I have enough clothing."

Ruth burst out laughing. "There's such a thing as doing laundry—even if we have to find a river and beat it on a rock." She chuckled and shook her head. "You really are hopeless, Dad."

Odd that she used that word. He felt hopeless sometimes...but never more than now.

"Is it safe to talk with you?" Fate's voice asked.

"No. That's it! I'm done with internet dating," Gaia announced to the ether.

Fate popped in and patted Mother Nature on the shoulder. "There, there. I'm so sorry it didn't work out with the basketball player. Let's try something a little different."

Gaia crossed her arms. "I don't know if I want to try anything at all."

Fate handed her a glass of white wine and instantly transported them both to a quiet terrace attached to a villa in Italy. "I've actually found someone for you myself. I think you'll like him and vice versa. He's an astronomer. A little older, but with that comes maturity. He's a bit of a geek, as they say, but these days, it's a compliment! He won't run around on you. Plus he's intelligent and loves the universe as much as you do."

Gaia scratched her head. "I admit, he sounds interesting. I think that's the way we should've gone about it all along. Please, no more internet dating."

Fate raised her hand, fashioning her fingers in a strange formation. "I won't, Scout's honor. But this date seems very promising. Will you give him a chance?"

Gaia reclined on the lounge chair and took a sip of wine, making it look like she was mulling it over. It might go well...or at least better than the other disaster dates.

They could gaze at the stars together. She knew the humans had named her constellations, and she hadn't paid much attention to those names for the most part. When they came out at night and twinkled hello, some were actually saying goodbye. The suns that had died long ago were still visible because their light took years to reach Earth—hence the term light-years. But of course, he would know that.

"Okay. I'll try one more date. If it doesn't work, I'm done."

"You can't guarantee the next one is the last one. If it is, that's wonderful. That's all we want. The one. But if it doesn't work out, don't give up. Please. You still need a companion, ideally a lover. I know you don't believe you do, but trust me. Once you've experienced the best sex there is, you'll want to be sexually active."

Gaia chuckled. "I look forward to it, if I ever get to that point with anyone."

"So you're willing to meet the astronomer?"

"I said I was, didn't I?"

"I just wanted to make sure, because he's waiting for you in his observatory now."

Gaia sat up straight and faced her sister head on. "Are you kidding me? You were so sure of my answer that you already set up a date?"

Fate shrugged. "I didn't know for sure, but I really hoped I could talk you into it. And now that I have, don't keep him waiting."

Gaia rose quickly and looked down at her toga. "What should I wear? I've been told my fashion choices are last century. Also that my hair is not a good color for dateable women and that my eyebrows are too full or something…"

"Who the hell told you all that?"

Gaia frowned. "The basketball player."

Fate sighed. "I'm so sorry. Maybe you're right, and the internet is not the place to find your dates. I'll scour the earth if I need to. But I think this guy might be the one."

Gaia nodded. "That's all well and good, but how do I look?"

"Like a goddess." Fate smiled.

"But I need to look like a human." Gaia spied a magazine on a nearby table and strode over to it. She opened the pages and flipped through until she saw someone who looked smartly put-together and adopted her outfit. "Okay, are these clothes all right?"

Fate appraised her from foot to head. Brown leather boots, tight brown pants with a pronounced pouch at thigh height. Plus a houndstooth jacket and a riding helmet.

"Oh wait. There's one more accessory." Gaia snapped her fingers, and a moment later she held a riding crop.

"Let me see that magazine."

Gaia walked over to her sister and handed the open magazine to her. Fate flipped back to the cover and laughed. "This is an equestrian magazine. And I'm sorry, but you look ridiculous. You would look better as yourself in a toga than in this getup on a date."

"Are you saying I should wear my toga?"

Fate laughed. "No, of course not. Oh my. Let's get Karma to dress you. She has great taste."

Before they could call her, Karma showed up. "I hear you need my help."

"Were you eavesdropping?"

Karma shrugged. "Li'l bit."

Gaia placed her hands on her hips. "Don't do that—even though it came in handy this time. So can you help me pick out an outfit to wear on a date with an astronomer?"

"Absolutely." She snapped her fingers, and Gaia looked down at an attractive dress in midnight blue with a pattern of stars all over it.

Gaia smiled. "It's perfect. Thank you."

"Any time. Now, have fun on your date. Oh! You need shoes." She snapped her fingers, and the brown leather boots disappeared. Gaia looked down at her feet and almost fell over. She was wearing the most ridiculous high heels. The silver shoes went nicely with the stars, but the heels... No way. She stepped out of the shoes, snapped off the heels, and put them back on. Her height dropped at least four inches, but they still felt uncomfortable and just looked wrong.

Fate said, "Let me help." She snapped her fingers, and the shoes became ballet flats. "There."

"Yes. Better. Now I'm ready. Where is he?"

"I think you'll be happy. He's in California. I know how you like that state because of its many geographical variations. Mountains, ocean, desert, lakes... everything."

"Terrific. I should get going."

Fate snapped her fingers, and Gaia stood outside the door of a large domed building.

She knocked, and the door flew open, revealing a bespectacled older gentleman with thinning gray hair and a toothy grin. He wasn't bad-looking, but he wasn't dressed as well as she was. His pants were corduroy, and his casual shirt was plaid. But who was she to complain if he was a nice man? Maybe Karma could help them both pick out a new wardrobe sometime.

"Welcome. I assume you're Gaia," he said.

"I am. And you are?"

His brows raised. They weren't groomed any better than hers. "Your friend didn't tell you my name?"

Gaia just shook her head.

"Call me Dr. Ned for now. That's what the kids call me when I speak at their schools." He stuck out his hand for a handshake.

She shook his hand and wondered when he was going to invite her in. "May I come in, or did you want to look at the stars outside?"

He slapped his forehead. "I'm sorry. Please come in. I'm not used to having company." He backed away from the door, and as he did, his corduroy pants squeaked.

"So you're a doctor," she said. "I know a doctor. He's a cardiac surgeon. Are you a cardiologist? Or a surgeon?"

He stared at her, incredulous. "No, I have a PhD, not an MD. I'm a doctor of astronomy, and my specialty is observational astronomy."

Mother Nature was puzzled, but she was getting used to that feeling as she learned more about human beings up close and personal. "Are the stars sick?" she asked.

He laughed. "You were joking. I get it now. Sorry, I'm not always skillful when it comes to recognizing jokes. Good one!"

He smiled, and she felt a little more at ease.

"Let me take you up to the observatory. I'm proud to say I have one of the most powerful telescopes on the West Coast."

"Really?" She wasn't much better at conversation than he was, but she'd give it a try—for now. Every time he moved, his pants squeaked. That was bound to drive her crazy before long.

When they finally reached his telescope, he asked, "Do you know much about the stars?"

She smirked. "Why don't you tell me what you want me to know, the same way you'd explain it to school children. I'd like to hear what you're teaching them."

He smiled. "Of course. We'll start at the beginning then. Take a look in here." He pointed to an eyepiece that magnified the night sky hundreds of times. "With so many stars in the universe, the night sky is a beautiful sight. But not all stars are the same. I'll explain the different types of stars so you'll know exactly what you're gazing at each night. First of all, what is a star? Do you know?"

Did he really want her to answer that? Of course she knew. She had created them, but how could she explain that? Fortunately, he continued his lecture.

"Stars are burning balls of gas, and from a far distance, they all look pretty much the same. But did you know that there are different *types* of stars? Here in my telescope, we can take a closer look at those twinkling stars you see way up high."

She couldn't help tuning him out. He droned on and on about things she already knew, but he took all the beauty and magic out of it.

He let his hand drop, and she realized she'd better start paying attention. Maybe she was supposed to ask a question or feign interest.

Much to her annoyance, he continued to lecture.

"Another type of star is the *white dwarf star*. This star forms from a red giant that loses its outer layers, leaving behind mostly carbon and oxygen, then shrinks into a very compact star. It's fairly cool, so it gives off a weak, bluish-white color. There's one up there called Sirius."

"Are you serious?" She winked.

"Ha. I see what you did there."

Pan hid among the scaffolding, out of sight. He had hoped this date would flop on its own, but it didn't seem to be failing. In fact, he was concerned about it succeeding!

Time for another teeny-weeny truth spell, only this

time, I'll put it on her! He almost laughed out loud and had to press his hand over his mouth as he considered the possibilities. *I can't wait to see this!*

—◆◆◆—

So far, this date seemed to be going pretty well. She really should ask a question or something. "That all sounds fine," she said. "Now, how old is the universe?"

"About fourteen billion years old."

"Correct. Do you know how I know that?"

He grinned. "No. Are you a scientist too? Or maybe a teacher? I never did ask what you do for a living."

She laughed. "I'm Mother freakin' Nature. That big bang that happened fourteen billion years ago? Yeah, that was me. I sneezed. Bet you didn't know that."

He took a step back. Then after a brief hesitation, he burst out laughing. "Oh. That's funny. You're making jokes again. Fate didn't tell me you were so funny."

"Fate? Oh, my sister, yes. Yes, she is the one who set us up."

"Yeah, I had never met her before, but she seemed familiar. I thought it was strange that she would walk right up to me and ask if I'd like to go out with someone."

"Is that what she did?"

"Yup. I was standing in Starbucks, waiting for my latte. She was right behind me, and she said, 'Hey, you look like a nice guy. Are you involved with anyone romantically?'"

Gaia snorted. "She said she was going to do this the old-fashioned way since internet dating wasn't working for me, but I didn't know she was going to approach unsuspecting strangers. I'm sorry about that."

"Oh! Don't be. I'm enjoying our date. Are you?"

Gaia shrugged. "I've had worse."

The doctor's face fell.

"Oh, don't be upset. It's just very, very difficult to find someone who can become an equal partner with Mother Nature. As you can imagine."

Dr. Ned tipped his head and eyed her carefully. "You really believe you're Mother Nature?"

Gaia laughed. "Of course, and I can prove it to you."

"Okaaaayyy…"

"Follow me outside."

The two of them tromped down the metal stairs, and Gaia took the lead, listening to his pants squeak behind her. *Squeak, squeak, squeak. Yep, that would drive me crazy.* She opened the door, and he followed her out hesitantly. It looked as if he might be thinking about slamming the door before he stepped through to the other side. But he eventually followed her out and closed it carefully behind himself.

"Okay, observe." She swept her arm across the lawn, and nothing seemed to happen.

"Am I supposed to see something?"

"Hang on." Gaia twirled her finger, and the sun rose. Green sprouts shot up from the grass. Then the lightest-pink buds on a tree opened and showed off their darker pink blossoms. Before long, they were joined by white lilies of the valley, yellow and purple pansies, and ferns, and then the yard was exploding with all kinds of flowering bushes and sturdy ground cover.

Dr. Ned staggered backward a few paces. "How? How did you do that?"

She placed a hand on her hip and frowned. "I told you… I'm Mother Nature."

Dr. Ned passed out.

"Oh, for the love of me."

Pan came trotting out from behind a rock, laughing and bleating, laughing and bleating.

"Okay, dipshit. What did you do this time?"

Pan could barely contain himself. He kept trying to talk but would burst out laughing and had to start over. Finally, he took a few deep breaths and said, "Just another little truth spell. Except this time, I cast it on you!"

As he rolled back and forth in the grass laughing, she grasped his scruffy beard and yelled, "Fate! Karma! Come here."

Pan tried to pull away, but she just grabbed him with her other hand and held him tight to her leg. "Oh no, you're not getting away this time."

Fate and Karma appeared simultaneously.

"What happened?" Fate asked.

Karma checked out the male figure facedown on the ground, saw Gaia with her teeth clenched, hanging on to Pan, and started to chuckle.

"It's not funny!" Gaia groused.

"It's kind of funny."

"How can you say that? *He* could be dead."

"He's not dead," Karma said, poking the doctor, still unconscious on the ground. "He's not even injured."

"He passed out. He could have been injured if he fell on a rock," Gaia said.

"How did it happen?" Fate asked.

"Ask this dumbass. Last time, he cast a truth spell on my date. This time, he cast the truth spell on *me!* Here I am telling the scientist all about the big bang because I was there!"

"And she said she sneezed," Pan added. "She caused the big bang with a big sneeze! She probably farted, since it was a gas explosion!" Pan laughed and laughed and laughed.

Mother Nature yanked his goatee and yelled, "Stop it. You're a menace."

Karma crossed her arms. "Do you mean to tell us you've interfered with her date?"

Pan smirked. "I don't know if I'd call it interference. I was trying to help. I think honesty is a very good policy, don't you?"

"Let's see how much you like it." Mother Nature kicked him and said, "Why are you doing this?"

"Because you insulted me. I volunteered to be your mate, and you all laughed. How would you feel if someone you admired laughed in your face?"

Fate sighed. "I see your point. Your feelings were hurt, but that did not give you license to interfere with and ruin her dates."

"What should I have done, then?"

Karma put her hands on her hips and leaned over him. "Oh, I don't know. Maybe *not* ruin her dates? Maybe tell us how you felt? Allow us to apologize for hurting you?"

"Okay. Here's how I felt. I felt insulted, slighted, disrespected, offended, outraged, snubbed, hurt…"

Gaia rolled her eyes. "We get it. You felt terrible because you were inadvertently insulted."

"Inadvertently? No. It was advertently! Very advertently."

"I assure you, we didn't set out to insult you," Fate said. "I just didn't feel you were a good match. I didn't mean to upset you."

"Well, you did. You all owe me an apology."

"If I gave you any false hope, I apologize. I am nothing if not extremely honest," Mother Nature said. "Sometimes a little tactless, but as honest as I can be without doing…that." She pointed to the PhD facedown on the ground.

Karma sashayed over to Gaia and leaned in. "I think we need to do something to teach Pan a lesson."

"I agree. Perhaps we should strand him on a desert island."

"No. Goats are good swimmers. He'll just consider it a vacation," Fate said. "How about stranding him on a high mountaintop? No. That wouldn't work. Goats climb huge mountains all the time."

"Leave this to me," Karma said. "I know exactly what to do." She narrowed her eyes at the goat god, and he started to shiver. "You can let go of him now, Sister."

As soon as she did, both Karma and Pan disappeared.

Gaia took a deep breath and looked at the body lying on the ground. "I don't know if I should be here when Dr. Ned wakes up."

Fate shrugged. "I don't think it'll hurt."

"He already thinks I'm a kook. I'll help you get him inside and lay him down someplace comfortable, but then I'm going to leave."

"Don't you think we should erase his mind first?" Fate asked.

"Well, duh. But only up to the place where Pan interfered. It was going well, and I don't want him to think my not seeing him again was because of anything he did wrong."

"Oh. You don't want a second date?"

"No. There's something missing. I think you call it a spark—the sexual attraction people feel for a potential mate."

"Have you ever felt it with anyone?"

"Um…I may have—once."

The two goddesses carried the poor man inside his observatory and laid him on his couch. As soon as they'd propped a pillow under his head, Gaia stood next to him and wiped his brow. His eyes fluttered open.

"Where am I? What happened?"

"You're on your own couch. I'm afraid you don't look well," Gaia said. "I called Fate to help me carry you to a comfortable place. I think you just fainted."

"Oh? I didn't know I was sick. I felt fine before. How long have I been out?"

"Not long. I don't think it's anything serious," Gaia said. "You'll feel better in a few hours."

He reached for her hand. "I'm glad you were here. Usually, I'm all alone."

"Thank you for a lovely evening. I hope you'll continue dating. You're a wonderful guy. I'm just too busy right now. My sister really had no business setting me up with anyone."

Fate frowned at her. "We're sorry to have wasted your time," she said. "Are you feeling better?"

"I feel fine."

Gaia smiled. "Good. We'll be on our way now."

The two of them walked out of the observatory, and as soon as Fate closed the door, she whirled on Gaia. "I guess that truth spell Pan placed on you is gone now."

"Thank goodness. Truth sucks. I had no idea the truth hurts so much."

Fate rolled her eyes. "Now do you see what you do to others *all the friggin' time*?"

Gaia hung her head and looked contrite. "Yes. Fine. That's all true. But I'll have to contemplate that later. We need to get out of here."

"Agreed. Let's go back to that villa in Tuscany and finish our wine."

"Sounds like a good idea," Gaia said.

But before the two of them disappeared off the California hilltop, Karma returned.

"What did you do with Pan?" Gaia asked.

Karma snickered. "I turned him full goat, and now he's the mascot of a college football team called the Rams."

Chapter 10

"SHE'S GETTING OUT," DAWN YELLED.

Luca rushed into the kitchen from the backyard. Glancing around the kitchen, he asked, "What? Where?"

"My mother's getting out of prison!" She waved a letter.

"Oh." He smiled. "I thought you'd trapped a mouse in a jar or something."

She laughed as Luca threw his arms around her, giving her a warm hug.

"Really? Your mom is getting out of prison? When?"

"It will be in time for our wedding!" Dawn said. "She's getting out in a couple of days."

"If it's an early release, she'll probably be on probation in Boston. Sorry, babe. I don't think she'll be able to attend."

Dawn stepped back and rested her hands on her hips. "She was released for good behavior, and she's going to a halfway house—not back to the old neighborhood. How can you just dismiss the possibility? She's my mother, and I want her at our wedding. If there's any way..."

Looking at the ground, Luca shook his head. "I'm sorry, babe. I don't think there is. Probation is all up to the judge. They can pretty much set the conditions any way they want. I doubt many of them would let her leave the state, never mind the mainland."

"Then I'll have to talk to the judge."

"You're going to call the judge in Boston from Puerto Rico and ask him to let your mother take a plane to a tropical island and promise to come back?"

Dawn gritted her teeth and tried not to spit out the angry words she was thinking. How could he not understand? She would do anything short of moving heaven and earth, and only because she didn't have that power—but she knew people who did. "I've heard of convicts allowed to attend funerals. She's out on good behavior. There must be some precedent? I know it sounds far-fetched, but I have to try."

Luca looked at her gloomily. "Of course you can try. I just don't want you to get your hopes up."

"I can do my best. And if that doesn't work, what if maybe you and I have our wedding in Boston? I would have waited to move here if I'd thought she could attend. My mom has been in prison for three years. I thought she was going to be there for five. Now she'll be out in time."

"I don't know, babe. This is sort of a last-minute wrinkle. I'm not sure who to talk to about it. My brother wouldn't be able to attend if it were in Boston, since everyone there thinks he's dead. Maybe I can call up one of my old buddies in the Boston Police Department— not that I have a lot of them. Captain Moore was pretty cool. Maybe I can ask her what to do to get your mom down here."

Dawn calmed down. She plodded over to their kitchen table and slumped down into a chair. "I know you're right. I didn't think it would be easy, but it would be so cool if we could have her here. Trying to relocate the whole wedding up to Boston at the last minute would be ridiculous. Unless…" Her face brightened.

"Uh-oh. I know that gleam in your eye. You're getting some kind of idea."

Dawn smiled sweetly at her fiancé. "What if we had two weddings? One up there and one down here?"

Luca scratched his head. "I don't know… One of the weddings would be legal and one would just be for show. We only have one marriage license. And we'll only be issued one marriage certificate."

"I want to talk to Gran about this. Are you okay with my doing that?"

"Of course, be my guest. I may want to talk to my dad too."

"Fine. You go talk to your dad, and I'll talk to my grandmother. They live in the same house anyway, so that's handy. Do you have time now?"

Lucas brows lifted. "Now? Like right now?"

"Yeah. Do you have anything going on?"

Luca checked his watch. "I have a client to meet in a half hour. You go ahead and talk to your grandmother. In fact, that might be better than us talking to different people. I honestly don't know what my dad would think, but you can bet he'll state his opinion and insist he's right. It's what you and I decide that's most important. If you need to talk to you grandmother to figure it out, fine. You two know your mother a lot better than I do."

Dawn nodded. "That's true. And Gran's a savvy woman who won't lie to me in any way."

"That's what I like about her." Luca smiled. "Whatever you and your grandmother decide, I'm fine with it, as long as all my brothers can attend."

"Okay, it's a deal. Everything goes off as planned, but we either get my mother here or have another wedding up there."

Luca nodded. "Yep. I can deal with either of those things. Just tell me where to show up and when to say 'I do.'"

Dawn kissed Luca and grabbed her purse, stuffing the letter inside on her way out the door. All she had to do was walk up the hill to see her grandmother and Luca's parents in their solid, cinder-block home. She just hoped her Gran was home and not off with the new man in her life. It would be nice if she was out with him, but Dawn selfishly hoped she would be seeing him tonight and not today.

When Dawn knocked on the door, Gabriella opened it. "Dawn, honey! Come in, come in. You don't need to knock."

"Well, I don't want to barge in on you and the others. I mean, what if you were having a big orgy or something?"

Gabriella burst out laughing. "Oh sure. That happens all the time. Come here, you." They shared a tight hug.

"Is Gran here?"

"Yes, she is. Let me go get her."

Gabriella strode toward the back of the house, and soon Dawn's grandmother, Annette, came bustling around the corner. She opened her arms wide.

"Dawnie!"

Dawn walked into her grandmother's embrace, and they hugged hard as if they hadn't seen each other for weeks when it had been maybe two days.

"To what do I owe the honor of this visit?" her grandmother asked.

"Oh, Gran. You're being silly. Although I do have some news, and I need to talk to you about it."

Her grandmother took her hand and walked her into the kitchen. "Have a seat, sweetie."

Dawn took an empty chair at the kitchen island and wondered where Mr. Fierro was. Chances were good he was out helping his sons rebuild homes on the island. If Gabriella was trying to stay out of the way so they could talk, it wouldn't surprise her.

"Can I get you a cup of tea or coffee?" Annette asked.

"Sure. Tea, please." As Annette put some bottled water into the teapot to boil, Dawn asked, "Did you get a letter from my mom?"

"No. Should I have?"

Dawn pulled the letter out of her purse and handed it to her grandmother.

Annette scanned it, and her jaw dropped. "Lissie's getting out early?"

Dawn grinned and nodded enthusiastically.

Annette read the rest of the letter and then placed an arm around Dawn's shoulders, squeezing her sideways. "This is good news."

Dawn leaned back and scrutinized her grandmother's face. "This is *great* news! You don't seem very excited."

"Oh, I am. I love and miss my daughter. I just worry that it may be another one of those times when she'll break my heart."

Dawn took a deep breath and reminded herself that her grandmother had picked up the pieces whenever her mother had let them down. Gran had basically raised her. Her mother had been pretty unreliable, even when she wasn't in prison. "I know, Gran. I was hoping she

could come to the wedding. Luca said he'd be cool with
it, but that she'd be on probation and unable to leave
the state."

Dawn's grandmother sighed. "That's probably true.
However, judges have been known to allow unusual
visits, and since she's been on such good behavior, perhaps her probation officer can ask the judge's permission for her to attend your wedding."

"That's what I was hoping. Is there any way we can
help make that happen?"

Annette shook her head slowly. "I wouldn't interfere
if I were you. But I would suggest you write her back
as soon as possible and tell her she's invited. Don't give
her too many details, and tell her you'd love to have her
visit and attend the wedding *if* she can get her probation
officer to agree. We don't want to do anything to get her
into more trouble."

Dawn's bubble burst. "You don't think she would
just take off and come here, violating her probation, do
you?"

"Lord, I hope not."

"We do want her to move down here eventually,
right? That's what we've been saying all along. And it
sounded like she wanted that too."

"Oh yes. I want your mother to have the fresh start
she deserves. She's worked really hard for that early
release, and she's been clean and sober, attending the
AA and NA meetings they have there."

"Yes, that's what she told us. Apparently, it's true, if
she's getting out early."

Annette nodded. "I would like to see her get a fresh
start here as much as you. But things have to be planned,

and she's not been the most patient person when it comes to planning, waiting, and doing things one step at a time."

"Don't assume she can't do it without giving her the chance to try," Dawn said.

"I'm not saying that at all."

The teapot whistled.

"I have some instant coffee, if you'd rather have that. There's not a lot of milk to put in coffee. Can you drink it black?" Annette asked.

"I'd rather have tea. Unless I can put lots of cream and sugar in my coffee, it just tastes bitter."

"I know what you mean. In a way, I'm glad you're getting this experience."

"What experience is that?"

"Not having everything available that you're used to. I think kids—I mean, young people of your generation— can get a little spoiled. You have at least a dozen choices of brands and flavors of everything on the grocery store shelves. Down here, you're lucky if there's two of something."

Dawn smiled. "Well, I guess. But it hasn't really bothered me. I understand the island has experienced a lot of losses. We're lucky to have a few well-stocked stores."

"I think I can better understand what my daughter's been through for the last few years," Annette said. "I'm sure there were plenty of things she wished she could get even one of."

"That's true. Maybe she won't have as difficult a time adjusting to Puerto Rico as we did. But who knows if she'll be able to come here to stay soon or if she'll have to spend another two years serving probation in Boston? I worry about her getting into trouble again up there. A lot of gang members were sentenced to twenty years or more for little Mandy's kidnapping, but there were some that had nothing to do with it. They're still out there and—unless I'm very wrong—still dealing drugs."

"Let's draft a letter together, Dawnie. We can let her know we're both excited about her progress and would love to see her, either up there or down here, whatever she's allowed to do. We'll make a visit happen either way."

"That's a great idea."

"I'll be right back with a pen and paper," Annette said.

Dawn sat at the table, letting her tea steep, wondering if she would see her mom before or after the big day. It would be nice to have her in attendance, but Luca was right. She shouldn't count on anything.

She sat bolt upright. Wait! Maybe there was a way!

—⁓—

"I'm done dating humans! Can you believe he fainted just because of a little truth spell?"

Fate sighed. "You *did* tell him you were *Mother Nature*. And when you proved it, well, what did you expect?"

Gaia took a sip of her wine and looked out over the vineyards from the villa's terrace. "Look, my point is humans are too frail. They couldn't possibly handle me. So I'm done with dating."

Fate threw up her hands. "Karma! Karma, come here."

Their redheaded sister appeared, wearing spike-heeled black boots, a black leather miniskirt, and some kind of animal-print top, not real, of course. "*Now* what do you want?" She folded her arms and looked upset.

"Are we interrupting something?" Gaia asked. "We don't really need you for this conversation."

Fate slapped her hand on the lounge chair arm and said, "Oh yes, we do."

Karma muttered something under her breath and pulled up a lounge chair. Settling into it, she said, "Okay, lay it on me. The latest bit of karma I have to dole out can wait. Sheesh, I hate mean girls."

"I don't blame you," Fate said. "There seems to be so many of them these days."

"Thanks to the internet," Gaia added. "Or so I've heard."

"Yes, but there's still hope. I've seen bumper stickers that say *Mean people suck*." Fate chuckled. "But let's get to the reason I called you."

"Yes, I'm curious about that too." The goddess of all ran her fingers through her long white hair and feigned disinterest.

"Gaia has sworn off humans. And I understand why. However, I do not want her to give up completely, so it seems as if we're going to have to talk her into dating paranormals."

Gaia leaned over and placed her head in her hands, then shook her head vehemently. "No. No. No. That's not a good idea."

"Why?" Karma asked. "It seems like the perfect solution. They're all aware of you, or most of them are. So why wouldn't that be an obvious solution?"

Gaia raised her head, frowning. "I've been so hard on them. Expected too much of them. I just know they think I'm an ass and I never apologize."

Karma laughed. "Well, it's about time you learned how."

"I don't think so. I'll lose all my authority, and some of them have some pretty serious powers. I *must* keep them in line. It's for their own protection!"

Fate smiled. "If that's all you're worried about, I'm sure we can work around it. They will still respect you. In fact, I think they'll respect you more. If you have something to apologize for and you do it sincerely, I really think they'll appreciate it and they won't take advantage of you because of it."

"Honestly, I believe that will inspire more loyalty if anything," Karma added.

"I'll think about it."

Karma rolled her eyes. "We know what you really mean when you say 'I'll think about it.' It means you *won't* consider it, but you just don't want to appear like a butthole."

"That's not true. Well, okay, maybe it is a little true or was in the past. I'm doing things differently now."

"Like what?" Fate asked.

"Are you kidding me? This whole dating thing is new and different for me."

"And you just said you're not going to do it anymore. So how are you doing things any differently?" Karma asked.

Gaia was silent. She rotated her glass and watched the wine swirl around.

Karma cleared her throat. "Gaia, you know we love

you. You know we wouldn't steer you wrong…on purpose. Fate is right. You owe the paranormals an apology for being too harsh. That kangaroo court thing you did, that was something you can apologize for. Start with that."

"Are you kidding me?" Gaia shot to her feet. "That's not something I did wrong. They violated my only rule! Never expose their powers to humans."

"Which is what you did with the astronomer," Fate reminded her.

"That wasn't my fault. I was under a spell."

Karma rose. "Think about it. How would you feel if you were yanked into a courtroom and put on trial for falling in love? That's all they did. They happened to fall in love with humans, and only after they knew they could trust them completely did they share their paranormal status. Nothing bad happened."

Gaia scratched her head. "I hadn't thought of it like that. Okay, okay. I'll think about apologizing. I'm not guaranteeing I will. But I promise I'll consider it."

"That's a start," Fate said. "I think you are changing for the better."

"Now, if only human beings would change for the better and treat my beautiful planet the way it should be treated, a lot of my anger would dissipate."

Karma put her arm around Gaia. "I know what you mean. We'll cross that bridge when we come to it. And we'll do it together."

―――

Gaia thought and thought about it. She sat on a rock overlooking one of her favorite spots in Maui. The water was warm and softly lapping at her feet. She was trying to ignore the volcano on the next island. So she went to the other side. "I had nothing to do with that," she mumbled under her breath. "That was all Pele."

Gaia was wondering if she should confront Pele or if the goddess had a good reason for blowing her top. Either way, she was tired of confronting everyone, especially now that she had done it badly and had to think about apologizing. It was something she had never done before. Of course, she hadn't lost it like that before either. She had never yanked a bunch of her special children into a courtroom, set them on bleachers in midair, and then unleashed a frightening tirade.

She dropped her head in her hands. "Okay," she sighed. "I guess I do owe them an apology. But for what? I have one rule, and every one of them violated that rule. Is my rule unfair? Is it too difficult?"

After pondering that, she decided it was absolutely not impossible to continue obeying her rule. Such a simple thing. *Just don't expose your powers to humans.* What was so hard about that?

Some paranormals had even found out what happened when they did expose those powers. A few years before in Boston, a merman had been captured in a net. A bunch of science nerds from the local university called MIT had kept him in a giant saltwater fish tank in a warehouse in Cambridge—and then did experiments on him! He had given them information on other paranormals, hoping they'd leave him alone and turn their attention to other, more powerful paras.

She had only met him briefly, but that was enough. He had spilled the Boston baked beans about the whole paranormal community. The nerds had invented a way to detect paranormal energy and found the bar on Beacon Hill called Boston Uncommon. Apparently, their meter had gone crazy as soon as they walked in.

Gaia had known that place was a bad idea and had suggested repeatedly that the owner shut it down. The vampire hadn't listened. He had insisted his staff, who were human, had no knowledge of their paranormal patrons. He had said if the paras got to know each other, they would get along better. His theory had proved somewhat correct. The tensions between shape-shifters and vampires had diminished significantly. There was much less possibility of humans discovering paranormals through some kind of local war where they might be tempted to use their supernatural powers.

But once the unusual creatures were discovered, they risked capture. The humans had discovered paralyzing drug darts would allow them to grab paranormals, stick them in a van, and bring them to their lab in Cambridge, where they had incredibly strong cages waiting. It had been a disaster.

It hadn't been until the still free paranormals had located the lab and chosen to work together that they had been able to dismantle it and completely erase all knowledge of the scientific findings—with *her* help, of course. That had been too close for comfort. Perhaps all she had to do was share that scenario with the paras who hadn't been a part of it. They would have to understand the importance of secrecy then, right?

She liked that idea—a lot. Not only could she apologize, but she could also express her reasoning for her one and only rule. If her concern made sense to them, they wouldn't mind following the rule as much. She

understood how hard it was to find love, and that made
her a little sad, but that was Fate's department, not hers.
All she could do was take responsibility for her own
mistakes.

She rose and gazed out at the hills. *I know what I'll
do. I'll have a party! A huge party where I can invite
everyone I brought to court that day. And then I'll be
able to apologize—just once—to everyone at the same
time, which shouldn't be too painful.*

Just the thought of apologizing to each one individually left her shaking, and a drop of sweat rolled down
her face. Then she squared her shoulders and continued
her thoughts out loud. "I can put their minds at ease.
I'll let them know that there's a good reason behind my
only rule."

It was for their safety. The danger would seem
obvious to her. But one thing she had learned was that
humans and paranormals alike didn't always get it without full and complete explanations. Even then, some of
them failed to learn before repeating mistakes. She was
just attempting to avoid a recurrence of the mistake that
happened in Cambridge.

*Okay, how do I go about inviting all these people? I
know! My muse of email can help! I will simply ask her.*
She looked up at the sky and called out, "Bliss! Bliss!"

A human riding a bike along the Hana Highway
glanced over and called out, "It really is blissful, isn't it?"

Gaia chuckled and wondered how many times her
modern muse had problems with a name like that. She
was happy to see that Bliss was waiting to appear. She
was obeying the law...*her* law.

As soon as the human had bicycled around the corner

where he could no longer see Gaia's spot, the brunette called Bliss appeared.

"Mother Nature! What can I do for you?"

"I understand there's a thing, some kind of card that can be physically mailed or emailed to invite people to an event. I guess it's a nicer way of doing things than just calling out like I usually do."

Bliss grinned. "You've come to the right place. I used to make cards for a living. What you're describing is called an invitation."

"Oh. That's perfect. Can you make an invitation and send it to the following people: Nicholas Wolfensen, your husband, Drake Cameron, and many Fierros? Let's see, there's Miguel, Gabriel, Dante, Noah, Luca, and Antonio. Yes, I think that's all of them. Those are the ones I caught violating the law who hadn't been dealt with yet. I brought them to the paranormal court and... well, I'm afraid I need to apologize for that."

"You regret calling your tribunal?" Bliss asked.

"Don't look so surprised. I can rethink my actions."

Bliss just bit her lower lip.

"So, the invitations. Can you do it?"

"Should I know what I'm inviting them to?"

"I guess it's sort of an apology party. But *I don't want to call it that*. Can you think of something appropriate? Make it sound like a celebration."

Bliss scratched her head. Then her eyes opened wider. "I know. How about Gaia's gala?"

"Gaia's gala. I like it. Okay, let's call it that, and how do we send these invitations?"

"There are several ways, but first I need to know where it will be held and what date and time to give out."

Gaia let out a long breath. "I don't know. What's a good time and day to hold these things?"

"Usually a weekend night works best. Most people don't have to work. I think the Fierros are all on the same shift…at least they were before most of them moved from Boston to Puerto Rico."

"I'll leave it up to you. See if you can find a date and time that works."

Bliss looked confused, her brow wrinkled. "I could probably ask Drake to find out. He knows them better than I do. And it wouldn't be weird for him to want to keep in touch."

"Okay then, do that. Just tell me when and where to show up, and I'll throw a very nice party for all of them."

"Would you like these invitations on paper sent in the mail or in electronic form sent by email?"

"What do you recommend?"

"I'm not sure what their email addresses are. How about if I find out what their mailing addresses are and I can send them a nice paper invitation? That would be the thoughtful and special thing to do."

"Okay. That sounds good. Thanks very much."

"Is there anything else, Goddess?"

"No, not unless you have something to ask or tell me."

Bliss paused to think and then said, "No. Everything is good. We're all fine. The job is going well. The baby is growing up quickly. He's three years old now. Walking and talking. You should see him running after his daddy, trying to be exactly like him. Of course, he'll never be a dragon, thank goodness. I'm just as happy that he's a little human being and *not* a baby dragon that I have to attempt to discipline."

Gaia laughed. "Very good. And of course you know my number one rule. He's never to know about your husband's paranormal powers. Or yours."

"Yes, Gaia. We are well aware of your rule."

"Perfect. That's all I ask. Thank you for sending the invitations. Just let me know where and when everyone is gathering, and I'll be there."

"Would you like someone to organize the party itself?"

"Who would you suggest?"

"How about if you leave it to Brandee and me? The two of us can do it together. Unless you have someone else in mind. I could ask my close friend who owns the tea shop on Beacon Hill to have it there. They usually close in the early evenings now. Maybe they can keep it open later and make it a private party."

"Is this a human establishment?"

"Well, yes. But that's why I suggested Brandee and I host it for you. We both used to waitress there. My best friend is the manager, and now she's married to the owner."

"That sounds fine. Who's your friend?"

"Claudia Cross."

Gaia planted her face in the palm of her hand.

"Oh, that's right…you know her. Do you think that might be a problem?"

Mother Nature laughed. "You think? Her husband violated my rule so damn much, I sent him to the top of the Matterhorn to think about what he was doing, but he still refused to close the bar. I finally had to make him human again and erase his memory. Let me tell you, it is not easy to undo vampirism!"

"I don't think it will be a problem after hours. Claudia and Anthony still know nothing about the paranormal world, and they might let us rent the perfect space. Brandee and I used to operate the equipment and could provide tea and coffee with already-made cakes and cookies, that sort of thing. I can *ask* about renting the place from her for a private party. All right?"

"Sure. See if that'll work."

"If Claudia is not okay with our taking it over completely, I can come up with something else. Maybe a private outdoor place under a tent? But I don't know any paranormal caterers, and then what do we do about food and drinks?"

"Do we have to feed and water them? What are they, cattle?"

Bliss chuckled. "No, but a party isn't a party without refreshments. Some folks are terribly shy, and just having something to do other than stand there looking uncomfortable is helpful."

"Yes. That's what I'll be doing. For this event, I think privacy is key. My muses can transport the guests wherever they need to be, so it doesn't matter where we hold this party, as long as it's secluded."

"Leave it to me. I'll find a good place and time where everyone can meet, then I'll design your invitations and show them to you before I send them out. How's that?"

Mother Nature smiled and patted Bliss on the head. "You know me well. You'd probably call me a control freak, but that's fine. It's just the way I am, and I don't think it's a bad thing."

Bliss smirked. "I wouldn't call you a control freak. At least not to your face!" The two of them laughed. Then Bliss continued in a sincere tone, "You're the goddess of all. And we're lucky to have you. You're looking out for us, even if not everyone realizes it."

"Thank you, Bliss."

Bliss disappeared. It sounded like the next and hardest thing to do would be coming up with the right words for her apology. How could she say she made a mistake without losing the respect of her subjects? Oh! Maybe she didn't have to.

"Now who can I get to say those words?" she mumbled aloud. Letting out a long sigh, she realized. "I know exactly who has to do it. Me, dammit."

Chapter 11

RUTH'S READING WAS INTERRUPTED BY THE FIRST SHARP pains of labor, and she began timing her contractions. Five minutes apart. It was time to call her father. She punched in her father's number and waited until it went to voicemail. *Dammit. He's probably off in the rain forest and doesn't have a signal. Thank goodness I have Kizzy as a backup.*

Rain was coming down heavily. She couldn't drive herself, since her dad had their rental car, so she'd have to take a taxi to Kizzy's place. She just had to be sure her sister was home.

After only a couple of rings, Kizzy picked up. "Hi, Ruth. What's up?"

"My *time* is up. I'm in labor."

Kizzy gasped. "Oh my Goddess! Where are you?"

"At the hotel. Dad was going to drive me in our rental when the time came, but he's probably off in the rain forest and unreachable. Of course, he has the car, so I'll take a cab or Uber. I don't want you driving in this rainstorm."

"I'll be right there."

"No! I just said I don't want you driving in this. I'll come to you."

"I'm at Gabriella and Antonio's place. Do you have the address?"

"I think so. Let me check my contacts." A moment later,

Ruth saw that she did indeed have the number and address of the Fierros' home. "Yes, I have it. I'll be right over."

Kizzy squealed with delight. "How much time between contractions?"

"Five minutes. Plenty of time."

"Okay, great. Firstborns usually take a little longer, so we're good. Do you want me to call the cab for you?"

Ruth laughed. "I'm in labor, not helpless. Of course I'll call my own cab. In fact, I can see one sitting outside the lobby. I'll be there in a few minutes."

Kizzy signed off, sounding as excited as Ruth felt.

—∾∾—

The cab ride was harrowing. Ruth didn't know if that was why her contractions were picking up or not. Maybe this kid just wanted to come sooner rather than later. The cab driver weaved in and out of traffic. In the torrential downpour, Ruth wondered how he could see anything. "You must have the roads memorized."

He didn't answer. Maybe he didn't speak English—or maybe he was deep in concentration.

If she got to Kizzy's safely, she'd be happily surprised.

A contraction hit just as they were pulling up to the Fierros' home. Gabriella and Kizzy ran out to meet her, carrying two open umbrellas. They threw open the door to the back seat. "You're here!"

"By some miracle," Ruth mumbled. "Let me pay the driver."

"I'll pay the driver," Gabriella said. "You and Kizzy get inside out of the rain."

Ruth rolled her eyes. "Thanks, Gabriella, but I've got

it." She handed the cab driver a $20 bill, and he thanked her for her generosity and wished her good luck.

Luck wasn't the only thing involved. She had cast a protection spell around the vehicle as soon as she realized it would be a dangerous trip. In other words, the minute he stepped on the gas.

Kizzy and Gabriella got on either side of her and helped her heave herself out of the back seat. The umbrellas covered her completely, and the other two were getting soaked. They walked her into the house as if she were a fragile doll.

"I'm okay, really."

They had just gotten her into the house and shaken off the umbrellas when she had another contraction. Suddenly, her water broke. "Yikes!" The gush added to everything dripping on the tile floor.

"Oh my God, did your water just break?" Gabriella asked.

"It would appear so," Ruth said. "I'm so sorry. Your floor…"

Gabriella laughed. "Do you know how many times I soaked our floor in Boston?"

"Seven?" Kizzy asked, smiling.

"Almost. I went to the hospital before my water broke with Ryan. He was my first, and I was nervous. After that, it was a piece of cake. Should we go to the hospital?" she asked.

"No!" both Kizzy and Ruth said at once.

Gabriella paused and then asked, "Oh. Is this a paranormal birth? Are you nervous about your unusual DNA or something?"

Ruth laughed. "No, this child is one hundred percent

human. Witch DNA doesn't look any different from yours. We're human, just not in need of a hospital—yet. I want my sister by my side. I'm not sure a hospital will let her into the delivery room, but I'll have the baby in the hallway if they don't."

Kizzy asked, "Can I get you a cup of tea? Decaf coffee? Perhaps an enema?"

Gabriella laughed. "I'll get her whatever she wants except that last item. You just stay by your sister."

Ruth bent over with a strong contraction. Her Lamaze breathing wasn't relieving the pain. "Kizzy." She grabbed her sister's hand. "I think something's wrong. The pain is too strong too soon. I thought we'd have hours to wait, but now I think this kid is coming."

"Oh my!" Gabriella exclaimed. "How exciting. We have an extra guest room, if that's where you would be most comfortable giving birth."

"Kizz, I think you should do a quick pelvic exam. I really think something's wrong."

"How can you tell?" Kizzy asked. "Is your psychic power alerting you?"

"Yes! I know my hips are small and this child is large. I guessed I might need a C-section, but I had hoped we could magically widen the pelvis. I figured we could work on that here, where we had some privacy."

"Is there time for that now?" Gabriella asked.

"Probably not." Kizzy helped Ruth back toward the door. "Let's not even bother doing a pelvic. Let's just get you to the nearest hospital or clinic. I can do a C-section. I just need the proper equipment—*sterile* equipment."

Ruth gazed at Kizzy intently. "Promise me if it comes

down to a choice between me and the baby, you'll save
the child."

Kizzy reared back. "My Goddess, you can't be
serious!"

"We are not in Brookline anymore. I know one of us
might not make it, and you can save only one goner per
day. I want it to be the baby."

Kizzy seemed to cover her shock by ignoring the
request. "We've got to get you to a hospital, now.
There's actually a clinic closer. Gabriella? Do you know
anything about that clinic?"

"Oh yes. I went there to get a splinter taken out when
we first got here. They were very professional and very
kind."

"Okay, then you'll have to drive, and I'll be in the
back seat with Ruth. She needs to lie down."

Gabriella's eyes widened. "But I…"

"Please! I know the driving conditions are terrible,
but we have to try to get there so I can save them
both!"

Gabriella took a deep breath and said, "Of course."

The two women braced Ruth on either side and
walked her out to Kizzy's vehicle. Kizzy handed
Gabriella the keys and helped Ruth into the back seat.
Gabriella seemed hesitant but eventually got behind the
wheel, turned the key, and revved the engine.

"I'm glad this is an automatic." Gabriella put it
in drive, and the three of them took off at a crawl.
Eventually, when Ruth began moaning in the back,
Gabriella picked up speed.

Ruth couldn't see what was going on, but Kizzy
would glance out the window at the road once in a while,

and her face said it all. Ruth quickly cast a protection spell around Kizzy's vehicle too.

The car zigzagged back and forth. At least they were getting to the clinic, even if they were all shaken like martinis.

"Geez, Gabriella, do you know how to drive?" Kizzy asked.

"Um, I never needed to drive in Boston. Antonio would drive, or I would take the subway everywhere."

"Do you even have a license?" Ruth asked.

"Not exactly. It expired years ago. I had to get a true ID to come here," Gabriella said sheepishly.

"Oh my Goddess!" Kizzy and Ruth exclaimed as one.

"Almost there," Gabriella called out. She careened into the parking lot and slammed on the brakes. If Kizzy hadn't been kneeling next to Ruth and bracing her, she would've wound up on the floor of the back seat.

"Thank the Goddess," Kizzy muttered under her breath. "We're here."

The two anxious women escorted Ruth into the clinic. The rain had let up a bit, but it was too late to get to the hospital. Her contractions were coming fast and furious now. This child wanted to be born immediately, and Ruth wanted her out just as badly!

Her. They had never asked about the sex of the baby, but Ruth just knew. She was about to have a little female witchette.

A young man in black pants and a white shirt came rushing to the door. The nametag on his lab coat said Dr. José Ortega. Just as Kizzy was helping Ruth through the door and into the clinic, Ruth collapsed. Dr. Ortega reacted quickly and caught her, preventing her from hitting the floor. He scooped her up into his arms and carried her, asking questions in Spanish over his shoulder.

"Do you speak English?" Gabriella asked.

"Yes. Quite well."

"My sister needs a C-section. I can do it. I'm a doctor," Kizzy said, following him through the double doors.

There seemed to be only one person behind the desk, and she stopped Gabriella, thrusting a clipboard and some paperwork in front of her. "Go on, Kizzy. I'll stay here and fill this out to the best of my knowledge."

Kizzy didn't think Gabriella would be able to fill out much except Ruth's name and Aaron's as next of kin, but she was grateful she wasn't detained. She had to stay with Ruth.

The doctor set Ruth on a gurney, then turned to Kizzy. "That's it. You can go no farther."

Ruth grabbed Kizzy's hand and cried out, "No! She's my sister and a doctor too. She goes with me. Do *not* take her away from me."

Kizzy smiled. "You heard the girl. I go where she goes."

"I'm sorry. You can't. I don't even know who you are. We have rules, not many, but those rules are important to protect our patients."

"*I'm* important to protect *this* patient." Kizzy hung on to Ruth's hand and gave her a reassuring squeeze. "I'm not leaving her. Not for anything."

"My sister really is a doctor, and I'm a labor and delivery nurse. I need her. Please."

The doctor just sighed. "Fine. Come with me." He rolled the gurney up to a pair of double doors where a nurse met him and helped them through. At last, they entered a clean-looking room. There was not much in there but a metal table, sink, and some basic equipment.

Ruth's eyes were half-closed, and she started mumbling. "Don't leave me, please."

"I won't. I won't leave you. Don't worry."

The doctor glanced at the nurse, who glanced back at Kizzy and then back at the doctor. "Give her a sedative. She can't be awake for this."

A quick look at the color draining away from Ruth's face alarmed Kizzy. She grasped her sister's wrist and checked the clock on the wall. "Her pulse is rapid and thready."

"If we had had more time to prepare, we could have arranged a better situation and she could be conscious, but it will take longer for a local anesthetic."

"I understand," Kizzy said. "Go ahead and put her under. And have your nurse show me where to wash up."

"Oh no, I'll be doing the procedure. My nurse can hand me the instruments. And you can stay by her side and keep your sister safe from us heathens."

Kizzy's jaw dropped. "I never said... I—I'm sorry. I don't mean to doubt you. I just know my sister, and this isn't the most ideal situation. Please let me assist."

The doctor nodded to his nurse, and she helped Kizzy wash up and put on a mask and gown. The doctor placed a mask over Ruth's nose and mouth and administered some gas, and Ruth was asleep in seconds.

Without monitors or anything but the basics, Kizzy knew it would be a risky procedure, no matter how she looked at it. "The baby's in distress. Ruth knew it before she went under."

"Why didn't you get her to the hospital as soon as she went into labor?"

"We…ah…we thought we had plenty of time. It's her first. She wanted to be comfortable at home for the first few hours. And she wants me with her for the whole thing."

"Are you a surgeon?"

"I'm an emergency room trauma specialist."

The doctor nodded. "That's good. That will help."

The nurse went to work getting Ruth's belly washed, and she sterilized the area as quickly as she could with some antiseptic solution.

Kizzy stationed herself next to the physician and held her sisters legs open. "How can I help?"

"Just do exactly what you're doing. Be ready when I hand the baby to you. I'll need to clamp off the vessels and sew her up. Meanwhile, you can care for the infant."

As he went to cut into Ruth's belly, it stilled, as if the baby was giving up the fight to get out. "Hurry!" Kizzy cried.

The doctor took a deep breath and moved his scalpel well below Ruth's umbilicus, then drew it across her abdomen in one sure slice. She would have a bikini scar.

The baby was limp. Kizzy saw the cord wrapped around the baby's neck, and the baby looked blue. "Oh my God and Goddess!"

The doctor glanced up at her. His thick eyebrows lifted, and his brown eyes caught hers for just a moment. When would she be able to say "Goddess" without people getting all wigged out?

Even after they got the cord away from the infant's

neck, it was clear the baby was not doing well. Kizzy also saw Ruth had lost a lot of blood and her face was extremely gray. "Save my sister!"

"I intend to." The doctor lifted the baby into Kizzy's waiting arms. She used her one *save*, and soon there was movement. Then at last, the baby opened her mouth and wailed. Her color grew pinker and her cries stronger.

"Thank goodness! Oh, thank goodness!"

"I need your help. Hand the baby over to my nurse and clamp off this vessel here."

Kizzy quickly but carefully gave the infant to the nurse, who had a blanket waiting. She grabbed the clamp and did as he asked.

Ruth seemed to be bleeding more than expected. The doctor said, "Here, put more pressure here." He looked up at Ruth and realized he was losing her. "Do you know how to close up?"

Kizzy was surprised he'd ask but didn't hesitate. "Yes. I can do it."

Dr. Ortega put his hand on Ruth's abdomen above the wound. Suddenly, the opening grew smaller. The blood stopped flowing. The placenta was delivered, and she was ready to be closed up, but she still didn't look good. Her skin was ashen.

He said, "I want to save your sister, but you cannot tell anyone what you see."

For some reason, Kizzy knew she could trust him, so she just nodded. Besides, what choice did she have?

The doctor placed his hands on Ruth's abdomen, and the small bit of pressure he applied knitted her vessels back together. He removed the clamps, and the color returned to Ruth's face.

Kizzy checked her pulse and was relieved to find it much stronger. She turned to the doctor, and after making sure the nurse wasn't listening, she whispered, "What are you?"

Answering her also in a whisper, he said, "The name on my island is Santeria. But I prefer not to use a label. I'm simply a doctor doing the best I can each day with whatever is available and within my power. I get to save one soul per day who wouldn't have made it. Today was your sister's turn."

Kizzy grinned. "I think we found a fellow witch. My sister is a nurse. Saving one patient who wouldn't make it otherwise is one of our powers. She made me promise to save the baby. I was so afraid I was going to lose her." She threw her arms around his shoulders. "Thank you. Thank you for my sister."

Then she walked over to the nurse, who had just finished cleaning up and wrapping the baby in a new warm, clean blanket. She settled the little bundle into Kizzy's arms.

Looking down, Kizzy sighed. "Hello, little niece. We were so lucky today. Thanks to this wonderful doctor, you and your mommy are going to be fine."

The baby opened her eyes a bit, and Kizzy could have sworn she saw a tiny smile.

———⟡———

Misty had been watching from the ether. Now that Ruth and the baby were doing well, she'd be off to locate Aaron.

She concentrated on his energy and found him up in the mountains in the rain forest. Odd place, she thought.

Regardless, she zeroed in on his location and appeared nearby. She walked through the trees and smiled when she saw him.

"Misty! What are you doing here?"

"I just came to congratulate you, Grandpa."

Aaron stood still, shocked. "Ruth had her baby?"

"She sure did. It was touch and go for a while. I was watching from the ether in case I was needed. But between Kizzy and the doctor at the clinic, everything went better than expected. Mother and baby are doing fine."

"Oh, thank the Goddess."

Surprisingly, the Goddess herself appeared. "Misty, can you give us a few moments?"

"Of course, Gaia. I'll be at the Fierros' home. That's where they said they would take her when she was ready to be moved. Take *them*, I mean."

"Wait!" Aaron said. "Is it a boy or a girl?"

Misty smiled. "It's a beautiful girl."

Aaron groaned. "Wonderful. Another female more powerful than I am."

The Goddess took a step back. "Seriously? You're upset with your daughters having more power than you?"

Aaron laughed. "Absolutely not. I was being facetious. I love the fact that my daughters are so capable and can take care of themselves. I worry less, but I still worry. They're my…well, they're my world."

Gaia nodded. She glanced at Misty, and Misty seemed to understand. "I'll see you guys later."

As soon as Misty disappeared, Gaia took a step toward Aaron and held out her hand. He took her hand in his.

"I've missed you," she said.

"I've missed you too. What should we do about that?" He smiled.

Gaia grinned. "Maybe we should kiss and make up? I hear that's what people do after having a disagreement."

Aaron's eyebrows shot up. "Well, some people do that. Usually people in a relationship. Are we in a relationship?"

Gaia stiffened, then relaxed. "I think…I would like to be. May I ask you out on a date?"

Aaron's jaw dropped, then he grinned. "You may."

Gaia cleared her throat. "I guess I should ask you out to dinner and a movie. I understand that's a common date night."

"I would like that very much. When should this date occur?"

Gaia tipped her head and thought. "I imagine you want to see your daughter and granddaughter first."

"Absolutely. How about tomorrow night?"

"Yes. I will plan for that—unless the earth decides otherwise. Until tomorrow night then," Gaia said and took a step back.

"Wait a minute. What about our kiss to make up?" Aaron asked.

Gaia smiled shyly. Her cheeks heated, and she knew she must be blushing. It was now or never. She stepped forward, draped her arms around his neck, and leaned in, closing her eyes and puckering up, as she had seen many mortals do.

Aaron met her lips with his own, gently applying pressure. After angling his mouth and with the gentle pressure of his tongue, he teased her mouth open. They swirled their tongues together, and Gaia felt as if butterflies had invaded her tummy. *So this is what everyone feels that I've been missing. No wonder love is so popular around the world.*

When they finally let their lips and bodies leave each other, they grasped both hands. "Until tomorrow night," Aaron said. "I need to drive back to the Fierros' house and check on my family."

"Drive carefully," Gaia said. "May I dry the road for you?"

Aaron smiled. "No need. Now that the rain has stopped, I can navigate the roads, and I promise to be careful."

Gaia nodded, wishing she could help, but she had made that mistake before. She was going to ask before she just jumped in to save him from minor inconveniences.

She disappeared into the ether and stayed there a moment to sigh privately. He was different from all the other people she had met. And she wanted the date to go well. She would have to figure out how to make that happen. There must be someone who had long-term relationship success.

Suddenly, a woman popped into her mind. Gabriella. Her new muse of parenting. She had certainly stayed in love with her Antonio, and it was very clear her love was returned tenfold. Gaia nodded to herself. "That's what I'll do. I'll talk to Gabriella." And then she remembered that everyone was going to the Fierro home to visit Ruth, the baby, Kizzy, and Aaron. The conversation would have to wait, but she would speak with her as soon as she could. This one relationship had to go well.

—w—

Aaron drove as fast as he could until he reached a place with some cellular reception. He pulled over and called Kizzy.

"Hi Dad, or maybe I should say Grandpa!"

"I just heard, Kizzy. How is she? And how's the baby?"

"They're good. We're still at the clinic and could use another driver."

He heard a giggle in the background. "Oh. Misty said you'd be at the Fierros'."

"Yes, that's where we're heading soon."

"I feel just awful I wasn't there. I'm sure I could've helped. I understand it was touch and go for a while…at least that's what Misty said."

"She's right. But everything's okay now. In fact, it's a little better than okay."

"Do you want to tell me what that means?"

There was a pause on the other end, and at last, she said, "I'll tell you when you get here. You can meet him."

"Him? Okay, I'll be there in ten minutes."

Aaron hung up and drove a little faster than he should have to get to the clinic. He had to know what happened. What does *him* mean? Did Gordon come looking for Ruth? Was she going to go back to him?

She'd better not.

Aaron never liked the jerk, and after dumping his eight-months-pregnant daughter…well, the guy was a coward. Thank goodness Ruth had erased his memory of their family's secret.

Pulling into the parking lot, Aaron saw Kizzy's car. He wondered why they would need another driver, but he'd find out in a minute. He slammed the car door and charged into the clinic.

"I'm Ruth Samuels's father. Can you tell me where she is, please?"

The woman behind the desk pointed to the double doors on her right.

"Thank you."

Aaron hurried through the double doors and checked the hall before he came to a room with three beds. His daughter and granddaughter were lying in one of them. Kizzy and Gabriella stood on either side.

"Hi, Dad!" Ruth handed the baby to Gabriella.

Aaron rushed over to Ruth, leaned over the safety rail, and gave her a big hug. "I'm so sorry I wasn't here, honey. Are you all right?"

"Never better. Do you want to meet your granddaughter?"

"Absolutely." He rounded the bed and met Gabriella at the foot of it. She handed him a little pink bundle of joy. The baby seemed healthy. Pink cheeks and a shock of brown hair and eyelashes. He parted the blanket a bit and saw ten tiny fingers. He was betting there would be ten toes under there too. "What a beauty. Well done, Ruthie. But who is this 'he' Kizzy mentioned?"

A handsome young doctor strolled into the room. Kizzy brought him over and said, "Dr. José Ortega, this is my father, Dr. Aaron Samuels."

José took a brief glance around the room and then whispered, "Is he a witch too?"

Aaron's jaw dropped. Before he could fumble the

baby, Gabriella grabbed her back and brought her to Ruth, who anxiously reached for her.

"You did the delivery?" Aaron asked José.

"Yes, I did. Your older daughter assisted as well."

Kizzy smiled and said, "Ruth wouldn't be here if not for Dr. Ortega. He saved her life."

Aaron's eyebrows rose. He extended a hand and shook José's hand. "I can't thank you enough, Dr. Ortega. That's my precious baby girl lying there, holding her precious baby girl."

"Thank heavens for both of you," Gabriella added.

José moved over to Ruth's side and asked, "How are you feeling, Miss Samuels?"

"Like I just won the lottery—and you can call me Ruth."

He smiled. "Have you decided what to name her yet?"

"I was thinking of a few different names, but there must be a perfect one. I just don't know what it is yet. I'm sure it will come to me."

The doctor nodded. "Well, let me know when you decide. We'll need to put something on her birth certificate before you can take her home."

"Oh, that's right. I guess I have to come up with something pretty quickly."

"You have about twenty-four hours. I want you here for observation, and it wouldn't be a bad idea to let your stitches heal a bit."

"That isn't necessary." Ruth put her hands on her own abdomen and closed her eyes briefly. "There. All healed."

"Wow."

When he'd gone, Gabriella asked, "What were the names you were thinking of?"

"Well, I wanted Kizzy, but she said no. Apparently, people have a hard time with it, and she didn't want my baby to go through the same thing."

"How about something that sounds like it but is a bit different?" Gabriella started rhyming names. "Lizzie, Busy, Dizzy…"

Kizzy held up her hand. "No. Nothing after me, thank you. She should have her own individual identity."

Ruth smiled down at her baby and said, "Or I was also thinking of naming her after Mom or Grandma."

"Mary or Ann?"

"Or both of them. I was thinking I could name her Mary Ann if she was a girl. Mitchell if she were a boy, since that was Mom's maiden name."

"Well, I vote for Mary Ann," Kizzy said.

"I like that too," Aaron added.

"All right then. Her name is Mary Ann Samuels."

"You don't want to give her Gordon's last name?" Aaron asked.

Ruth shook her head vehemently. "No. He doesn't deserve that honor. I'll use our last name, Dad, if you don't mind."

"I'd love that. Mary Ann Samuels. It has a beautiful ring to it."

"It does," Gabriella said. "So would you like me to go tell Dr. Ortega's secretary so he can fill out her birth certificate now?"

"Yes, please. Be sure it's spelled M-a-r-y space A-n-n. I'm sure he'll let me go as soon as the secretary has that information."

"Maybe not forever," Kizzy said and winked.

Ruth blushed and smiled down at her daughter. "Hello, little Mary Ann. My darling girl."

"So why do we need two drivers?" Aaron asked.

Kizzy groaned. "Well, don't get mad. Keep in mind that I had to be with Ruth in the back seat while she was in hard labor, just in case, and the only person left to drive my car was Gabriella."

"And that's a problem because…"

Gabriella strode back into the room. "Because I don't have a driver's license."

"What?"

"It's okay, Dad. We got here safe, and so did Mary Ann," Ruth said. "Now let's take her home."

"Home? You mean to our hotel room?"

"No, of course not. To *our* home," Gabriella said. "I've invited Ruthie to stay in our guest room."

"You may regret that at two in the morning," Aaron said.

Gabriella laughed. "I'm used to it. *Plus* I'm the new muse of parenting…or didn't you know?"

"And that means…you can get children to stop crying in the middle of the night?" Aaron asked.

"Absolutely not. But I can get up and feed them without losing more than half an hour of sleep."

Ruth laughed. "I'll get up with her, silly. She's mine, and I don't want to hand her over to anyone else." Then she gasped. "Oh! I didn't mean that the way it sounded, Gabriella. Of course I would trust her to you. It's just that I don't want her to leave my arms until she absolutely has to. I already love her so much."

"Of course you do." Gabriella squeezed Ruth's

shoulder. "I understand perfectly. I've been through it seven times. And you'll probably go through it again."

Ruth rolled her eyes, then her expression saddened. "I hope next time it's not without a husband."

Kizzy just shook her head. "Can we please get this one to toddler stage before we start talking about Ruth having another?"

"I think it's Kizzy's turn next," Gabriella said. "I want to be a grandma again! Soon!"

"Misty looks like she's ready to give birth to a whole football team." Everyone laughed. "Are you ready to go home?" Aaron asked.

"As ready as I'll ever be." Ruth handed the baby back to Gabriella, and Kizzy put down the safety rail so her sister could swing her feet out from under the sheet and onto the floor. She was wearing hospital scrubs.

"Where did you get the scrubs?" Aaron asked.

"One of the nurses had an extra set in her locker. I had my bag packed and ready to go and then forgot it in all the hoopla."

Aaron laughed. "It's usually the opposite of that in the movies. The frantic husband grabs the suitcase and leaves his wife behind."

"Well, this is a new kind of movie. Apparently, the sister and her mother-in-law grab the mother-to-be and take her on a wild ride through a torrential downpour, completely forgetting the bag."

Aaron pinched the bridge of his nose. "Don't tell me anything else. I prefer not to know."

Chapter 12

GAIA SMILED AS SHE STROLLED THROUGH THE FOREST, thinking about her date with Aaron. Suddenly, she came to an abrupt halt. *Oh no. I'd better check on Pan.* "Karma?"

Her sister appeared.

"Where exactly did you put Pan? I should check on him."

"Would you like me to do it?"

"No, I'd rather see him with my own eyes—not that I don't trust you, Sister."

"Of course not." Karma rolled her eyes, then muttered under her breath, "Once a control freak, always a control freak."

"What did you say?"

"Oh, nothing."

Gaia sighed. "You know I heard you, and I don't like that term."

Karma shrugged. "Okay. I'll try to think of some other expression that means the same thing. Power junkie? Control enthusiast?"

"Marginally better."

"Meanwhile, the school you're looking for is in New York. Fordham University. He's the mascot."

"Thank you."

Confronting her sister on her rudeness wasn't as important as her mission right now. She materialized at the college where Karma had deposited Pan. There was a football game going on. *Perfect. Mascots are always at the games, right?* Looking around, she didn't see him. *Oh crap.* She couldn't sense him either. *Double crap.*

She quickly copied someone else's outfit and stepped up to one of the players on the sidelines. "Where is your mascot?"

The player scanned her up and down. "Aren't you a little old to be a cheerleader?"

Gaia looked down at her outfit, which matched the girls who were jumping up and down on the sidelines. *Cheerleader?* She must have picked a uniform that didn't apply to her. Oh well. Tough.

She shrugged. "Never mind how I'm dressed. Where is your mascot?"

"You mean the goat?"

"Yes. The goat."

"Someone left the pen open, and he ran away. Which is fine with us, because he wasn't a ram. Our name is the Rams."

"What do you mean 'he ran away'? Where did he go?"

The player shook his head. "If we knew that, he wouldn't be missing. He'd be here on the sidelines, wouldn't he?"

Gaia was getting frustrated with this young man. If he couldn't tell her anything about where Pan might be, she should begin scouring the city. "Forget it. I'll look for him. If I find him, I'll bring him back."

"Don't bother. Coach is looking for a ram. An actual ram. Why do you want to know about the damn goat anyway? He was a complete pest."

She shrugged. "What does it matter? He isn't here anyway."

The kid just shook his head and walked away. She thought she better do the same thing, so she strode around to the back of the bleachers. As soon as she was sure everyone's attention was diverted by the game, she stepped into the ether.

Now what? If Pan was on the loose, he could still ruin her date. She'd about had it with his truth spells. But what could she do? He was a god and, as such, hard to manage. If she had been able to control her gods, there would be a lot less trouble around the globe. Especially with the horned ones.

She returned to her rain forest and hoped that some idea would come to her. Pacing, she racked her brain. *How can I keep him from ruining my date if he comes out with another truth spell? I really want this one to go well.* She snapped her fingers. *I was going to talk to Gabriella Fierro anyway. Maybe she can help me figure out what to do.*

As she neared the Fierro home, Gaia zeroed in on Gabriella's energy. She saw her in a nursery holding a beautiful newborn baby. *Oh yes, I remember. Aaron's daughter gave birth to his first granddaughter.* Gaia would love to see the child and congratulate the family. Since there was nobody in the house who didn't know of her existence—nobody awake anyway—she stepped out of the ether and into the room.

Gabriella jumped. "Oh, Mother Nature, you startled me."

"Don't be startled when I show up, just pleased. If you're going to be my muse, you'd better get used to it. I drop in from time to time. How are things going with this mother and infant?"

Smiling, Gabriella looked down at the tiny baby in her arms as Ruth was sleeping. "I can't wait to be the muse of modern parenting. I think I'm going to love the job."

"Has Misty told you how to perform your duties?"

"We were just getting started when Ruth went into labor. She went off to find Aaron, and I went with Ruth and Kizzy to the clinic. I was one of the first to hold this little bundle of joy."

Gaia smoothed the baby's dark hair back from her forehead. "She's beautiful, isn't she?"

"She absolutely is." Gabriella looked up at Gaia and grinned. "Some of your finest work. Naturally, my sons were your best."

Gaia melted inside. At last, someone who respected her creativity. "I worked hard to create the propagation of the species. I knew human infants would come with unique challenges. They're one of the few species that are completely helpless for a year or more. Occasionally, the parents are overwhelmed and underprepared. I just know that you will work hard to help them."

"I'm looking forward to helping in whatever way I can," Gabriella said.

"I'm glad. I had to make sure that love would often lead to sex and made sex pleasurable. Otherwise, humans would never do it. And then the love had to extend to the children…"

At that moment, Ruth stirred out of a sound sleep. When her eyes fluttered open, she looked over to Gabriella and then Gaia. "Mother Nature! How good of you to come."

"You know who I am?"

"Yes, my father explained you weren't a neighbor, that you were indeed Mother Nature. Is that true?"

Gaia smiled and nodded. "It is true. I'm glad your father told you. Eventually, I would have if he hadn't. There are times you might see me around." She cleared her throat. "Speaking of which, I'd like to talk to Gabriella, alone. Would you be willing to hold your baby?"

Ruth laughed. "More than willing." She reached for Mary Ann, and Gabriella placed the sleeping infant in her arms.

"How can I help you, Gaia?"

"I'd like to ask you something…if you don't mind." She was trying to be more considerate since her sisters said she could be selfish, rude, demanding, and whatever *blah blah blah* came out of their mouths. She was unwilling to hear most of it and tuned out.

"I don't mind at all." Gabriella took Mother Nature's hand and led her outside the home. "There's a lovely tree over here. We can sit beneath it on the grass."

"Yes, it's beautiful. But it needs one thing." Gaia snapped her fingers, and a wooden bench circled the tree.

"Oh, how wonderful! Now we can sit on a dry surface in the shade and chat anytime. Oh, provided we can keep it."

"Yes, of course you can keep the bench. You may need it sometime to talk to those you help. It's nice and private. Congratulations on your first client, by the way."

Gabriella looked surprised. "Client? Who, Ruthie?"

"Who else?" Gaia chuckled.

"Oh, I don't think she'll need much help. She's

a natural. And she loves this child like you wouldn't believe."

"It's good to start with a comfortable situation. They won't all be easy."

Gabriella nodded sagely. "I know. Unfortunately, some parents just don't understand what they can and cannot expect of children, and when they get frustrated, they don't know what to do. Sometimes, they do the wrong thing and make it worse."

"Exactly. And you will whisper in their ear to calm down, find someone else to watch the baby so they can get a break. Or if they're alone, you'll suggest other healthy ways to cope. Even if they can only find another place in the house to go and get a grip, it's better to leave the child in a safe spot like a crib or playpen and get away from the situation rather than harm the child."

"I understand. But what if they don't listen to me?"

Gaia shrugged. "You won't speak to them directly. You'll stay in the ether and whisper in their ears. They'll think it's the small voice inside their own minds and hearts. A conscience can do wonders to prevent abuse."

"But what if—"

"Misty will instruct you further. What I really wanted to talk to you about is my date with Aaron Samuels."

Gabriella sat up, and her eyes sparkled. "Date? With Aaron? How exciting!"

"Yes, I guess I'm excited too. I don't really understand what this feeling is. Sometimes, my stomach feels it's tied in knots and other times like my beautiful butterflies are flitting around inside. At least I'm not nauseated."

Gabriella chuckled. "That's exactly how you should

feel when you're attracted to someone. So that's a good sign. It means you care about Aaron. I'm glad. He's a nice man."

"Yes. I think so too. But I have a little problem."

"Oh? What is it?"

"There's this troublesome god who has ruined my dates with other people. I really want this one to go well."

Gabriella took her hand and squeezed it. "Aaron won't let anyone ruin your date, if he's half the man I think he is."

"You don't understand. This troublemaker is a god. And he doesn't need me to cast spells. He has the power to extract the truth from anyone. On one date, he cast a truth spell on the man. He wound up telling me all kinds of wayward behavior he'd participated in. It wouldn't have been unforgivable except that he admitted he intended to continue on the same path.

"On my next date, the pathological god extracted the truth from me! The poor astronomer fainted when he learned I was Gaia, the goddess of everyone and everything in the universe. At least Aaron knows me, and my identity won't come as a shock."

Gabriella smiled and said, "There's one way you can outsmart this god."

"There is?" Gaia asked. "What is it?"

"Simply beat him to the punch. Tell Aaron the truth and reveal any secrets you have. The god won't be able to blindside you, and Aaron will be prepared for whatever you might be tempted to hide from him."

Gaia tipped her head and thought about it for a moment. If Pan showed up and she had already told

Aaron everything she might want him *not* to know, would that be better or worse for them? It would be fun to see Pan's face when he was cheated out of his rival's reaction. But would Aaron have a negative reaction, even if he heard the truth from her first?

"It's better if he hears it from you," Gabriella reiterated as if she could read Gaia's mind—which, of course, she couldn't.

What sort of truths would she hide from a man on a first date? Ugh. There were too many things she wouldn't want *anyone* to know. She'd made many mistakes, especially when one added them up over the millennia.

As she ruminated, Gabriella placed a hand on her arm. "Don't be afraid to tell the truth. Lies take a lot more work."

"I understand. And being honest would be a good way to start a relationship, I suppose. I've heard that honesty is the best policy. However, what if he doesn't like the truths I have to tell? Will he be able to forgive me for my past mistakes?"

"He might need some time to process everything, but if he's worth your time, he'll come around. And you don't need his forgiveness. We all make mistakes. As long as he can accept you—flaws and all—you'll be on solid ground. And that goes both ways."

Gaia thought about that. She wanted him to be worth her time. She doubted any man or woman on earth was perfect, so why should he expect her to be?

"Thank you, Gabriella. I appreciate your input. I'm not sure exactly how much to reveal yet. I could start with the dinosaurs and work my way forward, but it might become a very long date. I have the feeling I could probably tell him anything and he'd be patient and listen without interrupting, but he may hear a lot of strange things."

"Give him credit. He's a doctor. He's probably heard it all. Well, maybe not about the dinosaurs…"

Gaia snorted. "Yeah, the Ice Age wasn't one of my finer moments. Maybe I'll tell him about the Renaissance instead."

"I may have found her a match," Fate said excitedly.

Karma's brows rose. "Really? I'd better check him out first. We don't want her getting completely discouraged."

"I know. That's exactly why I was coming to you."

Karma produced a pad of paper and pen out of thin air. "Okay, what's his name?"

"Um…I'm not sure. Abraham or Aaron or something. He's a doctor and a witch. He's always helping his fellow humans. But he needs someone too, a lot."

"A witch doctor?"

"Very funny. You're distorting this on purpose."

"No distortion needed. You're so vague, he could be anybody. What kind of doctoring and witching does he do?"

Fate shrugged. "Right now, he's helping his son-in-law build a she shed for his daughter. It seems pretty nice."

"What's a she shed?"

"Damned if I know. I guess it's something she wants, but they're building it as a surprise."

"How am I supposed to check him out if you don't even know his name?"

"I can take you to him—staying in the ether, of course."

"Of course. Our sister would have a fit otherwise."

Fate grabbed Karma's hand, and the two of them appeared near a construction site.

Karma stretched her neck, looking in every direction. "Where's the she shed?"

Fate looked around too. "I don't know. They were talking about it earlier, but this isn't a shed at all. It looks like it will become a rather large family home."

"Yes, and a sturdy one, thank goodness. This is Puerto Rico. Gaia must have had a hissy fit when she saw what happened here."

"You don't think she did it on purpose, do you?"

"No. She makes a lot of threats, but you know she doesn't carry them out. At least not the big ones. I heard her telling someone she was trying to keep California from having a huge earthquake and falling into the ocean at the same time. Naturally, she quipped a rude 'You're welcome' afterward."

Fate shook her head. "That sounds like her. You know, I'm not sure this guy deserves her."

"What do you mean? I haven't even checked him out yet. What did you see him do wrong?"

"Him? Nothing. He just seems to deserve better."

———※———

Aaron looked up from his blackboard where he was trying to break down the properties of the broken heart plant. Yes, that was what he'd been calling it until he had the chemical formula. Then he could come up with a better name.

Gaia stood there, a few feet to his side. *She looks beautiful.* Her long white hair had been gathered up behind her head with a few tendrils falling down. And someone must have given her a fashion stylist, because she was wearing a clingy dress that showed a moderate amount of cleavage. The color complemented her eyes, sky blue.

He didn't know where she was taking him, so he'd tried to dress for anything. Just some khakis and a white button-down shirt, nice and crisp. He had a tie with him in case that was something he would need for dinner. But it was too hot in Puerto Rico for a jacket, so he hadn't even brought one. Hopefully, she wouldn't want to go anywhere that fancy.

"You look stunning, Gaia. How are you tonight?"

"I'm happy, and you?"

Happy. That's so much better than 'fine' or 'well'. "Very happy. I have a new granddaughter, and I have a date with a beautiful woman."

Gaia actually blushed. He didn't think that was possible.

"Where are you taking me?" she asked.

"Oh! I thought since you asked me on the date, you had a plan. I hadn't made any reservations."

"Oh dear. Neither did I. Do we need reservations to do anything?"

"No, there are many places we can go without them. Why don't we figure out something we would like to do together. Do you enjoy the beach or the mountains or just walking down a country lane?"

Gaia smiled. "I like everything, as long as it's left natural. If they pave my country lane, that kind of ruins it for me. How about if I take us to one of my favorite places?"

Aaron wondered what one of her favorite places would be, since she had her choice of the whole world. "Sure. I'm up for everything. As long as I'm dressed appropriately."

She grinned. "I think you'll be fine."

He took her outstretched hand, and before he knew it, he'd stepped into someplace cool and foggy. Then a moment later, he was following her out of that and into a beautiful mountain valley with several other mountains all around it. He was chilly but not cold.

"This is beautiful. Where are we?"

"I think you people call it Switzerland. I just call it my beautiful, beautiful mountains. And I understand that dinner is something we should have on a date?"

"Yes, that would be great, but I don't see a restaurant anywhere."

Gaia snapped her fingers, and a table appeared, laden with every imaginable raw fruit, nuts, berries, along with other foods that were more or less man-made but not processed to the extreme. Some cheeses, some whole grain breads, and a bottle of red wine.

"This looks delicious," he said. "Shall we?" He held out her chair. She went to sit in the other one. "Oh, would you like to sit there instead?" Aaron quickly moved behind it, pulling the chair out for her.

Gaia put her hands on her hips. "Well, make up your mind. Which one do you want? I'll just pick the other one."

Aaron chuckled. "I was holding the chair out for you, because that's what a gentleman does. I was planning on pushing it in when you were seated."

"Oh? I guess that's very nice of you then. I'm not used to gentlemen."

Aaron tipped his head. "Not used to gentlemen? That's a shame. You should have met many of them in your long life."

As soon as she was comfortably pushed up to the table, he took the other chair and noticed the bottle of wine next to him was already open. There were two glasses, so he assumed she wanted some as well. He took her glass, poured it half full, and put it in front of her. Then he poured himself a glass. He had to try to remember that she wasn't used to dating, or etiquette for that matter. He wondered what else they would come upon that might be a tad embarrassing.

Gaia cleared her throat. "Thank you for the wine. And for agreeing to come out with me."

"I'm delighted you asked."

"You are? Why?"

Aaron grinned. "You have no idea what an honor it is for me to know you. Or how beautiful you are, do you? I hope we will be good friends if nothing else."

Gaia's eyebrows shot up. He noticed they had been groomed a bit too.

"You've already decided we're only friends?"

"Not at all. I just thought we would see how this goes. That's usually what happens on dates. People see how they get along first and foremost. If we enjoy each other's company, I'd like to spend more time with you."

Gaia's posture sagged. "I'm so hopeless at this stuff. I've never had to do dating. I hope you can forgive any mistakes I make."

Aaron reached over and took her hand. She wrapped her fingers around his, and he gave her a gentle squeeze. "Don't worry. I'm not judging. I'm just enjoying your company, and I hope you'll enjoy having dinner with me too."

Gaia just remembered something. He could tell from the look on her face. Then she coughed and hesitated a moment.

"There is something I need to warn you about."

"Oh?" He wondered what it could be. Were they about to experience an avalanche? "What is it?"

"I want to apologize in advance if somebody shows up and tries to ruin our date. It's happened to me before."

"Who would want to ruin your date?"

"A pesky little god named Pan. I rejected him, and now he's made sure nobody else likes or wants me."

"Well, that's not going to happen. I already like you." Aaron smiled and took a sip of his wine while she visibly relaxed. "What did he do to try and ruin your dates?"

"Well, the first time, he just showed up in his true form. He's a satyr."

Aaron's brows shot up, but he didn't comment, so she continued telling the truth.

"The next time, he put a truth spell on my date. Then the man told me all kinds of unethical things that he liked to do. It wouldn't have been so terrible except he let me know he had no intention of quitting his bad behavior. I was pretty unhappy after hearing that.

"And the next time, Pan put the truth spell on *me*. I wound up scaring the pants off my date—oh, not literally. But I did have to loosen his tie, because when I told him I was Mother Nature, goddess of the planet and whole universe, he fainted. Apparently, he wasn't used to powerful women."

Aaron laughed. "Well, I'm very used to powerful women. My daughters are both witches and they are far more powerful than I am. That's just a fact. It has never really bothered me, except when I was raising them alone and wasn't sure how much magic I wanted them to use. When they both became health professionals, it was clear their powers were going to be used for good. I was happy to let them be as powerful as they needed to be as long as it was to help others."

This time, Gaia reached for his hand and gave it a squeeze. "That's so reassuring. I was told it might be a good idea for us to share our truths up front, even the ones we aren't proud of. That way, if Pan shows up, he can't get the satisfaction of shocking us by putting a truth spell on either of us."

Aaron wasn't sure he understood her statement. It sounded like she wanted to hear anything and everything that he had ever done wrong. *Do I really want to confess everything? There could be a lot there, though most of it was not necessarily my fault. Going back to my younger years, however, would be embarrassing.*

"Okay. You want us to reveal all our past transgressions so that this god, if he shows up, can't surprise us with any truth we might be tempted to hide."

"Um, is that not okay?"

"No, it's all right... I get it. Usually, those things

come out over time. You just want to push up the timeline for getting to know each other—warts and all."

"You have warts?"

Aaron chuckled. "No. But if I did, would you like
me less?"

"No. Exactly my point. That's what I was hoping we
could do. I'll go first, if you like."

"I think I'm going to need more wine for this," Aaron
said.

———∿∿∿———

Gaia had launched into a long list of mistakes she'd
made—starting with the big bang. She had indeed farted
and caused an explosion that booted her out of the new
galaxy. Aaron had quickly stopped her and pointed out
that everyone has limited control over certain bodily
functions.

She felt a little better until she started contemplat-
ing the things she'd done on purpose. Sometimes, she
lashed out in anger. After that, she might try teaching
someone a lesson. But was that her fault?

"I'm confused," she confessed. "Some of the bad
things I did were a reaction to other people's bad behavior. Is that a mistake?"

Aaron scratched his chin and appeared to be thinking.
She'd vowed not to read his mind. Gabriella emphasized
that her power of telepathy wouldn't be fair to a mate
who didn't have the same ability. Aaron's only power,
according to his own admission, was invisibility—and
he rarely used it.

"I understand what you're saying, and *it's human*
to react to things other people do that make you angry,

but there are usually good and bad ways of coping with them."

It's human? Is that what I'm doing? Acting human? Now she was really embarrassed. She had always thought she was better than that.

"For instance," he continued, "if your actions are *overreactions* meant to get revenge or to dole out punishment that doesn't fit the crime, you might have been able to find a better way of handling it."

"Oh. Yes, sometimes my temper gets the best of me. And to be honest, I'm in a unique position. Some of my eruptions of temper are because of my own mistakes. I'm actually mad at myself."

"That's very wise."

"I wish."

Aaron leaned back in his chair and swirled his wine. "It sounds as if you have one major regret. Perhaps you should just tell me about that."

"Yes. I probably should. My worst mistake—the thing responsible for most of my bad behavior—is…" She took a deep breath and finally spit it out. "Because I created the human race."

Aaron sat up straight. "Excuse me? Did you just say the worst thing you've ever done is to create mankind?"

"Yes. And womankind. All kinds of humankind. You'd think the word 'kind' right in the name would provide a hint of what I'd intended to do, but no."

Aaron paused, then asked in a quiet tone, "Have you ever been tempted to correct that mistake?"

"You mean have a big flood and start over? No. It's too late for that. Humans would just get on their cruise ships and aircraft carriers. They're too damn smart now.

No matter what I'd do, they'd find a way around it. And what makes me mad as hell is that I gave them so many gifts! Free will and bigger brains to survive...and instead, they're using my gifts to kill each other! Their greed and misguided beliefs caused all these problems in the first place."

She could feel her temperature rising as her anger surfaced, but she was on a roll, and maybe this was the stuff he needed to hear. "Did my animals ruin my planet? No. Even lions and tigers respect my rules. They only kill so they can eat. Do the birds foul my air so that no one may breathe? No. They utilize the winds and currents and respect the sky. Do fish pollute the waters beyond their ability to live? No. No, they don't. But man...humankind, smart enough to share the land with my animals, share the sky with my birds, and share the sea with my fishes, they disrespect it all. They pollute it all. They ruin everything! Sometimes I wish I had never created them."

She slumped over with her head in her hands.

Her date was quiet. Too quiet. She was beginning to wonder if he had become invisible, then snuck off and run away. A lot of men would.

At last, she felt a warm hand on her back, gently rubbing in circles. *He didn't leave. He heard my worst mistake and all the regrets I've had because of it, and he didn't leave.*

Moisture gathered in the corners of her eyes. One tear leaked out and ran down her cheek. *What's happening? I don't cry. I never cry. Ever!*

She raised her head, and there was Aaron's face, close to hers. He swiped away the tear with his thumb.

He didn't try to tell her she was wrong or that everything would be all right. Smart man. Instead, he simply
adjusted his body and pulled her close to his chest,
enveloping her in a comforting hug.

"Wh—what is your biggest regret?" she asked finally.

"Not meeting you sooner," he said. And then he
pulled back just enough to kiss her.

It wasn't a friendly kiss on the cheek or an even
friendlier peck on the lips. No, it was a long, deep,
emotionally satisfying smooch that made butterflies flit
around her stomach again. Not only that, she liked the
way he opened his mouth and swirled his tongue with
hers. That was very intimate.

She didn't know how long their lips were fused
together or when they started running their hands over
each other's arms and backs. She just knew she liked it
and wanted it to last forever.

Chapter 13

GAIA HAD TOLD AARON SHE NEEDED SOME TIME ALONE TO think. She was having some *human* reactions, and that made her uncomfortable. He reluctantly let her pull him through the ether and return him to a private spot in the Fierros' backyard. Before she left, he pressed a kiss to the back of her hand. Her hand tingled in the most agreeable way. She hadn't felt anything special when Bruce had done it. The sweet gesture she had seen centuries before made her wonder why it ever went out of fashion. Perhaps humans weren't a complete failure as a species after all. Aaron seemed perfect. But according to him, nobody was perfect.

Eventually, Karma and Fate found her brooding a few miles away under a large leaf dripping moisture in the foggy Puerto Rican mountains.

"Hello, Sister," Fate said cheerily.

"Oh, it's you," Gaia answered, deadpan.

"I'm here too," Karma said as she walked out of the ether.

"Fabulous."

The two interlopers glanced at each other as if wondering why she was being sarcastic when they hadn't had a chance to annoy her yet.

"I was pondering the future of the planet. Whatever you have to say, say it and let me get on with my deliberations."

214 ASHLYN CHASE

"Hmph." Karma stuck her fist on her hip and said, "I don't know if you deserve to hear our good news. Not with an attitude like that."

Gaia sighed. "All right. I could use a bit of good news about now."

Karma gestured to Fate. "The floor is yours, Sister. Since it's your area of expertise, I'll let you go first."

Fate grinned. "We found a match for you!"

Gaia slapped a hand over her eyes. "Not this again."

"Don't be hasty. At least listen to what she has to say." Karma folded her arms.

Gaia sighed. "Fine. Go ahead, Fate."

"He loves nature, is trying to do something good for humankind, and is a dedicated family man. He's a widower with two grown daughters and a new grandchild whom he adores. Bachelor number one is Dr. Aaron Samuels."

Gaia reared back, laughing. The fog cleared, and sunshine warmed her.

Fate whispered to Karma behind her hand. "Why is she laughing? Ah! I know. She's glad we persisted and found her a match."

"Or she's just losing it," Karma said.

"No, I'm laughing because you're too late. I already found him."

"Really? How?" Karma began, then she smirked. "Never mind. It just proves Fate knows what she's doing...sometimes."

"And we give you our enthusiastic blessing." Fate clapped her hands.

"Well, thanks. I'm kind of glad you showed up and told me this. I was trying to think of ways to wipe the humans off the planet—but then I realized I'd be wiping out good people too, like Aaron and his children and the Fierros and their brood, as well as Dawn and her grandmother, who has been called Saint Annette by her friends."

Fate gasped. "You were going to wipe all the humans off the planet?"

"Wow. I did not see that coming!" Karma said, wide-eyed.

"Relax. I had already talked myself out of it as soon as Aaron kissed me."

"He—He kissed you?" Fate asked, giggling.

"Yes. What's so funny about that?"

"Nothing! I'm just tickled. You know we love you, right?"

Gaia raised one eyebrow. "Tickled?"

"It's an expression that means we're happy for you," Karma said.

"Well, thanks. I'm pretty happy too. I think."

"Only pretty happy? Maybe?" Fate's expression reflected concern.

"I'm still not happy about the rest of humanity. Well, many of them. I haven't taken the time to examine each and every person. In fact, I intended to stay away from them. Like you'd cross the street to avoid a bad smell."

"They don't smell bad anymore. Back in the day though…" Fate waved her hand in front of her nose.

Gaia sighed deeply. "No. That's not what I meant. I can't explain it properly. I've had to keep a careful eye on my paranormals. Maybe I let the humans fall through the proverbial cracks while doing my utmost to protect them."

"You're losing me," Karma said.

"I've been trying to keep the paranormals from revealing their existence to humans, knowing how badly people would behave if they found out. They can barely tolerate each other. Can you imagine how threatened they'd be if they realized there was a whole subgroup with superior powers?"

"Oh, I don't know," Karma said. "All of my clients are human, and they're assigned to some pretty powerful minor goddesses."

"But what happens when they find out the person you've assigned them to *is* supernatural? And superpowerful?"

"We give them a time period to adjust. If they can't or don't want to handle it, we wipe their memories."

"Hmm… If only I could wipe every human's mind and start over. I'd eliminate a lot of my gifts."

"What would you take away from them?" Fate asked.

"That's just it. I don't know. I think they need most of what I gave them, but some have perverted it."

"Are you talking about sexual perverts?" Karma asked. "Because I can help you with them."

"No. I mean, yes…but not specifically or *only* them. But this might be a useful example. I gave people a sex drive to be sure the population didn't die out. And yet, some have carried that too far."

Karma nodded.

"Listen," Fate said, "you can ponder the worth of your creation later. For now, we want to get you laid—I mean *shade*. We need to get you into the shade. Your fair skin will burn in the bright Caribbean sun."

Gaia stuck a hand on her hip. "Sure, that's what you meant to say. And that's another thing! My ozone layer is my sunscreen, and humans are blowing a hole in it. With every rocket, every jet, it gets worse and worse. Why can't they just leave my creations alone?"

Karma sighed. "It's okay, Sister. Everything will work out. You'll see."

"I don't know how you're able to be so optimistic. Don't you deal with the worst of them?"

"Yes, and I take great pleasure in busting their chops. Leave the offenders to me, Gaia. Take a little nap, and let me do the rest."

"Why do you get to have all the fun?"

"Oh? You want to get in on the revenge game?"

Gaia shrugged. "It beats trying to think of ways to blow up the whole human race while leaving my innocent animals."

"Why don't you just concentrate on the people you *don't* want to blow up?" Fate winked. "I think there's someone out there who is as lonely as you are. Maybe you should spend some more time with him?"

"I'm afraid I'll screw it up."

Fate choked, and Karma laughed. "Good for you, Sister. Now go tell him that."

Aaron looked up from changing his granddaughter's diaper. He seemed surprised to see Gaia.

"I thought you wanted to be by yourself to think."

"Yes, and I thought. I also had a chat with my sisters. I'm done now," Gaia said.

He grinned as he gently placed the freshly diapered baby in her crib. "So did you come up with any revelations? I mean—considerations?"

Gaia sighed. "No, but when Fate and Karma showed up, they gave me something else to think about—some interesting news."

"Oh? What was that?"

Gaia chuckled. "I'm not sure I should tell you. You'll laugh."

He straightened and gave her his full attention. "I won't if you tell me not to."

"Seriously? You really won't?"

He schooled his features and hoped he wouldn't burst out laughing. But with Gaia, who knew what she might find humorous? "Sure. If there's something you want me to know, you can tell me."

"It's just this silly thing. Fate has been looking for somebody to keep me company, to make me laugh, someone I can spend quality time with. She thinks it will make me less annoying."

Aaron's brow furrowed. "Oh? Did she find someone?"

"Yes, as matter of fact she did. She told me to go spend some time with him."

"I see. So I guess you're here to tell me you won't be around much anymore."

"Really? Why would you assume that?"

"I'm confused."

"It's *you*, silly. They said I should be spending time with *you*."

Aaron's smile grew. "I see. I'd like that." He placed his arm around her waist and said, "What should we do with our quality time together?"

"I thought maybe I could help you with the plant you want to make into medicine. We haven't talked about that for a while."

"It's true. I still want to explore that possibility, and now that I'm here in Puerto Rico, I can. Since plants can't be taken off the island, I guess I have to take myself to the plants. I was thinking of moving here."

"Really? You'd give up your lovely home in Brookline?"

"It would be hard. I have so many memories of my daughters growing up there. But if it's something important, yes. I think this might be very important, and I'm sure they would understand."

Gaia placed her arm around his waist too. "So you want to mend shattered hearts... I think that's a lovely thing to do. Sometimes it makes me sad to see so many brokenhearted people."

"I'll bet. How do you deal with it?"

"I try not to look."

He chuckled. "Well, now that you're aware there's something that might be able to help, you won't need to be afraid to look anymore."

"True. Although I'm not sure how to help you. I could whip up a greenhouse and put a few hundred plants in there for you, just to get you started. I haven't the faintest idea what you're talking about when you say things like 'analyzing compounds' and 'finding the best delivery systems,' but I can grow plants all day long!"

Aaron looked thoughtful, gazing at his feet, then looked up at her and said, "No. This is something I should do the human way. I can't let you do everything for me."

"Oh. But I could really help..."

"You probably can, but I need to know the process can be duplicated *without* supernatural help. First, I'll have to find a place to build the greenhouse, and it should probably be close to the area where they grow naturally so we're not changing the conditions too much. There are so many different climates here. I guess I'll need to find a piece of land near that mountainside. I'm just not sure if the rain forest is for sale."

"Okay, how can I help with that?"

"I don't think you can. I'll need to speak to someone who knows about owning land all around the island—and I have a strong feeling that a lot of rain forest land is probably protected, never to be built upon. But *if* I can find a spot that works, you can help me build the greenhouse—by hand."

"Build it? You mean from bricks and mortar?"

"Yes, so to speak. I imagine I'll use metal and plastic, but with a kit or plans, I can probably put it together myself. That's how everything starts, right? Even things you do must start with a plan."

She tipped her head side to side a couple of times. "I suppose so. I got a little lazy and just made it so each generation's DNA would vary a bit, and then whatever species I was tweaking comes out just a little differently—but the same in most ways. I don't have to build the whole item from scratch over and over as you do."

"Yes. It must be nice to put something in motion that will self-replicate. But when it comes to inanimate objects, like buildings, I can't do that. In other words, I don't *want* your help in that way."

"Hmph. *Don't want* my help… Here. Let me show you something…"

"It's not that. I'm just not sure how much I should

depend on you. I could get so used to your doing things for me that I'd no longer want to do anything for myself."

Gaia sat down and hugged her knees. Aaron sat beside her but didn't say anything.

At last, she looked over at him and asked, "Do you really think I would make a mistake like that? Let you use me? Or make you dependent on me?"

"I hope not. But I have to confess… I don't always understand you. I would like to though."

"That makes two of us." Then she smiled. "What would you like to know?"

"I—I don't even know where to start. Where did you come from?"

She shrugged. "I've just always been here. Not necessarily here *here*. Not even on this planet before your concept of time."

"Really? So there was no one before you?"

"I'm not sure. I don't think so."

"Is there a God?"

Gaia laughed. "There are lots of gods."

"No, not those guys. I mean, one big guy. Up there." He pointed to the sky.

Gaia looked up, then gazed at him in wonder. "I think I know who you're talking about, but he's not up there."

"Where is he then?"

Gaia let out a deep breath. "I don't know. We don't see each other very often. Sometimes our paths cross, especially if it looks like a huge disaster might impact both of us. Lately, I've been trying to get in touch, to advise him that we need to intervene before man destroys this planet and maybe others as they try to escape and start over somewhere else. Plus, with all the space junk they're leaving up there, they could be blocking their own way out.

"We met a few years ago. I warned him that humans were creating a climate change I couldn't fix by myself."

Aaron sat up straight. "What did he do?"

"Nothing. He just wanted me to wait and see if the humans could figure it out for themselves. I was angry. Incensed is more like it. I think he's avoiding me now."

Aaron put an arm around her shoulder. "Do you think he's still waiting for people to figure things out for themselves?"

"I imagine so. Although it's getting harder and harder to leave this problem alone. I'd ask him again, except I don't think I would get a different answer. He really doesn't like to encroach."

"I can understand that. I'm not sure I'd want to interfere either. Self-created human problems can be very confusing and complicated. Mostly because everyone thinks they're doing the right thing."

"It doesn't seem that hard to me." Gaia rose and paced. "It's pretty simple, actually. People used to teach their children, 'Do unto others as you would have them do unto you.'"

Aaron nodded. "Yes, the Golden Rule."

"Golden Rule?"

"That's what we call it. Most children learn about that idea very young but seem to forget it. Sometimes when they need it the most."

"Exactly. How do you get them to remember it *always*? To have that in the forefront of their minds at every moment?" She held her hand out to him.

Aaron grasped it and rose. "If I knew the answer to

that, I could probably cure a lot of the world's ills. But unfortunately, I'm just one man. I hope I can cure *one* ill. Even that might be quite an undertaking, but I'd like to leave the world a better place by making that one thing possible."

Gaia continued to hold his hand. "I'm glad Fate picked you out for me, although"—she chuckled—"I told her I had already picked you out for myself."

Aaron grinned but looked down so she couldn't see his eyes.

"Was that too forward of me?"

"No. That was just perfect. I needed to hear it. If it's not too forward of me, I'd like to say something too."

She smiled prettily and said, "Of course! Say whatever you wish."

"I hear you've been a little hard on some of the paranormal–human couples. I think if we're going to make this work, you'll need to accept them for making the same choice we're making. Otherwise, you'll be called a hypocrite."

At first, she stiffened, and her eyes rounded. Then she shook her head and let out a sigh of resignation. When she relaxed, she said, "I know. I know. Someone already spoke to me about it. I just wasn't sure if it applied to me. When I realized it did, I wasn't sure what to do about it. Eventually, I decided I should host an apology party— but we're not calling it that! We're calling it Gaia's gala. I have to maintain some semblance of dignity."

Aaron smiled. "Perfect. I'm proud of you. It might not be easy, but I'll be right there at your side."

—◦◦◦—

Gaia eavesdropped through the floor of the vacant second floor over the party venue—a tea room. Bliss had managed to get her friend to reopen after business hours for a private function.

"Who sends out invitations to a party that starts in an hour?" Gabe asked.

Misty leaned into him and whispered, "It can only be one person, hon. My boss."

Kizzy overheard and exclaimed, "Gaia herself will be here? And by the way, where are we?"

The goddess decided she needed to make an appearance quickly before thirteen tables full of guests whipped themselves into a tizzy. She floated down through the ceiling to the small stage that had been set up for performers at the Boston Uncommon Tea Room.

"Welcome, one and all. Welcome. I'm glad you could all make it to my party."

"Did we have a choice?" Antonio asked.

Gaia held her tongue and gazed out at the crowd. So many familiar faces. So many humans mixed with paranormals, and it *wasn't* the horror show she'd thought it would be. She did a quick count and noted five phoenixes—three with human partners, two with modern muses—a werewolf with another one of her muses, a wizard and vampire couple, a human waitress with a shapeshifting coyote, two muse and dragon couples, and a handful of witches among the humans. A veritable smorgasbord of humanity and paranormal beings, all sitting together like…friends! Who knew?

Aaron rose and joined her on stage, putting his arm around her waist. Gaia sighed and laid her head on his shoulder.

Some of the couples looked at each other with eyebrows raised.

A disembodied female voice said, "Oh, come on. Don't look so surprised." Fate stepped out of the ether and gazed at the crowd. "You all knew I was looking for a mate for Mother Nature. As you can guess, I succeeded."

"Where the heck are we?" Ruth asked, holding her infant dressed in a pink onesie.

"Some kind of restaurant, I think," the male witch next to her whispered.

"I can see that. I want to know where *the building* is," she said.

"You're back in Boston!" a pretty brunette said as she entered from a door on one side. She carried a large, steaming teapot. "For those unfamiliar with the place, you're at the Boston Uncommon Tea Room. My name is Bliss. I'll be serving tea, and someone is coming right behind me with coffee. Simply ask for what you want." She pointed to each table, and a cup and saucer appeared in front of each guest. Then she began making the rounds with the hot water. She offered a choice of teas, and whatever the guest asked for appeared in front of them.

Another young woman, carrying a tray with a pot of coffee and an assortment of sweeteners and creamers, entered behind her and said, "Welcome back, most of you. I'm Angie. I'm an actual waitress here. Bliss is just helping me today. So are a few others you may not know, like my boyfriend, Tory." She pointed with her thumb behind her. A tall, muscular black male came out carrying two trays with three tiers each. The three silver levels were laden with scones, cakes, and tiny sandwiches. The appearance of a big man with small delicacies was incongruous but cute.

Tory set them down on two tables, then rushed back for more. Another young man, also muscular but shaved bald, passed him carrying two more of the same triple-tier trays and set them on two more tables. Before long, each of the attendees had a cup of tea, a small plate, and an assortment of goodies in front of them.

Once everyone was settled, Gaia cleared her throat. "Welcome to Gaia's gala! I know it's probably not what you expected, but I thought this would be cozier then a raucous party with a dance floor, a DJ, and all those crazy buffet lines."

Another goddess walked out of the ether. Karma was wearing studded stilettos and leather from head to toe. She smiled at everyone. "For the few of you who don't know me, my name is Karma. And you're all here because"—she looked over at Gaia—"*somebody* has something to say to you."

"Wait a minute. I was going to let people fill their tummies and have some pleasant conversation first."

"There's no time like the present, Sister." Ah, Fate chimed in.

Gaia shifted from foot to foot. She looked over at Fate and said, "I would have gotten around to it."

Fate just raised one eyebrow and folded her arms.

"Fine," Gaia sputtered. "You're all here because, as Karma hinted, I have something to say."

Her words were followed by a long silence. Eventually, Aaron gave her a little hip check. She narrowed her eyes at him and said, "I'm getting to it." Then she took a deep breath and let it out on a sigh. "I'm here to say I'm sor—I mean to say, I may have made a mis—" She cleared her throat and said, "I'm trying to apol—apol—I'm trying to say, I may have been—"

Everyone remained silent but glanced at each other, looking confused. They were clearly waiting for her to finish her sentence.

"Okay, let me try this again," she said. "I apol—I mean to say apolo—"

A young, handsome god appeared out of nowhere with his arms crossed and his legs apart.

Oh shit. It's Apollo.

"Did you call, Great-Grandma?"

"Apollo! I told you never to call me that."

Apollo shrugged. "Well, I'm here now, Goddess. You called me. What do you need me for?"

Gaia shut her eyes and slapped her own forehead.

Fate leaned over to whisper in his ear but everyone heard her say, "She's trying to *apologize*, but it's not going well. She could only spit out 'apolo' and then stopped."

Apollo laughed hard, then leaned back and watched as Gaia struggled again.

"I'm trying to say I'm sor—sor—"

Apollo jammed his hands on his hips. "What my beautiful great-grandmother—I mean, Goddess—is trying to say is she's sorry. She wants to apologize. I don't know what for, but I can't wait to find out. This is a first!"

Gaia pointed to him. "Yeah, that."

Aaron tipped his head and looked at her with narrowed eyes. "You're going to let him do it for you?

Are you sure you can't say it yourself? I think everyone
would rather hear it from you."

Her posture deflated somewhat. Then she straightened her spine and announced, "I'm *sorry*. I may have
been *wrong* about not allowing paranormals and humans
to mix. I can see how difficult it was to expect paranormals to only match up romantically with other paranormals. Some managed to do it, but it was rare."

Aaron kissed her cheek. "You did it. I knew you
could."

She let out a sigh of relief. "Yes, I did. And now I can
rest easier, knowing that I'm not going to be a hypocrite
by dating you."

There were surprised murmurs from the crowd.

Mother Nature faced the group and said, "Yes. I may
have found a human mate. Just like many of you did.
That's why I called you all here. Bliss was kind enough
to arrange for this lovely tea party and send out the invitations. She was once human, and after falling in love
with a dragon, she's now a modern muse. This is how
I started getting around the whole paranormal/human
thing. I had to make some humans supernatural."

Bliss joined the god and goddesses at the front of the
room. "It was my pleasure, Gaia. And I can honestly say
it was worth it. But I wasn't the first."

"Oh! That's right. Where is Brandee?"

"Here, Goddess!" A redhead hurried through the side
door, wiping her hands on a towel. "I was doing all the
prep. Is it time to take pictures?"

Bliss shook her head. "No. We were just talking
about how Gaia solved the problem of humans mating
with paras by making us muses."

"Oh!" Brandee giggled. "Yeah. My werewolf marked me, so there was really no going back. And I wouldn't want to. As a reward for taking the position, Gaia made one of my fondest dreams come true."

"She did that for all of us," Bliss said. "Even though my modern muse job can be difficult at times, it's worth it." She looked at the crowd. "I'm the modern muse of email. I lean over people's shoulders and whisper, 'Don't send that boneheaded reply.'"

Many chuckles and laughs erupted.

Gaia smiled. "I didn't catch everyone. Brandee's mate, Nick, has a twin brother, Konrad, who flew under my radar when he met his mate, Rosalyn. They were very quiet about it, so I never confronted them for doing what came naturally. Falling in love and taking it to the next level. There may have been a few others I missed. However, those of you that I did challenge a tiny bit…"

Karma interjected, "She means threatened, punished, or otherwise intimidated."

"Yes, yes. All of that." Gaia huffed, glaring at her sister.

Karma just chuckled.

"Anyway, I managed to find a way to make everyone happy, including myself. I do love my modern muses. They address problems the original muses couldn't understand. Brandee is the muse of modern photography and videography."

Brandee joined Bliss at the front of the room and said, "I've had to do everything from rescuing photographers from dangerous situations to making it difficult for people to upload certain recorded acts of stupidity, then whispering, 'You might want to think twice about

sharing that. You were told not to try it at home.' Kind
of like Bliss does with email."

More chuckles filled the room.

Mother Nature smiled and said, "There are a few
other modern muses who are not here, because they are
paranormal and always were. Dragons Chloe Arish and
Kristine Scott for instance. They both found paranormal
mates—phoenixes Ryan and Jayce Fierro."

"They also did not get dragged into your courtroom,"
Fate reminded her.

"Right. That. However, as muses, they have been
instrumental in helping me with modern problems that
the old muses were useless at. Pardon me. I mean the old
muses were *struggling with*." She looked to Aaron, and
he nodded, smiling.

A witch whispered to her neighbors, "I think she's
trying to be nice now."

"Nicer," Gaia said. "I was always nice as long as
humans cooperated with me. As they became less and
less cooperative, I became less and less nice. But it seems
as if my sisters were correct. Not only are my muses
helping me and thus making me happier in this modern
world, but finding Aaron has also helped tremendously.
Looking around at all of you, I've become reacquainted
with my own initial intentions when I invented love."

Many of the couples gazed at each other or held
hands or kissed.

"That said, I would like to introduce you to our
newest modern muse, Gabriella Fierro. Gabriella, would
you please come up here?"

The diminutive matriarch of the Fierro family stood
and trotted up to the front of the room, joining Apollo,

goddesses Karma and Fate, and minor goddesses Brandee and Bliss.

"She is taking over for Misty as my muse of modern parenting. It no longer 'takes a village to raise a child'. Apparently now it takes playdates, pediatricians, parenting books, and a lot of Disney movies."

Again, laughter filled the room.

"It was too difficult on my darling daughter-in-law, Misty," Gabriella said. "She has her own tiny ones to birth and raise. I've raised seven sons and welcomed many daughters-in-law. And they all turned out beautifully. I couldn't be prouder of my family. I hope to use what I've learned over the years to help parents deal with their own frustrations without taking it out on innocent children who are just being children."

"And what about Misty?" someone said from the back of the room. "Is she going to be human again?"

"Well, no," Gaia said. "Misty initially wanted to be the muse of dance, and I already had one of those. Terpsichore is her name."

Another goddess appeared. She swirled around the room, holding her long, flowing skirt out on either side, dipping gracefully every few steps. "You called on me, Goddess?"

"Ah, no. But you can stay if you wish." Gaia refocused on the group at large. "Apparently, there are whole new categories of dances. Some even involve acrobatics. And some of these new types can get dancers hurt! Misty is going to be the muse of modern dance. She'll make sure people know when something is too advanced for them and suggest they try it only with expert supervision—or not at all."

Misty rose. "I couldn't be happier. Thank you, Gaia." She turned to the crowd and explained, "I always wanted to dance professionally, but I developed MS, which spelled the end of my own dance career. I'm very fortunate to have been given the gift of complete health as my reward for taking the muse job. Now not only can I dance again, but I can enjoy watching others without envy or sadness. Again, Gaia, my heartfelt thanks."

Gaia bowed slightly. "You're welcome. It's a pleasure to do things for those who appreciate it." She gazed around the room. "And by the way, for those of you who thought I didn't particularly like you—well, you were wrong. I love all my creatures, great and small and dorky."

Aaron gave her a little side squeeze. "Perhaps now that you told everyone what you needed to, we can eat!"

"Oh! Yes, let's get this party started!"

"Yay," a few voices called out, and they dove into the sandwiches and sweets.

Chapter 14

"Hello, darling." Aaron strolled up to Kizzy as she stood admiring the home Noah was building for them.

"Hi, Dad!" She gave him a hug and a kiss on the cheek.

Noah walked out the front door. "Hey, look. Two of my favorite people."

Aaron's gaze dropped to the ground. At last, he met his son-in-law's eyes. "I'm not sure why I'd qualify as one of your favorite people. I haven't always treated you well."

"The way you treat me doesn't matter nearly as much as the way you treat my wife. You raised her to be an incredible woman, and she adores you. That's enough for me."

Aaron shook his head. "You see? It's that kind of philosophy right there that makes you head and shoulders above the rest."

"That and his being so tall," Kizzy said. They all laughed, which defused whatever tension may have been left over from their dating days.

Aaron hadn't thought a firefighter was a good fit for his doctor daughter—until that firefighter had saved her life. He had felt like somewhat of a heel ever since.

"So, to what do we owe the pleasure of your visit?" Kizzy asked.

Aaron cleared his throat. "Well, I'm glad you're both

here. I have some news, and I hope you'll be on board with it."

"Does this have anything to do with dating Gaia?" Kizzy gave him a teasing grin. "Mother Nature herself?"

He smiled but shook his head. "No. I've learned relationships aren't anyone else's business. Even close family can't possibly know how another couple feels. Actually, I wanted to let you know the property up the hill from yours is available, and I was thinking about living there."

"There?" Kizzy pointed. "But there's nothing there to live in."

"I know. The only thing left is a concrete pad. I was looking to build a hurricane-proof structure on it—unless you object to having me so close."

Kizzy glanced up at Noah.

"No objection here," Noah said. "In fact, I'd like to help you build it just as soon as I finish here. We're in the home stretch, so to speak."

Aaron couldn't have been more grateful. Not just for the help but for his son-in-law's obvious forgiveness. "You wouldn't mind living next door to your in-laws?"

Noah chuckled. "As long as Kizzy's happy about it."

Kizzy hugged Noah, then her father. "I'd be delighted to have you and Ruthie as neighbors, Dad! I missed both of you when I first got here and left you back in Massachusetts."

"You didn't just miss your sister?"

She snorted. "I missed you both, dummy."

Aaron reared back and laughed. "Well, I guess I've been put in my place. Again."

"Don't worry, Dad. I'll keep a pin handy to puncture your ego whenever you need it." Kizzy hugged him again, then stepped back to wrap her arm around her husband's waist.

"Let's see what you've been doing inside that house of yours," Aaron said. "Maybe you can give me some ideas."

"Sure. I'd like to show off a little." As he led them into the home, Noah pointed to the floor. "We just put down vinyl plank flooring. It's waterproof."

"It looks like real wood."

"Yup. It's wider than normal wood planks. We added thick weather stripping at the bottom of both doors too. That's where water usually gets in."

"Good. Good. What about windows? How do you know they won't break?"

"Double-paned glass. So thick a karate expert couldn't break it."

"Really? They look just like normal windows."

"That's the idea."

"Impressive. So what's next?"

"Kizzy picked out our cabinets and countertops. We're waiting for those to be delivered now. When they get here, if you'd like to help, I could use a steady hand holding the uppers in place while I attach them to the studs."

Uh-oh. He said a steady hand. Did he notice my tremors? Aaron changed the subject with a dumb question. "I'd be happy to lend a hand. How do you know exactly where the studs are? The drywall is covering them."

"He has a stud finder," Kizzy said.

"I thought that was every woman's superpower," Noah joked.

Kizzy slapped his arm playfully. "Way to sound sexist, hon."

"Sorry. The joke was right there. I had to."

Kizzy rolled her eyes.

"So, what kind of cabinets did you order?" Aaron asked her.

"Solid wood. MDF swells with moisture."

"Listen to you. My daughter knows more about construction than I ever will."

"Not if you build your own home," Noah said.

She chuckled. "I've picked up a few things just by hanging around with my handyman here." She gazed up at Noah lovingly. There was no missing the joy shining in their eyes when they gazed at each other.

"Well, I'm glad you don't mind my living up the hill from you. Because I already bought the land."

Kizzy's dark eyebrows shot up.

"That's great!" Noah said.

"I plan to build a greenhouse too. But first, a safe home for my younger daughter, newborn granddaughter, and myself."

Kizzy smirked. "Where is Mother Nature going to live?"

Aaron laughed. "Wherever she darn well pleases. At least I'm betting that's what she'd say."

"You're probably right. Just do me a favor, Dad."

"Anything."

"When Ruth starts dating, stay out of it. Okay?"

He stuffed his hands in his pockets, looking sheepish. "I'll try."

"Try hard. Remember, she is the most psychic one of the three of us."

"True. And I'm the least. Have you been getting any vibes about her doctor friend? What was his name? José?"

"Yes and yes. There's attraction there, and you don't have to be psychic to see it."

"Is he a good man?"

Kizzy shrugged. "As far as I can tell, yeah. I—I think there's something you should know about him though."

"Uh-oh. What is it?"

"Relax. It's nothing to uh-oh about. It's just that he seems to have the same power I do. When it looked like Ruth and Mary Ann might not make it, I saved the baby, but only because Ruth made me promise to." After a brief pause, she said, "José saved Ruth."

"You mean—magically? I thought he just did the C-section."

"He did, but she was on her way out by the time we got there. He carried her in, then had to scrub up and put on a sterile gown, mask, and gloves. All that would have taken more time than she had. He saved her."

"So he's a witch too?"

"Santeria," Noah supplied helpfully. "The way of saints. We looked it up."

"It's white magic...mostly," Kizzy added.

"Mostly?" Aaron's alarm bells went off.

"It's fine, Dad. He's a good guy. Every religion has their rogues, but I'm betting he's not one of them. He took the Hippocratic oath just like we did."

"Sheesh, Kizzy, don't scare me like that."

"Sorry." She rubbed her father's back in a soothing gesture.

"So when are you going to start building?" Noah asked, probably trying to change the subject.

"The cinder blocks are arriving tomorrow. I hired a company to clean up any remaining debris today."

Kizzy's jaw dropped. "And what would you have done if we said 'Hell no. We don't want you to live next door'?"

Aaron shrugged. "Not sure. I probably would have reminded you this is part of the USA, so a free country. Or I'd say I taught you to ride a bike, kissed your boo-boos, and sent you to college…"

"No, you wouldn't have."

"You're right. And I was pretty sure you wouldn't say no."

"Hell no. Welcome to the neighborhood!" She gave him a big hug, and Noah shook his hand.

A few days later, Gaia zeroed in on Aaron's energy and took a peek around the area from the ether. Good, there was no one else nearby.

She knew he had bought a lot next to Noah and Kizzy with one half acre of available land for his greenhouse. He'd learned he could duplicate the rain forest conditions so the plants would grow where he wanted them to. However, the home had to be built completely from the concrete pad up.

Mother Nature popped in a few feet from him.

Aaron looked up from where he had been laying a big concrete block, brushed the sweat from his brow with the back of his hand, and squinted into the sun. "Gaia! Great to see you."

"I hadn't heard from you in a couple of days, and then I remembered I didn't have one of those cell phone things. I did have one, but I started receiving recorded messages for stupid things like my credit report. I don't even have a credit card, so I threw the phone away. I've always been more of a 'Don't call me, I'll call you' kind of girl."

Aaron laughed. He strode forward and met her halfway. He took a kerchief from his pocket and swiped it over his face, then gave her a quick peck on the lips. The sweat coming off his neck and back indicated he had been at work for quite a while. She hoped he wasn't pushing himself too hard. Humans needed rest.

"Can you take a short break with me?" she asked.

Aaron looked over at the concrete slab with the cinder blocks setting up. "I really should continue while the mortar is still wet enough to work with. If it dries, I'll have to throw it out and mix more."

"Why are you bothering with all this building? I can whip something up for you to live in."

Aaron returned to his short wall and placed another cinder block. "I know you can do that, but you shouldn't."

Gaia took a step back. "Shouldn't? You still don't want my help? Why? Are you afraid I'll do it wrong?"

Aaron bolted upright. "No. That's not what I meant. You're more than capable, but there's this supernatural being I know of who doesn't like humans to notice things out of the ordinary—things that only a paranormal has the power to do—such as snap her fingers and create a building where there wasn't one a few moments before."

Mother Nature rolled her eyes, and one side of her mouth quirked up. "Are you talking about me?"

Aaron grinned. "Only if you're the goddess who made the rule." He slapped some more mortar on the top cinder block and spread it around the edges.

As he was about to place the next block on top, suddenly an entire concrete structure appeared in front of him. "Whoa!" He stumbled backward. "What the hell?" His gaze flipped around to where she stood with her arms crossed.

"Oh, this wasn't what you were going for? I thought you'd like it."

"It's not that I don't like it. I like it fine, but I didn't build it. You did. I need to do this for myself."

Gaia let out a *pah* sound and strolled over to a nearby tree stump, then plopped down onto it. "So you won't even let me help?"

Aaron wiped his hands on a towel and strolled over to her. "Gaia, there is helping, and there's doing it for me. That was just a perfect example of doing it for me. I could never have built that so quickly with my own two hands."

She pointed next to her, and another tree stump appeared. He looked at it and looked at her. She crossed her arms and stared at him.

Sinking down onto the second tree trunk, he sighed. "I appreciate your wanting to help, but—"

"But it's taking too damn long. Do you know how long it would take you to build this whole structure, one single block at a time, by yourself? I calculate it would take several weeks."

"Noah said he would help as soon as he's through building his own home down the hill. He said it's almost finished." Aaron pointed to another concrete square structure about half a mile down the sloped road.

"Okay, so that's only a couple of weeks with a young, strong phoenix at your side. It's still too long," she said.

"What's the rush?"

Gaia dropped her head into her hands. "I…I just want to spend some time with you." Lowering her voice, she said, "I miss you."

Aaron smiled and bumped her with his shoulder. "You miss me?"

She frowned at him, and then her frown slowly turned into a smile. "Yes, I miss you. From what I understand, people who like each other miss each other when they're apart. Don't make it weird. Don't you miss me too?"

Aaron smoothed her long, white hair over her ear. "Of course I miss you, honey, but we both have important things to do. I understand that. I can't just sit around and watch other people working hard day in and day out to rebuild their homes and businesses, then expect you to come along and snap your fingers to create the same for me."

She sighed, then stood abruptly. "Fine. I'll take it all down." With a wave of her hand, the structure she had built disappeared, returning to the short concrete wall he had started.

"Would you like to lend a hand?" Aaron asked. "I could use an extra pair of hands until you're called away."

Her eyebrows rose. "You want me to what? Hand you blocks? One at a time?"

"Yes. That would be very helpful. Then I could just mortar them in place…unless you get tired. They're fairly heavy. Then I can take over and do it myself, albeit a little slower."

Gaia reared back and laughed. "You think this will make me tired? Try grabbing a hurricane by the tail and unraveling it before it roars all the way to the North Pole. A few hours of that and I might get tired. This? This is nothing. Let me at it."

Aaron smiled. "I was hoping you'd say that. You might need to change your clothes though. You don't want to get mud all over your beautiful white gown."

She looked down at her gossamer robe, which she always belted with a vine, and her silk toga beneath. *Now what should I wear?* She had been teased mercilessly by Karma for her out-of-date fashion choices. She took a brief look around and said, "Are there any females working in construction on the island?"

"I'm sure there are. I don't know where though."

"I'll be right back." She snapped her fingers and disappeared into the ether.

"Karma," she called out.

Her sister showed up with her hands on her hips. She was wearing a short, sparkly red dress and black high heels with red soles. She also wore an annoyed facial expression.

"What do you want, Gaia? I was dancing at a diplomatic ball in Prague."

"Sheesh. I was just about to ask you for a little fashion advice."

Karma's jaw dropped. "Really? Sure! Of course. What's the occasion?"

"I have a construction date."

Karma cocked her head. "A what now?"

"I'm helping Aaron build his house, and he said I needed something else to wear. He didn't want me to ruin my clothes." She produced a breeze to ruffle her soft, white garments.

"Hmm... Yes, you're not dressed for heavy labor." Then she laughed. "Come to think of it, the only heavy labor I've seen you in was when you gave birth to the Giants. The whole universe heard you scream, and I had to hold your hand."

"No. I was holding *your* hand so you wouldn't go looking for the father who knocked me up with Giants."

Karma covered her smirk. "Whatever. That was a long time ago. So now you have a date with a lovely man, and you want something cute to wear that can stand up to mud. Is that right?"

"Yes. Precisely."

"No problem." Karma snapped her fingers, and Gaia looked down at her strange outfit.

"Thanks?"

"You're welcome. Have fun!"

Gaia returned to the construction site wearing blue-and-white pinstriped overalls with a pink T-shirt underneath. She had no idea if this was what female construction workers wore, but the outfit seemed less heinous than she'd expected.

She yanked up the pant legs and noticed a pair of work boots and thick socks protecting her feet. They were clunky and ugly, so she snapped her fingers and turned the boots into high-top sneakers and the heavy wool socks into white cotton socks. "There. Not too shabby." She piled her hair up on top of her head like she had seen some women do and turned it into a bun. Then she stuck a stick through it to hold the bun in place.

"Okay, I think I look fairly normal." Then she slowly shook her head. "Gawd. What I do for this man. Making myself look normal? Who would've ever thought."

She reappeared and handed Aaron his first block. He glanced up. "Thank you, Gaia. Cute outfit." He laid the mortar on all sides and set the block. She held onto the next block, waiting until he'd spread the mortar, then she set the block next to the one he had just laid. "Is this where you want the next one?"

"Yes. That's perfect."

She thought it might be easier to go all the way up first and then do the next row to the top. Oh wait. That would make columns. She rolled her eyes at herself. She liked columns, but they didn't use those much these days.

What the heck. She could try it and see what he thought. She dropped the next block on the one below it.

"Um. I need to put some mortar down first. That will hold the block in place when it dries. And since I'm staggering the pattern, I need to go horizontally, not vertically."

She let out a quick breath of frustration, but he didn't seem to notice. He just plopped down some more mud and spread it out. Then she put her block on top of that.

"Now you're getting it."

What a frustratingly slow process! But at least she got to spend time with Aaron. At this rate, a lot of time.

"How did you learn to build a house? You're a doctor."

"The same way everybody does nowadays. I watched YouTube videos." He chuckled. "And then I went to a building supplies store and talked to the experts there. Before I started anything, I bought a set of plans and hired someone to take the debris away, because I didn't have the equipment to do that."

"Oh. So you're just learning how to do this? For the first time?"

Aaron shrugged. "Yes. I'm sure I can do some of the grunt work. But I will have to hire other people when it gets to the more specialized areas like plumbing and electrical needs. As soon as I have four walls, I'll need to add interior framing and a roof. I don't think I can do that all by myself either, but by then, Noah will be helping me."

"I see." She put another block on top of the mud he had just spread. "So you're going to do this all day?"

Aaron grinned at her. "Probably."

She let out a long-suffering sigh. "This is going to get boring."

"Not if I have your beautiful face to look at all day."

She laughed. "I see. You'll be entertained by my face, and I'll be entertained by your charm, is that it?"

"I could think of worse ways to endure a little boredom. Later, after we're finished for the day, I'll take you out to dinner."

"Okay. Let's do this, but maybe a little faster." She began speeding up the process. He kept up with her, slapping the mud down, letting her place the next block on top, then he scraped the excess mud off. They repeated this process, laying down new block after block, and before she knew it, the whole outer shell was complete up to the window openings.

At last, Aaron said, "I need a break. How about you?"

Gaia stopped and realized even though she could have gone on, she would like to have something cold to drink and put her feet up for a little while.

She snapped her fingers, and two Adirondack chairs appeared with a small table between them. A pitcher of lemonade appeared on the table, then she held out her hands, and two glasses with ice in them appeared. She handed one to Aaron and gracefully sashayed over to one of the chairs.

"Is this okay? Is anyone going to notice a couple of chairs that weren't here a moment ago?"

"No, but it could be a little less conspicuous. Tell you what, let's use these." He tipped over three empty buckets and set the cold drinks on the one in the middle.

She rolled her eyes. "Fine." Snapping her fingers, she made the patio furniture and lemonade disappear. She plopped her butt down on one of the buckets and replaced the one in the middle with a cooler.

Aaron joined her on the other free bucket and took a peek inside the cooler. "Ah! A nice cold beer. Perfect." He removed two, popped off the caps, and handed one to her. Raising his bottle, he said, "To hard work."

Oh, this must be one of those toasts they do. She clinked his bottle with hers and was about to ask why he would dedicate his drink to hard work, but his smile as he admired his half-finished shell of a house said it all.

Then he took a long pull from his beer. His Adam's apple bobbed as he swallowed the liquid. The sight fascinated her, and she momentarily forgot everything else.

Then he smacked his lips and said, "Ah." A moment later, he placed the bottle against his sweaty forehead.

She never would've thought hard work was sexy. But this man made it look that way. She took a sip of her own beer and appreciated the earthy taste of the cold drink. She placed the glass bottle against her forehead and was instantly cooled by it. "This is a nice refreshing break."

"Yes, it is. And look how much we accomplished." He pointed to the four walls they had already completed, minus a few spots for windows and two larger holes that, when completed, would leave room for doors.

She saw the pride in his tired eyes. They shone with more gratification than fatigue.

"I guess we did pretty well for having to lay one block at a time over and over and *over* again. All. Day. Long." She let her tongue loll out the side of her mouth and hoped he knew she was teasing.

He set down his drink, rose, and pulled a handkerchief out of his pocket. He mopped the sweat off his face, then wiped off the back of his neck and tucked the handkerchief back into his pocket. "I need to shower… and so do you." He winked.

Aaron reached for her hand. She rose, watching him curiously. He pulled her toward him and clasped the back of her head, bringing her in for a gentle but long, meaningful kiss.

She could have stayed like that all day if he didn't insist on building that damn house block by block. But he did, and she respected him for it. For some reason, she'd thought he might let her deviate from her own rule. But that wasn't the kind of guy he was. And that was one of the things she liked most about him.

One block at a time, with his own two hands, he would build his house. He would probably just call it necessity, but she called it integrity.

Chapter 15

AARON COULD HAVE SWORN HE HEARD TRICKLING WATER and felt droplets of cool spray on his arms. Opening his eyes, he took a step back and stared in shock. A whole new location had appeared around them. One that included a rocky ledge, a grotto, and a waterfall.

"What the..." Aaron began.

"You said you needed a shower."

He shook his head in amazement. "I don't think I'll ever get used to this."

"To what? My listening to your needs?"

"I—I guess. Where are we?"

"Still in Puerto Rico."

A sly smile quirked up his lips on one side. He leaned over the grotto and asked, "How deep do you think that water is?"

"About fourteen feet deep."

"Okay. So nothing bad will happen if I just—" Aaron gave her a shove, and she landed in the natural pool with a splash.

When she surfaced, glaring at him and sputtering, he couldn't help laughing. He knew he was in for it but couldn't imagine her really hurting him.

"Very funny." She rose from the water and disappeared.

"Oh no." He was afraid he'd upset her and she'd desert him there—which would be inconvenient, since he didn't know where he was. He might still be in Puerto Rico, like she said, or she could have transported him to Hawaii for all he knew.

At last, she reappeared next to him, perfectly dry and dressed in her silk toga. Her long waves of white hair, also dry, ruffled in the breeze.

"Oh, that's not fair. I thought we could shower together," he said when he'd collected himself.

She shoved him off the rock ledge and into the cold water.

When he came up sputtering, she chuckled. "What were you saying about something being unfair?"

He laughed and swam to the rocks in front of her.

Something about Gaia stirred his senses on a level he couldn't even begin to explain. So far, he'd tried to keep it casual. She was too into her work, and quite frankly, so was he…as usual. He needed to learn to relax and get his priorities straight. He had always wanted to explore the chemistry between them, but the timing had never seemed right. Until now.

Right now, there wasn't anywhere else he wanted to be. There wasn't any more important undertaking he wanted to do.

Some would probably claim kismet. They'd say something about the stars and moon being in perfect alignment. That was when true souls connected—or something like that. Aaron didn't believe in all the cosmic mumbo jumbo, but he did have to admit there was something perfect about this evening. About this unexpected opportunity that had magically presented itself.

He pulled himself out of the water and watched her eyes grow as she saw the rivulets of water cascade down his body. His T-shirt stuck to his hard chest. He was in his late fifties, but he didn't feel old. He had kept himself in shape, and apparently she'd noticed. She licked her lips.

She opened her mouth to say something, but no words came out. Aaron fought the natural desire to chuckle at her speechlessness. Perhaps he'd stunned her into silence.

He wondered how Mother Nature herself would respond to sexual pleasure. He imagined she was a powder keg of passion, waiting to be ignited. And tonight, he had the overwhelming desire to light the fuse.

"Tell me," he said in a low tone as he reached her. He leaned forward and rested his palm on the rock wall behind her. His body practically curled around hers, his erection pressing against her hip. His head dipped so he merely had to whisper in her ear. "How do you like to be touched, sweetheart?"

He heard her body humming with a curious vibration that seemed to leave her seriously off-kilter.

"Calm down," she muttered.

"I'm sorry, I—"

"Don't be sorry. I was talking to myself."

These were definitely uncharted waters, at least for him. Maybe for both of them. Finally, she smiled, took a step back, and produced two martinis in her fists. She handed one to him and took a generous sip of her own.

"Is this some sort of stalling tactic?" he asked.

"Why on earth would you think that?" She rolled her eyes. As he was deciding if she was being sarcastic, she continued, "Why are you wasting your time trying to seduce me when there are probably hundreds of beautiful girls that would love to get their hands on you?"

"Only hundreds?" He grinned at her, his eyes twinkling with mischief. At least he hoped so. He wanted her to know he was toying with her. Then he whispered, "I'm only interested in you. I want only you, darling."

Gaia sucked in a breath, her nipples tightening behind the flimsy swath of silk that barely covered her breasts.

"What's it gonna be, Gaia?" He set his martini on the ground and moved away from the rock wall and closer to her. His fingers toyed with the top button of his faded Levi's. They were still wet, and she stared at how they were plastered to his muscular legs. It looked like Gaia's mouth was practically watering.

"How about if I help you decide?" he said, a teasing smile playing on his lips. He clenched his fist full of wet black cotton and tugged the hem of his T-shirt from the waist of his jeans, then up over his head. Gaia's gaze dropped to his abdomen as he peeled the material from his body, exposing a wide expanse of taut muscle and damp skin.

An unbidden sigh escaped her lips.

But dammit, he was human. Aaron Samuels was a doctor and a decent human being, but human nonetheless. And she was Gaia, Mother Nature, goddess of all. How could they be a couple?

And yet, some mystical inner force had brought them together. She reached out her hand toward Aaron's chest. Her fingers just barely skimmed his well-defined abs. He stayed perfectly still and let her run her hands up over his pectoral muscles and then step into his embrace.

He was equally enraptured. He liked the way she touched him. The pad of one finger just barely skimmed his nipple, and his jaw clenched.

He knew if they continued, they wouldn't stop with mere touching. But common sense had long since abandoned him, and now what ruled was passion in his usually sensible brain.

Taking one small step forward, he closed the gap between them. Their thighs brushed. Their torsos slowly melded together. The hand that had previously touched his pecs now rested on his forearm as his own hand gripped her hip and yanked her that much closer to him.

A burst of minty breath escaped her body. Her gaze was smoldering, yet she was not the least bit intimidating.

He wanted her, but he didn't want to unnerve her with the intensity of his desire. Aaron kissed her jaw, then moved lower, his lips brushing her throat. "I want you," he said. It seemed like such a simple statement, yet his deep, intimate tone packed one hell of an erotic punch. Wondering where the growl that followed came from, he decided it didn't matter. To him, it really was as simple as that. He wanted Gaia, and she wanted him.

He hoped she would let him make love to her. They'd been friends first, but he didn't want to get stuck in the friend zone. It was now or never.

—◆◆◆—

Gaia looked deep into his eyes. "I've seen every side of love and sex. I've seen hopes of love. I've seen players played by another and left shattered. And I've seen the most incompatible of couples discover the one thing about the other that makes them whole." She shook her head.

She continued on, saying, "I have no delusions about anything, Aaron. I can't afford to. I want people to see past physical attraction and find something solid to hang onto. Starting a relationship is simple. But maintaining one, well…"

Aaron paused thoughtfully. At last, he said, "I don't have the answers either. But I do know I want to explore whatever this is between you and me. I would consider it an honor if you would allow me to do that, but more than that, I need you to try *with* me. I don't want to navigate these tricky waters alone. Everyone needs someone."

"And you want me to be your someone?" Gaia asked.

"I definitely do," he said quietly.

They hadn't resolved squat. What this might or might not mean didn't matter any longer to Gaia. All that mattered to her was that he consumed her mind. Making love to Aaron was the only thing she could think of now. The only thing she wanted to do. She wanted to please him. She wanted to drive him wild, hear him moan. She wanted to make him come and come hard.

The desire gripping her intensified until an insatiable hunger took over her body. One hand plowed through his hair, holding his head in place as she captured his lips in a deep kiss.

Maybe it was the martini. Maybe it was Aaron. But Gaia had never felt so freely uninhibited before, so lost in the moment. She wanted more than anything for Aaron to be buried deep within her warm, wet depths. His hands shifted, and he clasped her toga in his fists. Pulling the soft material upward, he broke the kiss so he could haul the garment over her head, then tossed it beside the pool.

"Oh my," she gasped. "You want to have sex here?"

Aaron grinned at her, but he backed her up against the rock wall, and when she was trapped between him and the rock, he said, "Why not?"

Why not indeed?

He slid his hands slowly down her arms, along the outer swells of her breasts, and over her rib cage. He let out a low groan as he took in her areolae and nipples, which were becoming a darker shade of dusty rose. The pebbled centers begged for his touch. She wanted more than anything for Aaron to take each sensitive bud into his mouth and lave it with the teasing pressure of his tongue.

His head bent, his lips seeking hers. She let out a soft whimper, and his mouth sealed to hers as he engaged her in another slow, sensuous kiss. He pressed his body against the length of her. His hands eased over her bare skin, and she tingled. Actually tingled. She felt the rise and fall of her chest against him. As he moved his lips lower, she sucked in a breath. Cupping her full breasts, he gave them a gentle squeeze. Gaia's soft, lusty moan heralded her slow surrender. At the same time, her heart melted a little more, knowing how completely she was ready for him.

"I'll give you everything you want, sweetheart," he whispered in her ear. "Everything you need. You may just have to tell me what feels good and give me a little guidance."

Her body trembled, and she heard her own breath catch as he latched onto one nipple and sucked. He leaned in closer to her, pressing his body to hers. His long leg wedged between hers, forcing them farther apart. His hands moved over her rib cage to her back. He broke the pressure on the first breast, and then he moved to the other one.

Oh! I feel really good! And he'd barely even touched her. But the night was still young, and she intended to make the most of every minute with Aaron.

What was most stunning to Gaia wasn't how incredible Aaron's hands felt on her body. She'd known he'd overwhelm her senses and drive her crazy with wanting him. But what surprised her most was how wantonly she responded to him. All inhibition seemed to melt away as his fingers eased over her burning flesh. As his lips worked their way back up and grazed her neck, she became just a little more undone.

His strong hands on her body, his tongue gently teasing her skin, his clean, wet scent mixed with his male heat turned her on more than anything she'd experienced. True, Mother Nature hadn't engaged in such a primal heated encounter before. Usually, it was just *Wham, bam, thank you, ma'am. Have fun giving birth to Giants.*

The air around them was sexually charged. With every breath she took, he infiltrated her senses all the more, making her even more excited and very wet. Swiping her sensitive center with the pad of his finger elicited a sharp cry from her. Her eyelids fluttered closed. The combination of his warm breath around the shell of her ear, her breasts pressing against his chest, and his talented fingers pressing against her most sensitive bud made her pulse race and her insides seize up. The throbbing between her legs intensified. *Oh, sweet torture...*

Maybe she wasn't Aaron's usual type, and maybe seduction was all new to her, but this wasn't just a wild impulse brought on by the full moon or basic physical needs. She had to admit it was Aaron himself. A passion-induced haze took over, shadowing all doubt and uncertainty. All reservations slipped away.

She cared deeply for him. And she knew he cared for her, as only he could. Faithfully. She knew the kind of person he was, and she would bet anything he was a one-woman man.

He leaned slightly away and gave her breasts a squeeze, then slid his hands down to her stomach. His fingers deftly worked the button and zipper on his jeans. He eased the denim over his hips and down his legs. He stepped out of the thick material and kicked his jeans aside. His hands went on a loving exploration of her legs, starting with her calves, and his fingers grazed the backs of her knees, teasing the sensitive flesh before moving higher up to her now quivering apex. He grinned at her, bestowing on her a sweet yet oh so sexy look that made her insides burn and her heart soar.

She sucked in a breath and gave him a small nod.

"Don't worry, sweetheart. You're going to enjoy every second of this."

"I'm not trembling because I'm nervous. It's just the way you touch me. The way you look at me. It makes me feel…" She searched her jumbled brain for the right words. "Sexy," she whispered.

Aaron stared at her. "You *are* sexy, darling. Damn sexy."

Gaia had never thought of herself that way. But tonight, she felt completely desirable. All because of

Aaron. She shook her head. "I can't even think straight right now."

Aaron winked at her. "Stop thinking, sweetheart. Just feel."

He trailed his hand from her stomach to her pelvis and down until the heel of one hand covered her mound. He applied just the right amount of pressure to make her whimper in need. As he massaged the sensitive area, desire caressed her insides...her heart and her soul. Her toes curled. His finger entered her slowly, gently, testing her wetness.

A moment later, he positioned himself right below her opening and thrust upward gradually but firmly until he was fully seated. "Are you okay?"

She sighed. "Never better."

He began the age-old rhythm of thrusts and partial withdrawals. Intense sensations rocketed through her body. She gasped. Her grip tightened on his shoulders.

He kissed her temple, cheek, and her ear as he made love to her.

She had never known such intimate pleasure. No god or man had ever made love to her this way. And she innately knew no one else could make her this hot, this restless, this in need of release.

He lifted one of her legs and draped it around his waist. He began stroking her clit with his finger while he continued thrusting with his cock. His eager cock increased the speed of their rhythm, and her hips matched him thrust for thrust, as all the while he murmured encouragement.

He continued giving attention to the swollen nubbin between her legs. Gaia rushed toward what was sure to be a powerful orgasm. Her heart thundered in her chest, and heat lightning lit the sky. Ripples of sheer joy rushed through her body until, at last, she erupted in a bright shower of stars.

What Aaron did to her body was more sizzling than she'd dreamed possible. Pleasuring her in a way that made her lose all control—now here she was *again* careening toward another release. She had never experienced multiple orgasms. Intense sensations consumed her, heightening her arousal to a nearly unbearable degree. But she wanted to see how high and hard she could climax.

"More," she whispered on a sharp breath. She whimpered encouragement, wanting Aaron to know how much she loved his intimate touch. Wanting him to know how crazy with desire he made her. As he pushed his cock deep into her core and intensified the pressure on her clit, she was done for. Another climax tore through her. The sensations were electric, intensifying to an overwhelming degree before the fiery heat and pleasure lit up the sky above them.

"Aaron!" she cried out. Bursts of light flashed behind her closed eyelids. Her heart slammed against her chest, and her entire being embraced the erotic sensations that surged inside her. She held onto the endless moments of rapture, her inner walls squeezing tight around Aaron's thick cock, holding him captive as she clung to his shoulders. She could have stayed in this glorious place forever. Nothing had ever felt so wonderful. So right.

Aaron's breaths came in shallow pants as he stared down at the place where their bodies met. Suddenly, he shuddered from his core.

His release seemed timed to her vaginal contractions. They came together, Aaron once, Gaia for the third time.

At last, he collapsed against her and braced his forearms against the wall behind her as if it were the only thing holding up both of them. Perhaps it was.

"I luuu—" she began. Could she do it? Could she say the words? "Luuuuv—"

Aaron pushed his upper torso from the wall without uncoupling them. His lips turned up in a smile. "I love you too, Gaia." And he sealed the words with a sensuous kiss.

Mother Nature summoned her sisters to the ether. Fate appeared first. Karma materialized close behind. They looked like they had been out partying, both wearing sparkly short dresses and spiky high heels.

Gaia just looked at them and shook her head. "Sorry to interrupt your fun. Listen, Sisters. I can't believe I'm asking you this, but I need your help, and I've no one else to ask."

Fate stepped forward and put her hands on Gaia's arms, looking at her with compassion. "Oh, Sister, what happened? How can we help?"

Karma stood behind Fate. "We're listening. Sort of." With a smirk on her face, she placed her hands on her hips.

Gaia took a giant step back and said, "It's not anything terrible, Fate. In fact, I think you'll be pleased. It's just that I need a little advice in the dating area."

Fate clapped her hands. "Oh! I knew it! You and Aaron. Is everything okay?"

Gaia smiled and nodded. "I think you're both right. He's as close to a soul mate as I'll ever find."

Fate ran back to Karma and squeezed her arm. "See? I told you she would be able to handle the idea of dating a human...if it was the *right* human."

Karma raised her brows and stepped forward. "So why do you need our advice, and why can no one else help you?"

Gaia blushed. "I...um..."

After a long hesitation, Karma said, "Just spit it out. We're all adults here."

Gaia took a deep breath and tried. "I'm just... I mean, he's just so... I mean...so very..."

Fate cocked her head. "We can't read your mind, Gaia. Unless you want to remove the shield you've put there to keep us from knowing your innermost thoughts."

Gaia thought about it and realized showing them might be a whole lot easier than telling them about her concerns. She placed her hand a few inches below her chin and ran it up over the crown of her head.

Then, with her shields removed, she thought about the night she had just spent with Aaron by the waterfall. Specifically, the time against the rocks and all the heat lightning and meteor showers.

Karma took a step back, and her eyebrows shot up. Then she grinned. "Wow. That was some passionate lovemaking."

Gaia let out a long breath in a whoosh. "You can say that again."

"Wow. That was some—"

Gaia held up her hand. "You know I hate literal

humor. Look, I just need to figure out how to enjoy that incredible feeling without, you know…"

"Causing an earthquake?" Fate provided.

"Yes. Exactly. I'm wondering, can I possibly contain this, especially if he gets any more passionate?"

Karma nodded. "I can think of one way. When you can't stand it anymore and know you're going to scream, shake, and have an out-of-body experience, you'll have to pop both you and Aaron into the ether. What happens in the ether…"

Gaia turned bright red and covered her face with her hands. "Stays in the ether," she mumbled.

Fate rubbed Gaia's shoulder. "Don't be embarrassed, Sister. You created sex to be enjoyable. Why shouldn't you enjoy it yourself?"

Mother Nature snapped her fingers, creating a fainting couch and two overstuffed armchairs.

"Oh, is this going to be a long conversation?" Karma asked.

Gaia flicked her fingers, and one of the chairs disappeared. "Not if you don't want to stay. I can puzzle out any remaining concerns with Fate."

"Okay then. I have someone waiting for a good swift kick in the butt, and I was just excusing myself to go to the bathroom."

Gaia made a dismissive wave. "Go. Punish. Have fun."

Karma sang "Ta-ta," and vanished.

Gaia sat in the chair and allowed Fate to have the couch. Fate was kind of a softy, and as Gaia expected, she stretched out on the lounge. "So that light show last night was you?"

Gaia sighed. "Yes, and it's fine to happen once in a while. People can call it a fluke, but what if…"

Fate rested her head in her cupped hand, getting even more comfortable. "Ah! What if you got together in a committed relationship and it happened almost every night? Hee-hee. Scientists would be going crazy trying to explain it. Imagine if they ever discovered the truth. Now that's an image and a half!"

Gaia slapped her forehead. "Shoot, I forgot to close down my mental shield."

Fate chuckled as Gaia moved her hand from the crown of her head back down over her forehead and nose to her chin.

"So can you think of any other way to *not* interrupt the mood and, you know, keep the earth from…"

"Detonating? Erupting? Imploding?" Fate giggled. "Why don't you just re-create the spot you're fooling around in, right in the ether? He won't even know you've relocated. You can do it before you start getting too involved to think about where you are."

"Sure. Like preventative protection."

Fate chuckled. "You could call it that. I'm sure to humans 'preventative protection' might sound like something else. And that's okay. You don't want him to know about the ether and all that, right?"

Gaia flopped back on the easy chair. "That's another problem. I've showed him some of what I can do, but there's so much more. Also, I don't know how much to tell Aaron about the other paranormals. He's familiar with the phoenixes, but should I warm him about the others? Vampires, for instance? What about some of the more powerful gods and goddesses? I mean, he's met

Apollo, you, and Karma. But there are others who could scare the pants off the bravest human. It was so much easier just to leave humans in the dark completely."

Fate shrugged. "I guess you just have to figure it out like all the other paranormals do. From what I understand, they tell their partners nothing until they're one hundred percent sure their lover can be trusted."

"But you said Aaron was my soul mate. I can trust him completely, right?"

Fate gave a weak smile. "I don't know. You might want to ask him how much he wants you to share. Now, if you don't need me anymore, I should get going too before I'm missed. I was working with Karma to redirect a wrong relationship to a right one."

"Why don't you adjust time like I showed you?"

Fate smirked. "I don't want to. You're on your own, Sister." And she disappeared.

"Wait! I didn't ask my most important question!"

When no one reappeared, she flopped onto the fainting couch to pout.

At last, Fate's voice reached her from somewhere outside the ether. "Try asking a happily married woman for the answer to your last question."

Chapter 16

GABRIELLA FIERRO HUMMED TO HERSELF AS SHE WASHED THE breakfast dishes. Her husband was out, helping with one of Habitat for Humanity's many projects. Her friend Annette Forest was at the senior center with her boyfriend, Diego. Gabriella thought to herself how funny "boyfriend" sounded when talking about men of a certain age. She didn't know how old Diego was, but if she had to guess—

Suddenly, Gabriella was standing in a flowering meadow, dirty dishwater dripping from her empty hands. "What the...?"

"Greetings, Gabriella!"

The goddess herself appeared from behind an apple tree and strolled toward her, holding a ripe red apple in each hand.

"Gaia?"

"Indeed! I thought it would be a good time to get to know each other better, since you're going to be working for me."

"Oh yes. I suppose it would be."

"I didn't take you away from anything important, did I?"

Gabriella chuckled. "Not at all. You can take me away from doing dishes anytime." *And my own silly thoughts.*

"Your thoughts aren't silly. In fact, I'd like to know your thoughts on something."

Gabriella took a step back. "You can read my mind?"

"Only when you think too loud."

"Oh. I didn't realize… Can Misty teach me how to think softly?"

Mother Nature smiled. "She probably can. I don't hear many loud thoughts from her now that you're taking over the job that left her panic-stricken."

"Panic-stricken? Oh dear. I knew she was uncomfortable being the muse of parenting since she just became a parent herself and now she's pregnant again. But will the job really be that hard?"

"Not for you. I should have realized a more experienced parent would take a lot of things in stride. But I think she's happier now. Is that right?"

"Oh absolutely. She's delighted watching dancers from the ether. She wanted to teach dancers, you know. Now she becomes that little voice of reason when they're about to attempt something stupid. Pardon me…I mean beyond their athletic skill. It's perfect for her."

"I'm glad."

"So am I. She's such a sweet, sweet girl. I watched her grow up. She was always like the little daughter I didn't have."

"Well, we're not here to discuss your daughter-in-law. I'd like to talk about you, Gabriella."

"Of course. I'm anxious to know something too. May I ask you a question?"

"You can ask…"

Implying she might not answer. Well, here goes nothing… "Why do you need a modern muse of parenting? Parenting is pretty much the same as it's always been. You feed, clothe, and protect your child while teaching them right from wrong. That doesn't change."

"Ah. But modern times have made it more of a challenge. Have you heard the phrase, 'It takes a village to raise a child'?"

"Yes."

Gaia sighed. "Well, the village is a thing of the past. People are increasingly cut off from each other. Parents face more distractions and financial pressures than ever before. Not to mention the internal pressure they put on themselves to raise a child who excels in some way, making it seem as if they're superparents. Sometimes, it's a way to cover up the fact that they're barely parents at all."

"So this isn't just about kids being raised by kids who don't know the first thing about parenting because they never had a good example themselves?"

"Oh, it definitely is. But it's not only that. Bad parenting crosses all economic and cultural lines. You know the difference, and I don't think you'll be shy about telling a parent to back off or step up when necessary."

Gabriella laughed. "Not at all. You have no idea how many times I've wanted to brain some obnoxious mother or oblivious father in public."

Gaia grinned. "I'm delighted. It seems as if you're prepared for it."

Gabriella shrugged. "Well, I'd rather give someone a pat on the back for good parenting, but I'm looking forward to helping the next generation however I can."

"You can absolutely give a parent praise when it's deserved. There isn't enough of that either."

She smiled. "Okay then. Between Misty telling me how to use my new powers and your pep talk, I think I'm ready. When do I start?"

"Ah, well, there's another reason I wanted to talk with you."

"Oh?"

"Yes." Mother Nature paced in front of Gabriella while she spoke. "I know you've been happily married for over thirty years, correct?"

"Thirty-six wonderful years."

Mother Nature smiled and halted her pacing, turning to Gabriella. "How? How did you do that?"

"Excuse me?"

"I believe you heard me. I'm asking how you accomplished thirty-six years of contented togetherness."

"Yes, I heard you. I'm—I'm just not sure *how* Antonio and I have stayed together and been happy for all these years. We just...have."

Mother Nature cocked her head and put her hands on her hips, as if waiting for the magic secret to be spilled.

Gabriella let out a long breath and scratched her head. "I really don't know how. It just happened naturally. We like each other. We're best friends. I can't imagine trying to cope, never mind enjoy life, without him. We rely on each other. We trust each other. We understand each other. Does that help?"

Gaia placed her clasped hands behind her back, then started pacing again. "I...I think so. You're saying you were friends first? And still are?"

Gabriella smiled. "Yes. Best friends."

"This friendship thing has me a bit confused. I don't know who or what to believe. I see couples trusting each other and being betrayed. I see friends enjoying each other's company, then having a fight and walking away, never to return. I just don't know how to avoid the things that ruin a relationship. I'm…I'm afraid I'll do something to ruin the one I have, which is just beginning."

"With Aaron?" Gabriella guessed.

Gaia nodded, snapped her fingers, producing a bench, then sat down and stared off into the distance.

Gabriella cleared her throat. "Well, you have maturity on your side."

Gaia burst out laughing. "Yes, you could say that."

Gabriella chuckled too. "I find that if Antonio and I disagree, we truly try to work things out. We don't stomp off like children. It helps sometimes to get a little distance from each other, but you should say that's what you need and assure your partner you'll be back to discuss it later. Good relationships happen when people try to give each other what they need."

"So you're saying if we have a fight, we shouldn't walk away, but we should give each other space."

"Exactly!"

"You've lost me."

"I'm not answering your question very well, am I?"

Mother Nature shook her head. "Not so far, but what I've learned about humans is I should probably just wait until you explain it in a way I'll comprehend, and we can talk until it makes sense. I don't need space. I need to understand what the secret is to staying together."

Gabriella brightened. "See? You just did it. You just told me you needed clarification. And you didn't need to walk away or get angry. That's a big part of successful communication. Just being honest and explaining how you feel, what you need, as well as what you're thinking. If the other person understands where you're coming from, they can correct any misunderstanding or miscommunication."

"Okay. I think I get it. So I should just treat Aaron as I would treat you or anyone who was trying to help me."

Gabriella reached over and took her hand. "Yes. And don't forget to use those three little words…"

"I love you?"

Gabriella grinned. "Those too, when appropriate, but I was talking about 'please' and 'thank you.' Be grateful for the times when he helps you or encourages you to do or keep doing something important to you. Or even when he just does his own job."

Gaia looked down at their clasped hands. "Now I'm confused again."

Gabriella heaved a sigh. "I apologize, I'm not explaining myself well. But thank you for being patient with me."

"All right. I think I get it. You're expressing gratitude for my…well, I don't know what I'm doing, but it sounds like I'm doing something right."

Gabriella let out her tinkling laugh. "Yes, you are. And actually, it's really quite simple. Let me just say this: treat each other with respect. That's all."

"That's all?"

"Basically, that's what it all boils down to. Like, love, and respect."

Mother Nature nodded slowly, gazing out at the meadow. "All right, I think I understand. But I may have some difficulty with that. To be honest, I haven't given human beings much respect in the past."

Gabriella patted her knee. Gaia looked down at the hand touching her. It seemed as if Gabriella was comfortable around her. That was new too. All these new thoughts and experiences, well…they were comforting, confusing, and sometimes downright baffling.

Gabriella straightened her posture. "There's one more thing."

Gaia quickly focused on her and paid attention.

"Forgiveness. A successful relationship requires endless forgiveness."

"Endless, like they're never going to stop needing forgiveness?"

Gabriella chuckled but nodded. "Unless you change our basic makeup, human beings are never going to stop making mistakes. Hopefully, with age and maturity, those mistakes become fewer and farther between. I know they have been for Antonio and me."

"Okay. So any time Aaron makes a mistake, I need to forgive him. No matter what he does?"

Gabriella nodded. "Yes. But don't tell him that."

Gaia leaned over and dropped her head in her hands. "Gawd. I'm never going to get this."

Gabriella put an arm around her and gave her a side squeeze. "Relax. You'll get it. Like, love, respect. That's all you have to remember."

"So what if I love and respect him, but he does something I don't like? Or I do something he doesn't like? Does that ruin the whole 'like, love, respect' thing?"

"No. But if you're in a committed relationship, you wouldn't need to worry so much. You can rely on love. You can dislike the other's actions without losing the love between you. You can love him and not like what he does. Do you understand what I mean by that?"

Gaia thought a minute. "Oh yes. There was that time when he didn't trust me. I didn't like that, but that didn't mean I didn't like *him*. I liked him a lot, and that was why his not trusting me hurt."

"Exactly! You've got it. Love always, and like the *person* if not always the behavior. And about respect… that's how you treat each other, no matter what."

Gaia rose. She reached for Gabriella's hands. Gabriella immediately placed her hands in the goddess's and rose. Gaia smiled. "Thank you, Gabriella. Thank you for a very important, very confusing, but very smart lesson. I will remember the main points. I may forget some of the bizarre ways you got there."

Gabriella giggled. "I wish you would. Hey, why don't you and Aaron come to Luca and Dawn's wedding? The officiant usually has some words of wisdom for the couple, and he will be much more well-spoken than I am. Plus a wedding usually brings out the romance in attending couples."

"Really? They won't mind?"

Gabriella smiled. "They'd be honored. Besides, Antonio and I were told we could invite whomever we want. It's an outdoor wedding, so size doesn't matter."

"That's another saying I've heard regarding couples…"

Gabriella smirked. "Oh, that. Well, you love him, so I think you're beyond that part. Besides, if you don't like the size you gave him, that's on you."

Mother Nature scratched her head. "I really don't understand what you're saying sometimes, but I think you're telling me not to worry about it. Okay. I'd better go now."

Gabriella blew out what sounded like a breath of relief.

———~~———

Dawn had landed at Logan Airport and was taking the subway to her mother's halfway house in Brighton, Massachusetts. Lissie had been sprung from prison early for good behavior. Dawn had mixed feelings. She knew her mother was clean and sober and really wanted to stay that way. Still, Dawn had heard it before and couldn't help worrying.

She arrived at the large, three-story brick house. It was several miles from the place she grew up. That took care of a major worry. Her mother got in trouble by being part of the neighborhood gang. Dawn had managed to extricate herself but not without difficulties. She knew how hard it was. When the gang felt they had you, they thought they owned you. That was *not* going to happen to her mother again if she could do anything about it.

Dawn strode up the old, faded brick steps and rang the doorbell. Lissie was the one to open the door, and she practically threw herself at Dawn, squeezing her tight.

"Oh, my beautiful Dawnie. Thank you so much for coming all the way from Puerto Rico to see me. I can't wait to spend some quality time with you. I've missed you so much."

"I've missed you too, Mom. I want to tell you something right up front."

Lissie's eyes widened. "Oh no. What's wrong?"

"Nothing. In fact, something is very right. I can't stay in Boston long because I have a wedding to go back to. Mine! I'm getting married!"

"Oh! Dawn, that's wonderful. Come in, come in. We don't need to stand on the stoop all day."

Dawn followed her into the big home's foyer and wondered how she was managing the challenge of living with other addicts. "How are you doing, Mom? Really."

Her mother threw an arm around her and gave her a squeeze, then escorted her to a living room. "Sit down, hon. I'm doing great. Can I get you something?"

"I don't suppose you have beer here?"

Lissie laughed. "Honey, this is a sober house. No alcohol allowed."

Dawn almost sagged in relief. "That's good. In fact, that's great. I'd just like an ice water, please."

"Are you sure? We have Pepsi, juice, milk…"

"Water is good. I need to drink more water anyway," Dawn said. "I forget to rehydrate in a hot climate. It's not as hot here, but establishing a good habit takes practice." She hoped she wasn't being too transparent or too preachy.

"You got it, hon." Lissie hurried off to another room, and Dawn figured it must be the kitchen. She looked around. There was a bookshelf with loads of AA and NA books. Two full-size couches and a loveseat were grouped around a large coffee table which displayed numerous pamphlets. The only decorations on the walls were banners proclaiming *One day at a time*. *Live and let live*, and *But for the grace of God*. It seemed as if Lissie had landed in a good place.

She wondered how some of the people she knew in the old neighborhood were doing, but she thought better of going to call on them. Most of the people she knew there had drug and/or alcohol problems and/or mental imbalances.

Her mother hurried back with her ice water and another glass filled with what looked like soda.

"So tell me about this wedding, and more important, the groom!" Lissie said.

"Oh, Mom, he's my dream come true. Luca Fierro is the most wonderful, smart, handsome guy ever. I feel incredibly lucky."

"And his family?"

"They're awesome!"

Lissie looked a little crestfallen. "I wish I could have been there for you." Quietly, she asked, "And how's your grandmother?"

"She's great. Her broken hip is all healed. You'd never know she broke it. And guess what? She's actually dating a wonderful man. She loves Puerto Rico."

"I was surprised to hear she wasn't coming back. I never thought you'd get her to leave her house."

Dawn laughed. "I know. It was the Fierro family who convinced her. And I refused to go without her. That would've kept Luca away from his family, because he wouldn't go without me. I think Gran knew how close he was to his family. She didn't want to be the cause of any rift there, and they've been so good to her. When she broke her hip and we had to take her out of the hospital, they took her in, and Gabriella fussed over her while she healed."

Someone interrupted by clearing her throat. Dawn and Lissie looked up, and Dawn recognized her karma officer, Lynda. She jumped up and ran into her open arms. "Lynda! I didn't know you were coming."

"You know my probation officer?" Lissie asked.

Dawn grinned. "Yeah. In a way, she was mine too."

She pulled Lynda aside. "Does my mother know about your other job?"

"Yes. She's a client."

Dawn squealed and pulled Lynda into the living room. They sat on the couches near each other, but Dawn took a seat next to her mom.

Lynda beamed. "You look wonderful, Dawn. I just knew Luca would take good care of you."

"We take good care of each other." Dawn took her mother's hand and squeezed it. "I wish I could introduce him to you. You would love him."

"Actually," Lynda said, "that might be possible. I pulled a few strings and got special permission for your mom to attend your wedding."

"You did?" Dawn jumped up and hugged Lynda, then returned to her spot on the couch and hugged a stunned Lissie.

"How did you manage that?" Lissie asked.

Lynda winked. "Karma and I have our ways. Plus, your hard work and great attitude helped!"

"I haven't always had the best attitude."

"We're not talking about the past. We're watching you demonstrate a genuine psychic change now. That's what second chances are for."

Luca Fierro and Dawn Forrest had picked their wedding venue carefully. It was on a beach at the foot of an old fort. The mood was casual. Their guests were able to sit on a concrete wall overlooking the small beach. The couple stood on the sand, wearing their new wedding clothes. Dawn was stunning.

Both wore white. "Virgins don't have a monopoly on bright white," Gabriella had said, and Annette agreed. Leave it to those two to be appropriately inappropriate.

Dawn's short, strapless dress boasted loads of lace and tulle, adding some volume to her slim body. She had complained that women envied her fast metabolism and hated that she could eat as much as a man without gaining an ounce. She was a little self-conscious of her small breasts and would have liked to put on a few pounds, but Luca thought she looked perfect.

They had no maid of honor or best man because there were too many brothers and sisters-in-law to choose from. They were each other's best friends, so they'd decided to do away with one more tradition. It was just the two of them and the officiant standing on the sandy beach.

The preacher wore a long, black robe over his clothes and stood nearest to the shore—about four feet away from the gentle waves lapping at the sand. Luca hoped he didn't stumble backward.

Luca gazed at his beautiful bride, who took his breath away. Dawn's brown hair had grown out from the initial spiky hairdo she had sported when they met to a short Audrey Hepburn kind of look, with her bangs scrolling to one side, by the time they had their first official date. Now, she had enough length to actually make an updo. A few strands had escaped and blew in the wind, but that was Dawn. Her energy could not be contained, and he loved that about her.

"Is everyone here?" the reverend asked. Dawn and Luca glanced at the guests sitting on the wall, making a semicircle around their spot, and agreed that yes, everyone they were expecting had arrived.

So many people were not only family but friends to both of them. They had decided early on that no matter where they had their ceremony, they didn't want aisles with a bride's side and a groom's side. Dawn's side would have been nearly empty and Luca's overflowing.

Dawn's mother sat with her grandmother right in the center. They were already weeping tears of joy. Diego handed Annette his handkerchief.

Luca's mother and father were sitting next to Lissie. His brothers and their wives filled in the rest of the spots on either side. Dante and Mallory, Jayce and Kristine, Miguel and Sandra. Gabe and a very pregnant Misty chose to stand on the walkway immediately behind the wall, their son, Tony, sitting atop Gabe's shoulders. Most were sitting on the edge of the wall, feet dangling.

At one far end sat Luca's eldest brother, Ryan, and sister-in-law Chloe, all the way from Ireland.

And at the opposite end, Luca saw Noah and Kizzy and her sister, Ruth, holding her baby girl, and Ruth's new beau, José, plus Dr. Samuels and a woman he didn't recognize.

Then realization struck. Oh my God...dess! It was Mother Nature herself!

She held hands with Aaron Samuels, Ruth and Kizzy's father. How on earth did they get her to come? Luca glanced at Dawn and wondered if he should tell her. Would that make her more nervous?

"Go ahead, Padre," Antonio called out from the attendees. "Nobody's getting any younger up here." A few chuckles followed Antonio's inside joke.

The minister nodded. "Dearly beloved..." He started in the usual manner and spoke the familiar words of a traditional wedding, but what Luca and Dawn had planned right after the ceremony was anything but traditional.

They faced each other, holding hands, and he couldn't help grinning at her from time to time. She always returned his grin with one of her own plus a giggle or two.

The minister had a message long before the *I do*s, and Luca liked what he heard.

"Love is endless forgiveness," the reverend said. "This I say because you're human and *will* make mistakes."

Luca raised one eyebrow at Dawn, who bit her lower lip and looked like she was trying to stifle a laugh. They were not exactly human, but yes, they would still make mistakes.

"When you make those mistakes, be it forgetting to do something or doing something you hadn't intended to do, don't let it divide you. Face all situations together. Work it out together. Compromise when you should. And always, always forgive and love each other." He droned on with a few more bits of advice for couples in love, and Luca couldn't help glancing over at Gaia. She was staring at the officiant with rapt attention.

She and Aaron holding hands wasn't news but still struck him as amazing. A lot of the other couples were holding hands too, of course. His parents, his brothers and their wives, even Dawn's grandmother held hands on both sides. Her left hand curled around Lissie's, and her right was enveloped in Diego's. He was glad the older woman had found happiness. She deserved it after doing such a wonderful job raising Dawn when her mother couldn't.

The reverend eventually got to the vows.

Finally! Luca didn't think he and Dawn could wait much longer for their surprise. The vows were simple but personal, promising to love and respect each other, to help each other grow, and to support each other as they reached for their dreams.

The reverend turned to Luca and asked if he had the rings. Luca took the rings out of his pocket, handed his larger one to Dawn, and held onto her smaller one. "Ready when you are, Padre."

The officiant said, "Do you, Dawn, take Luca to be your lawfully wedded husband, for richer or poorer, in sickness and in health, for as long as you both shall live?"

"I do," Dawn said. She placed Luca's ring on his finger without waiting to be told to do so.

The reverend smiled.

"Do you, Luca, take this woman to be your lawfully wedded wife?"

"I sure do—unconditionally," Luca said, not even waiting to hear the "for richer or poorer" part. Everyone chuckled. Luca didn't think it was necessary when talking about unconditional love. Happily, the reverend just went with it and didn't back up or correct him.

"Place the ring on her finger."

He slid the simple gold band on Dawn's ring finger. It looked perfect, even with the diamond ring that was already there—just like how the two of them suited each other despite their wildly different backgrounds.

The reverend pronounced them husband and wife, and after a long kiss and enthusiastic applause from their guests, they were ready for their surprise.

As soon as their lips parted, Dawn whirled around, letting Luca unzip her wedding dress, which fell to the ground while everyone gasped. The crowd giggled or groaned when they saw she was wearing a white strapless bathing suit beneath.

Then Luca threw off his tie, and rather than unbuttoning his shirt, which would take too long, he just ripped it open, then unzipped his white pants and stepped out of them. He too was wearing a white bathing suit beneath. The two of them held hands and ran into the ocean.

Laughter and applause followed them as they swam out to deeper water. As they bobbed in the waves, Luca looked up, as did Dawn, and saw the entire guest list standing along the wall laughing and waving. They grinned and waved back.

Antonio called down, "Did you two feel like you needed to be baptized on the same day?"

Then a speedboat appeared from the other side of the rocky shore, slowing the engine and maneuvering to pick up the couple. Luca helped Dawn onto the boat's ladder, then jumped up and followed her.

"No, Dad," he called, finally answering the elder's question. "We just couldn't wait to get started on our honeymoon."

Dawn pointed to two carry-on bags. "We're all packed and ready to go!"

He sat next to Dawn and kissed her with all the passion he could safely unleash. Then he put his arm around her, and they sped off into the sunset.

—∾—

Gaia picked up some unusual energy, then she looked over at Gabriella's red face and realized she was livid.

"Don't they realize we have a party planned for them?"

"You're the one who wanted to surprise them with a big thing." Antonio just shook his head and laughed. "I think the surprise is on you!"

Gabriella threw her hands in the air.

Antonio put his arm around her. "The boy has always done things his own way, hon. Why should his wedding be any different?"

Gabriella sighed, then faced the attendees and announced, "There's still a party back at our house, without the bride and groom unfortunately. But that doesn't mean we can't have a lot of fun with good food, music, and dancing. There's even a flamenco dancer waiting to teach us some moves!"

Lots of the attendees seemed excited about the party and grabbed each other's hands, racing off to their various vehicles.

"When is this going to take place?" Gaia asked their hostess.

"Right now," Gabriella said.

"We'd better get going, or everyone will beat us back there," Antonio called out. Then he and Gabriella ran for their car too.

Gaia looked toward Aaron. "Is this something you want to attend?"

"I think I should. And I would like to bring you too, if you're available."

"But I wasn't invited."

Aaron chuckled. "I don't think anyone received

formal invitations. You're here at the ceremony and heard them invite everyone to their house for a party. I don't think it's a very formal, sit-down thing where the number of guests matters." Then Aaron placed his hands on both her shoulders. "But first, I have a surprise for you. Wait right here. I've hidden it in the fort."

"A surprise, for me?"

Aaron grinned. "I didn't know if I could pull off a surprise, but I figured I'd try. I'm glad you don't know everything I'm going to do so I still can surprise you once in a while."

"Is it a nice surprise?"

"I hope so." He placed a finger under her chin and looked deep into her eyes. "I hope to have only nice surprises for you." He leaned over and gave her a gentle peck on her cheek. Because they had an audience, he didn't follow up with the passion that shone in his eyes.

He stepped away and said, "Okay, I'll be back in a few minutes. Wait right here."

As everyone else was getting into their vehicles, he jogged across the street and up the hill until he disappeared into the fort. Gaia sat on the wall and wondered what he could have hidden to surprise her with.

As the guests were driving off toward Antonio and Gabriella's house, she couldn't help wondering if she was really welcome or not. She had been so bitchy... She wouldn't be surprised if most paranormals wanted to avoid her. Humans who knew who she was also feared her. Most of the time they didn't have a clue so it didn't matter, but most of these people, except maybe one or two, knew exactly who she was.

Ruth had finished strapping her baby into the car seat

in the back of José's car and was just about to get in when she noticed Gaia still sitting there by herself. She bent down and said something to José and then closed the car door and walked over to Mother Nature.

"Aren't you coming?"

"I...I don't know if I'm invited or not. Your father said to wait here. Apparently, he has some kind of surprise, and he hid it in the fort. We might stop by later."

Ruth grinned. "That is so *unlike* my dad. You must be very good for him. I don't think I've seen him this happy in a long time."

Gaia nodded. "I'm more relaxed too because of him. I guess we're good for each other."

Ruth surprised her by leaning over and kissing her on the cheek. "Thank you."

Gaia leaned back and looked at her with surprise. "What are you thanking me for?"

"For making my father happy. Like I said, I haven't seen him this happy and relaxed in years. I was too young to remember much about the time when my mom was alive, but I seem to remember he was pretty happy then. For most of my life he's seemed a little sad and withdrawn. He's finally acting like his younger self again. I think some men are just lonely without realizing it."

Mother Nature nodded and let her eyes wander off toward the fort. Was Aaron like that? Lonely without even knowing it? Had he never had another woman since Ruth and Kizzy's mother died? She didn't want to bring that up right now. Ruth was on her way to a party, and it wouldn't be a good idea to bring up her deceased mother. Besides, she could always ask Aaron when they had a few moments alone.

"Well, I'll see you at the party," Ruth said.

"I guess so." Gaia smiled and waved.

She watched as Ruth and her date drove away. Ruth's baby in the car seat just completed the happy family picture. Even though the relationship was new, Gaia knew it would grow and flourish.

She leaned back and let the sun beat down on her face. It was another one of her beautiful days. She was able to do a few things for this devastated island. She made it sunny during the day and let the gentle rains fall at night. People didn't usually notice things going well, but that was good. She hoped nobody noticed her little blessings. It was better if they didn't.

After waiting nearly half an hour, she became concerned. Where had Aaron gone? She closed her eyes and tried to zero in on his energy. *Tried to* being the operative words. She couldn't feel him. Anywhere! He wasn't hiding. Even if invisible, he didn't have the power to hide his energy.

Suddenly realizing something was very wrong, she charged off into the fort to look for him. Retracing what was left of his energy signature, she came upon a small potted plant hidden behind a large stone. Picking it up, she recognized the little heart plant, but there were two of them, growing out of the same stem. Odd. Did he discover the anomaly and think of them? Two hearts sharing the same nutrients?

She cradled the plant to her breast as tears sprang to her eyes.

Chapter 17

AARON CAME TO, TIED TO A TREE. AS HE LOOKED AROUND, his vision cleared, but he wasn't sure he was seeing properly yet. Amid an Alpine forest, a furry figure that couldn't actually exist smirked at him.

"Who the hell are you?" Aaron demanded of the strange half goat/half man.

"You've never heard of the god Pan?"

Aaron frowned. "Are you telling me you're a god?"

"Yes. What's so hard to believe?"

"Gaia told me you were causing problems for her, but that was quite a while ago. I thought you had probably come to your senses and moved on."

Pan laughed. "Come to my senses? If anyone needs a reality check, it's you, mortal. You think you're good enough for the goddess of all?"

"She seems to like me."

"For now. She will get tired of your limitations before long."

"How do you know?" Aaron pulled at the ropes binding him to the tree. They held fast. "Gaia?" he called out. "Gaia!"

"Aww. You need her to rescue you, don't you? What a shame that you're so helpless and she doesn't know where you are."

"Where am I then?"

"I brought you to my own personal forest. It doesn't

exist on earth, so she'll never be able to find you." He laughed maniacally.

"If I'm not on earth, where am I?"

"We're in a galaxy far, far away." He giggled.

"Okaaaay… If there's no one around to help me, why do you have me tied up?"

"It's for your own protection. If I untied you, you'd run away, and you could fall right off the edge of my planet."

Aaron almost laughed. He'd heard of flat-earthers. They were people who insisted the earth was flat, took things literally—and if they couldn't see something with their own eyes, they refused to believe its existence, and that was that.

"Tell me, is there day and night in this place?"

"Of course. I need to sleep."

"So if it's daytime now, it's because we're facing the sun. How does it become night if the planet isn't round and rotating on its axis?"

Pan laughed. "It flips, dumbass. Fortunately, I'm able to add gravity to my little cave or poof to the other side right before the sudden shift. You, on the other hand, might *prefer* to be stuck to that tree. Otherwise, you'll fall off."

Aaron didn't know if this god was just toying with him or what. He had to be. In that case, arguing logic with him was a waste of breath. Even if Pan believed what he was saying, Aaron was still wasting his breath. "So how long are you going to keep me here?"

"So many questions!" After a considerable pause, he finally said, "I don't know. She'll forget all about you eventually. Perhaps when she gives up and allows me to court her, I'll let you go."

That wasn't very encouraging. Aaron was pretty sure he and Gaia had something real. A love that would never die. In other words, he'd perish here.

Suddenly, his hands began to shake. He was hoping Pan couldn't see his tremors, but the satyr's eyes widened, and he strolled around Aaron's back.

"Ha! You're shaking like a leaf. Try not to wet your pants, human."

"The tremors are caused by a medical condition."

"Oh really? You humans…so frail. You're always falling prey to something or other. What was she thinking?" He leaned against the tree, studying his human hands and crossing his lower hooves. "I could have just waited a few minutes and you'd probably die on your own. Then I could have stepped in and comforted her, eventually taking your place."

"Then why don't you do that?"

"Because I don't wanna. And I'm a god, so I don't hafta."

Aaron realized why Gaia was none too fond of the gods. She had inferred that they were selfish, spoiled brats. She clearly knew what she was talking about.

"So what is this medical condition, human? What is it called?"

"At first, I thought it might be Parkinson's disease, but now it's looking more like ET."

"Extraterrestrial? Like ET phone home?" Pan cracked up as if that were the funniest thing he'd ever heard. "I guess you could be considered an *extraterrestrial* on this planet."

Aaron blew out a breath. "It doesn't stand for extraterrestrial. It stands for essential tremors. It's a non-life-threatening condition that usually runs in families. It used to be called familial tremors."

Pan stopped laughing and planted his fists on his hairy hips. "You mean you shake because your parents shook, and they shook because their parents shook?"

"Well, not all of them, but some of my ancestors must have had the condition."

"So were they called Shakers? Is that what those museum villages are for? Did they corral you all in one place so you wouldn't spill everything on unsuspecting people?" Pan burst out laughing again.

"What?" It took Aaron a second to realize he was talking about the Shaker villages in the Northeast and Midwest. Whether he was serious was hard to tell.

"I asked you a question…"

"Uh, no. They weren't called Shakers. That was a religion that forbade men and women touching. The way they danced looked like shaking. They died out several years ago."

Pan reared back and laughed some more. "Gee, I wonder why? Well, mortal, there is one advantage to having you around. You amuse me."

Aaron just smiled. He really had no other recourse while tied to a tree.

"Aren't you the least bit curious about me? You haven't asked me one question about myself."

Aaron fished his memory for anything he'd learned in his mythology classes. "Pan is a nature god. The god of the wild, shepherds and flocks, mountains, and rustic music and companion of the nymphs. You have the legs and horns of a goat, just like a faun or satyr."

"Not bad. Actually, I'm the most famous of the satyrs

and a son of the god Hermes, also known as the messenger of the gods, and the nymph Penelope."

"And I suppose you're sending a message to Gaia as we speak."

"No. I won't be giving her any information about your disappearance. She'll probably assume you got scared and ran off when you realized how much more powerful she is than you."

Aaron had been around powerful women all his life. His mother and wife were witches. His two daughters were witches, both with the power to heal and one with psychic power. Maybe Ruth could pick up on his psyche and make the connection. But if he was truly in another galaxy or wherever... He was a witch too, but his power was fairly useless. He could become invisible. Big whoop. How could that help him now? Even if he disappeared from view, the ropes wouldn't let go. He'd have to look for another way to escape.

"Excuse me, but is there a stream nearby? A place I might be able to get something to drink?"

Pan tipped his head back and looked down his nose at Aaron. "Hmm... That's right. You humans have to hydrate regularly. And relieve yourselves." He heaved a deep sigh. "How inconvenient. Fine. I'll untie you. There's a stream right over that ridge. Don't think about taking off though. Like I said..."

"I might fall off the edge. Yes. I get it." Aaron mentally rolled his eyes as the cloven-hooved god stepped behind him and untied the ropes.

"You're not shaking anymore."

"It comes and goes."

"Sure it does," Pan mocked sarcastically. Then he

cautioned him as he walked toward the river, "Don't forget to come back. The forest flips in one half hour."

Aaron just smirked and kept walking without turning around.

He found the river where Pan said it would be. He splashed some water on his face and then cupped his hands and drank heartily. It tasted fresh and clean. He hadn't noticed any forest animals and hoped the stream was as clean as it looked. Large flat rocks lay in a path across the water. It was possible to cross, and even though running from a god seemed like a fruitless effort, he could say he was exploring.

Aaron couldn't help being curious what was on the other side of the river. He tiptoed across the flat rocks and found a rise that would give him a good view. Striding toward it, he wondered if this god was for real. He was sure the creature was not human, but something seemed really off about him. He didn't know much about gods. Could they create their own planets? He thought that was Gaia's department.

If the world was supposedly going to flip in one half hour, why was the sun straight overhead? Perhaps it was simply a large disc, made to look like a planet. This place didn't make any more sense than the person who'd brought him here.

Hopefully, Gaia could zero in on his energy. He climbed the steep ridge until he reached the top and was able to gaze farther. He was shocked to discover a cardboard cutout using perspective to make it look like mountains far off in the distance.

Aaron gasped. "I'll be god damned."

There beyond the artwork was what appeared to be

the jagged edge of the world. It was easy to see that Pan was right. There was just dirt and then nothing. If indeed this place was going to flip in half an hour, he had about ten minutes to get back. He turned and rushed toward the forest, jumping from rock to rock as he crossed the river again, then charging up the hill. Just as he neared the trees, he felt his feet leaving the ground and the forest floor tipping. He reached for the nearest tree and managed to grab a branch before he floated off into nothingness.

Suddenly, it was night, and Aaron was hanging upside down from the tree branch.

Pan trotted over to him. "I suppose you'll be wanting my help now."

The god was able to clop over to him without falling off the surface. Apparently, he was able to control gravity under his own hooves. "Being tied to a tree might be a real treat, don't you think?"

Aaron just eyed the little sucker. What could he say? The god would make fun of his puny human status no matter what he said. "Look, Pan, you're right. I didn't believe you. But I saw for myself that what you said was true. There was an edge, and it looks like I was lucky to have made it back this far. But I would really prefer not to hang upside down all night. Is there anything you can do about that?"

"Certainly. Would you like to be tied to a tree or transported to the other side?"

"I'd like to be on solid ground with gravity aiding me."

"A wise decision, my friend."

Aaron didn't correct him about the friend part. It was

clear the god had the upper hand, and anything he might say to anger the god would be foolhardy. He had to play along. But how could he beg for his freedom? Escape was impossible. Pan seemed to want what he wanted and didn't care what happened to anyone. Aaron simply had to stay alive and hope for some kind of rescue.

He knew not to lie...he wasn't very good at it. And who knew if gods had built-in lie detectors? "Listen, I have to ask you something. If you let me go and I leave Gaia alone, will you allow me to live out my life in peace? I have a family."

Pan's expression turned to one of surprise. "You're willing to break up with the goddess just to save your own neck?" Then he snickered. "Ah, but here you are hanging on for dear life. Things look a little different right now, don't they? You must not really love her if you're not willing to hang onto her."

"I didn't say that."

Pan crossed his arms. "Oh, I think you did."

"All right. You got me. I am begging for my own life, but I have other loved ones who need me. I have two daughters, one of whom is a new mother and depending on my help to support her until she gets on her feet."

"Well, if what you say is true, perhaps you would be missed..."

"I most definitely would be."

"So they would be looking for you, but they would never find you. That is, if I left you here."

"Yes, exactly. You would be ruining a lot of lives, not just mine." Dare he hope? Did the god have a conscience after all?

Pan shrugged. "I have no desire to ruin lives. I just

want to enhance my own. Hmm, I'll have to think about that." He began to wander off.

"Wait! I'm still hanging onto your world by a tree branch. My arms will tire soon."

Pan just gave a casual wave over his shoulder as he clopped away toward his upside-down cave.

Gaia wanted to sound the alarm, but how did she do that without upsetting everyone on this special occasion? Besides, humans couldn't really do much except keep an eye out for him. Aaron… She hoped he knew that wherever he was, she wouldn't stop looking for him. She could tell he was alive, but his energy was faint, that was all she knew for sure.

She didn't know why this was happening, but she could guess who was behind it. She set down the plant, put her hands on her hips, and called her sisters. "Fate! Karma!"

The other goddesses appeared quickly. Karma was carrying a surfboard and wearing a bathing suit, while Fate was in a fluffy bathrobe and looked like she had been at a spa or had just awakened. Either way, two cucumber slices fell off her eyes.

"What's the matter, Gaia? You look awful."

"Thanks, Karma. I needed that like a hole in my head. Aaron's missing."

Fate and Karma glanced at each other in shock. "Missing?" they asked at once.

"Yes. I can tell he's alive, but very, very far away. I can't lock onto his energy. I don't know where he is." She dropped her gaze, and tears welled up.

"Oh, Sister." Fate stepped into her personal space and enveloped her in a hug. Gaia didn't usually hug, but the welcome gesture was exactly what she needed. She just held onto her sister for a moment while she thought of possible explanations.

When she stepped away, she looked over at Karma. "It's got to be Pan's work. Correct?"

Karma snapped her fingers, and the surfboard disappeared. "Yes, I'm sure of it. Unless there's someone else you pissed off with the power to shield your lover from you…"

"Not as far as I know." Gaia let out a long sigh.

"Well, how do we find him?" Fate asked.

Gaia said, "Take my hands, Sisters. And then take each other's hands. We need to form a triad. Our energy combined is stronger. All of us need to reach out toward Aaron's energy signature and concentrate on locating him."

Karma and Fate did as she asked without comment for once. Gaia couldn't help being grateful right now to have sisters who would help. Hopefully, they could. She wished her powers were enough, but since that didn't seem to be the case, she dearly hoped the three of them together could find him. Aaron meant everything to her.

They let their minds meld and radiate out farther than they could have alone. Each one's mental forces reached out like tendrils feeling their way through the atmosphere, circling the globe, looking for any tingle of recognition. They stood that way for several minutes, searching, probing, until finally, Gaia dropped their hands and leaned over. "It's no use."

She slumped onto the earth, and her sisters grabbed her arms before she fell backward.

"Gaia." Karma shook her. "You can do this. We can do this. Don't give up."

Fate was rubbing her arm and looking concerned and sympathetic. Two very different approaches, but at this moment, she preferred Karma's tough love. Gaia stood up straight and tall. Raising her chin, she announced, "Yes. We can do this. He is somewhere. We will find him. Even if you leave, I won't stop."

Fate squeezed her hand. "I'm not leaving. I'm here for you as long as it takes."

Karma put her arm around Gaia's shoulder. "As am I. The jerks of the world can wait until we deal with the biggest jerk of all. How do we find Pan?"

"Sisters, we were locking onto the wrong energy. Let's lock on Pan. Wherever he is, I'm sure he knows where Aaron is."

The women reformed their triangle, held hands, closed their eyes, and concentrated again, this time letting their energies reach for and locate the little horned god they were all familiar with. Gaia suspected he would probably be having an orgy with nymphs in the mountains, but she had to wipe out any preconceived notions and just open her mind and let the energy take her to where he was, not bring him to where she thought he should be.

It took a long time, but eventually, she locked onto Pan's energy signature. "I've got him!"

Her sisters cried out, "Yes, he's..."

"Here!" Pan said from down a tunnel-like walkway. He clopped toward the three powerful goddesses.

"You're looking for me." He said it as a statement, not a question. "I assume you've come to your senses and realized a human is not worthy of your affection. Whereas I"—he swept his torso into an exaggerated bow, then straightened and looked her in the eye—"I am at your service. I would be delighted to show you the kind of relationship you deserve."

Gaia laughed. "What did I do to deserve you? And how do I undo it?"

Pan folded his arms. "Insult me all you like. Soon, you'll discover I'm the only one left who can tolerate you."

"Where is he, Pan?"

"Where is who?" he asked, trying to look innocent.

"I'm out of patience with you!" Gaia shouted. "Tell me where Aaron is right now, because if he dies, you die!"

Pan snickered. "I'm immortal. I can't die. Another point in my favor, if you ask me."

"I didn't ask you, and for your information, I can make your immortal life a living hell. I can trap you in the bowels of the earth. You'll never see another sunrise or snowcapped mountain, never speak to another living soul—and you'll never be found by gods or nymphs."

"You wouldn't. I'm one of your beloved creations, right? You wouldn't hurt me. Besides, being with me would be so much more fun than being with your frail human."

"If anything happens to him, I will *hate* you. You wouldn't want to be with someone who hates you so much they'd rather destroy you than look at you."

"Sister." Fate leaned in close to her and whispered, "Aaron's energy is fading rapidly."

"Pan! You have thirty seconds to produce him, or you will be surrounded by rock and molten lava—forever!"

"You wouldn't."

"I would." Her eyes narrowed to slits.

A staring contest between Pan and Gaia ensued, with Karma counting down the last ten seconds. "Nine, eight, seven, six, five, four, three, two…"

Pan half disappeared, but a moment before he could get away, Gaia latched onto his hairy leg with both hands and held on tight as he dragged her through the universe.

———

Aaron caught sight of something hurtling through space, coming right at him. Was it an asteroid? A meteor? No, it was…Gaia and Pan?

She clung to his leg and yelled furiously, "Where is he?"

"I'm taking you to him." Then the satyr snickered. "But soon, you'll have to make a choice. Him or me." He pointed toward Aaron, whose hands slipped a little farther down the tree branch.

Gaia zeroed in on Aaron and called out, "I'm coming for you. Hang on!"

Pan laughed. "You'll have to let go of me to catch him. He's falling, you know. Any second, he'll drop off the surface of my upside-down forest."

She furiously hurled the goat into a tree and grabbed Aaron just as his hands slipped off the branch altogether. He grasped onto her in a hug, and she gently floated him back to the surface, creating a small patch of gravity where they needed it.

"Thank goodness I found you, darling!"

"Thank you. I felt like a bat hanging upside down in the dark like that."

"This was no fault of yours." She glanced up at the tree, where Pan was holding on to the trunk with his two arms and sitting on smaller branches with his hooves dangling. "You think you got away with it, don't you?"

"I kind of did. When the world flips over, I'll drop to the surface and be just fine."

"Yeah, about that. I can't let you leave this place. You're not welcome back on Earth."

"And how are you going to accomplish that?" he asked.

She let go of Aaron just long enough to shoot giant spider webs toward Pan. They wound up covering the tree.

He laughed. "Is that supposed to contain me? A spider web?"

"It's from a Darwin's bark spider from Madagascar. It's ten times stronger than Kevlar. Go ahead. Try it," she said.

He rolled his eyes.

Gaia slipped her arm around Aaron's waist and waited.

Eventually, Pan edged his way to the apex of the tree where he could get a grip on the web. He pulled hard. The web stretched, but it didn't break. Then he held onto the tree with his knees pushed together and grabbed another fistful of the web, pulling it in the opposite direction, probably figuring it would split down the middle. Not only did it not split, but he couldn't hold onto the tree with his knees anymore and fell, landing in a cradle of sticky silk. "What the..."

Gaia looked into Aaron's eyes. "Are you ready to go home, darling?"

"More than ready."

Mother Nature snapped her fingers and produced a spaceship. It was small and reminded Aaron of the vipers used by the TV fighter pilots on *Battlestar Galactica* episodes.

I never thought I'd get to ride in one of those!

She swept her hand through the air in an upward motion, and the hatch opened. Holding Aaron's hand, she floated the two of them over to the shuttle. "Climb aboard," she said, smiling.

"Ladies first."

She kissed his hand and said, "You'd better go first, just in case you lose your balance and float away."

"You wouldn't catch me?"

"Of course I would—eventually."

He scrambled down the metal ladder, slid into one of two empty seats, and strapped himself in. She followed right behind him. As soon as they were situated, she waved her hand in a downward motion, and the hatch closed over their heads.

"Do you know how to fly this thing?"

"No. Do you?"

"No." Aaron's hand began to tremble.

"Are you cold?"

"I don't think so. I'm pretty sure this is pure fear."

She looked offended. "Why? Are you afraid of my driving?"

"I thought you said you didn't know how to fly it."

"Not to worry. I borrowed some stuff from a new Tesla. It's now a self-driving, GPS-equipped vehicle with an automatic braking system."

Aaron couldn't help teasing her a bit. "What kind of mileage does it get?"

"We'll see, won't we?" She pushed a button, and the ship roared to life. She pointed, and they shot off in the direction she had come from. Aaron gazed with amazement as stars streaked by.

"Gaia?"

"Yes?"

"What are we going to do when we reach Earth's atmosphere? Won't we burn up?"

"Don't worry. I can cast a hard protective shell around the ship."

Somewhat relieved but always erring on the side of caution, Aaron asked, "And what do we do if once we're in Earth's range, we're reported as a UFO—or worse, shot down?"

"You know that power of invisibility you have?"

"Yeah?"

"Does it extend to objects?"

"If I'm touching them, I can make objects invisible. That's why you don't see a suit of clothing walking around with no head."

She chuckled. "That's good. So if you place your hands on the ship, can you make it and all its contents invisible?"

"Probably."

"Great! Then we're all set."

"But what about—"

She interrupted him. "But what if we crash into space

junk?" Then she sent him a teasing smirk. "Automatic braking, remember?"

He grinned, leaned back in his leather seat, and finally relaxed.

She reached over for his hand. "I love you, you know. I would have looked for you until the end of time."

"I was almost at the end of time—my time anyway. Thank you for saving my life."

"Always. Thank you for saving mine."

He tipped his head and gazed at her, but she just smiled.

"There's something I've been meaning to ask you, Gaia."

"Sure. What is it?"

"I know my life is a drop in the bucket compared to yours, but do you think you could spend the years I have left living with me? Loving me? Letting me love you?"

Gaia placed her hand over her heart. "I can't think of anything I want more. Wait—there is something more I'd like, if you'll allow it."

"Anything."

"Can I give you a few godlike powers? Just so you have a long, long life—and a fighting chance if you come up against any other jealous gods."

He laughed. "I'm in."

They undid their seatbelts and floated above the controls. Removing their clothing and letting toga, pants, and shirt drift away, without words they decided not to wait until returning to Earth's gravity to make love.

Aaron took her hand and yanked her toward him. Weightless, she landed in his arms and grabbed onto his shoulders. He sucked in a breath, and her tongue darted out to lave across his skin. He placed the pad of his thumb on her lush red lips.

"Wait. Let me look at you," he said. He let go of all but her hand, and she floated a few feet away. He took a moment to enjoy the view, loving the sight of her hourglass figure, plus some surprisingly muscular arms and thighs.

She too looked her fill and nodded. "Some of my best work."

He chuckled. "I'm glad you approve. I've done my best to maintain the gift you gave me. Not just this bag of skin that contains all my muscles, bones, organs, and blood, but my life itself."

He had never had someone risk so much for him. She had faced a crazy god, dragging her who knows where through the universe. Then she had to conjure up some kind of vehicle to get him back to Earth. He almost choked on the love that welled up in his heart.

Taking his time, he put his mouth on every part of her, suckling her fingers, kissing lightly up to her neck, then down to her breasts, tasting the tight buds of her nipples. *His* woman, he thought, running one hand down along the outline of her body. She expelled a breathy sound—a signal she needed more than just slight petting. What she needed was something only he could give her. Only him.

Suddenly, need overwhelmed him, snapping his control and wrenching a growl from his throat. One part of his brain, the part that still retained its sanity, told him to calm down, to get a grip on his emotions.

He struggled for breath around the force of it. She widened her legs. He placed his cock at the apex of her thighs, and in one thrust, he slammed it home. His rational thoughts deserted him, overcome by something so powerful he struggled for breath around the force of it. He grasped her long hair and twisted it so he could make her meet his gaze. Wide, sky-blue eyes blinked at him, filled with desire.

"Only me, Gaia. Promise it." His voice was so ragged, he didn't even recognize it.

She seemed stunned.

"Say it."

"Only you, Aaron. How could you doubt it?"

Desire glazed her eyes, and she lifted her legs, twining them around his body, deepening his thrust even more. He clenched his jaw and concentrated on not coming until she did, but he teetered on the edge. The pressure building at the base of his spine was enormous. It made his whole body shake with the need for release. Her body had gone tight, every muscle contracted, and he knew she hovered on the edge.

"Please, Aaron," she whispered. She didn't have a chance to finish her thought. She arched her back, and her orgasm rocketed through her.

It triggered his own, which blasted through his body like an exploding nebula. There were no words for it. Just, perhaps, perfect.

Gaia brushed Aaron's shaggy hair from his face, meeting his gaze. Without even meaning for it to happen, the bond had been completed. She hadn't promised she'd be his *permanently*. But she'd done something much more powerful. She'd acted on the promise in their hearts and given him immortality.

Now the bond between their souls was sacred. Joy

washed through her, knowing that no matter what, they would both survive.

She hadn't realized how good it would be to have a mate. The bond was something she hadn't guessed she needed before. Even though she'd survived without it, she hadn't felt complete.

Now she did.

Epilogue

Two months later.

GABRIELLA FIERRO HADN'T THOUGHT ABOUT KNOCKING AS she entered the greenhouse until she saw Gaia and Aaron locked in an amorous embrace. They jumped apart.

"Oh! I'm sorry. I didn't mean to intrude…"

Gaia grinned. "Hi, Gabriella. Don't worry. We only get naked inside the house now that it's finished and we can lock the doors." She and Aaron held hands and strolled down one of the long rows of fragrant heart-shaped plants to meet the Fierro matriarch. There was one large silver-and-gold pot, and it housed two grander heart-shaped plants growing out of the same stem.

Gabriella hugged Gaia, then Aaron. "What's this?" She pointed to the metallic pot. "A different plant? It looks so much bigger than the rest."

Gaia smiled at Aaron. "It's very special, because it was a gift from Aaron to me. We don't know why it grew so much larger than the others."

"I believe it grew exponentially as our love for each other grew," Aaron said.

As if they couldn't help it, the couple shared a tender kiss, which grew passionate before her very eyes.

"At this rate, it will reach the ceiling in no time." Gabriella couldn't help but giggle. Then she cleared her throat, and the couple sprang apart as if they'd just remembered she was there. "Well, I just stopped by to let you know Misty had her baby—babies, actually. Twins! A boy and a girl."

"You didn't know she was carrying twins?" Aaron asked.

"She and Gabe knew, but they didn't tell anyone else. They wanted it to be a surprise."

Aaron chuckled. "And no one got suspicious when they saw two cribs and two highchairs?"

"Misty, because she's a muse, let Gabe build the crib and then just zapped up a duplicate when they brought their little bundles of joy home."

"How is Gabe handling it?" Gaia asked. "As I recall, he wasn't planning to have children—ever. Now he has three!"

"He's the proudest papa you'll ever meet." Gabriella's eyes twinkled. "And that's not all. Guess who else is expecting?"

"Dawn," Mother Nature said matter-of-factly.

"Well, yes... You knew?"

Gaia rolled her eyes. "Of course I knew. I'm Mother freakin' Nature."

All three of them laughed.

Gabriella glanced around the greenhouse. "It looks like your plants are thriving. When do you plan to start testing its chemical formula or...whatever else doctors need to have documented so they can prescribe the medicine?"

"Never," Aaron said and smiled, surprising her.

"What? But I thought—"

"I know, I know." He tucked his hands in his pockets. "Truth be told, Gaia finally convinced me it was in everyone's best interests to leave it alone. All the pharmacological rigmarole, that is."

Mother Nature slid her arm around his waist. "The plant is perfect in its original form. If he alters it, the advertising people will have to come with all those warnings you see on TV when they ask people to buy their medication."

"You've been watching TV?" Gabriella gasped. "I thought you didn't like TV."

"Well, occasionally I tune in to something, just to learn more about blending in with modern society. But there's no avoiding those commercials. To be honest, the medication warnings frighten me. The side effects are much worse than whatever condition the pills are supposed to treat."

Aaron mocked the voice-over actor. "Stop taking Banishtheboogie and call your doctor if you notice symptoms of anal vomiting, spontaneous tap dancing, or if your penis falls off."

Gabriella burst out laughing.

Mother Nature just smiled lovingly at him. "Isn't he fun? I never get bored when he combines his irreverent sense of humor with his intelligent mind." They gave each other a peck on the lips.

When Gabriella had stopped giggling, she asked, "Then why are you bothering to cultivate the plants? It sounds like you're not going to do anything with them."

"Ah, that's not true. We're just not going to alter them," Aaron said. "They can be added to flower arrangements, and the scent will help alleviate the sadness of a broken heart. People will simply attribute the lifted mood to the thoughtful gesture and the fact that somebody cares."

"Or," Mother Nature added, "if someone buys the flowers for themselves, they'll attribute the happy effect to bringing the beauty of nature into their homes."

"That's wonderful," Gabriella said. "I love the idea of treating heartbreak in the most natural way possible. A quick fix doesn't allow for learning and growth."

"Of course," Gaia said quietly, "if you know someone whose heart is breaking and desperately needs a full dose, you can give them a cup of tea made with a couple of the plant's raw leaves."

"I can? You're going to allow me to use it?"

"As you see fit," Gaia said. "I trust you and will share the offer with all my modern muses."

Gabriella covered her heart with her hands. "I—I don't know what to say. I'm honored by your trust."

Mother Nature and Aaron gazed at each other. "We're learning a lot about trust these days."

"That's wonderful. I knew you two could make an unconventional relationship work! So I guess my explanation about like, love, and respect helped?"

"Oh no," Gaia said. "Your explanation was shit."

Gabriella's tinkling laugh filled the greenhouse.

Aaron stroked his lover's arm. "Gaia learns what she needs to know about relationships from watching successful couples like you and Antonio," Aaron said. "Every day, you show each other what no one can put into words."

"You're both so happy," Gaia added. "I notice you enjoy spending time together, but you also spend time with friends or doing other things you enjoy individually.

That type of freedom to be yourselves—to be your best selves—is rooted in trust and love."

"Thank you, Goddess. I'd never thought about it that way, but you couldn't be more right. What about you, Aaron? Do you watch other couples to pick up relationship tips?"

He smiled. "I'm afraid that even though I can use my power of invisibility to lean over people and eavesdrop, I'd feel like a voyeur, but there's plenty of good inspiration around. Your sons, for instance."

"Oh my, yes!" Gabriella agreed. "That was my entire goal as a mother. I wanted to see my boys grow up to be healthy and happy. To me, that includes finding and keeping alive a loving relationship."

"Well, you've accomplished your goal," Aaron said.

"I knew as soon as Luca, our youngest, started dating Dawn that every son had found lasting love. Antonio wanted to retire down here in the Caribbean long ago, but I wouldn't leave our sons until I knew each one of them had found their mates."

"And now all but your two oldest have come with you!" Gaia said. "What does that mean?"

"I think it just means we're a close-knit family—even as large, boisterous, and wildly different as we all are. We can completely rely on one another, and the boys do enjoy one another's company. Even the two eldest, who live far away, wouldn't miss Sunday dinner for the world."

"That's because I made their mates modern muses, and the minor goddesses can travel through the ether in the blink of an eye. Ah! That reminds me… I always grant my muses some kind of retention bonus. Basically, it's your chance to ask for anything you want."

Gabriella thought and thought. Eventually, she said, "I can think of something."

"Name it."

"Can you make it so all my sons' marriages continue to be as happy or happier than they are now?"

Gaia laughed. "I don't have to make that happen. It's going to. All I can do is assure you it's true."

"That's all I could possibly ask for. Thank you, Goddess!" Gabriella's expression became serious for a moment. "Oh, one more thing… I wanted to ask you about the phoenix gene. Will that be passed on to our grandchildren?"

"Since they'll only inherit one quarter of the gene, it's doubtful. Of course, if you happen to have any phoenix genes on your side, there's a greater chance."

"Do you know if I have any phoenix ancestors?"

Mother Nature just laughed. "My paranormals used to listen to me and wouldn't have mated with a human. But I may have missed a rebel on your side."

Gabriella smiled. "You don't seem angry about that anymore."

Gaia gazed into Aaron's eyes. "How could I be? Now I know love can override any stupid rule."

Acknowledgments

I would like to acknowledge all the people who helped me research and publish four trilogies with Sourcebooks. They include editors Deb Werksman, Cat Clyne, numerous line editors and proofreaders, agents Natanya Wheeler, Nicole Resciniti, plus a plethora of firefighters, police officers, and fellow authors who acted as critique partners. Special thanks to my beta reader Peggy McChesney who created my series bibles so I wouldn't mess up little details from previous books. Also, special thanks to Joanna D'Angelo for brainstorming with me when I got stuck.

Strange Neighbors started it all, and led to the spin-off series Flirting with Fangs, which inspired the Boston Dragons spin-off series and finally the Phoenix Brothers series spin-off as well. This is the 13th book and wraps up the entire world my imagination created. The whole grouping was greatly improved greatly with their help.

Thank you all!

About the Author

Ashlyn Chase describes herself as an Almond Joy bar: a little nutty, a little flaky, but basically sweet, wanting only to give her readers a few fulfilling smiles.

She holds a degree in behavioral sciences, worked as a psychiatric RN for fifteen years, and spent a few more years working for the American Red Cross. She credits her sense of humor to her former careers, since comedy helped preserve whatever was left of her sanity. She is a multi-published, award-winning author of humorous erotic and paranormal romances, represented by the Seymour Agency.

Ashlyn lives in coastal Florida with her true-life hero husband who looks like Hugh Jackman if you squint, and they're owned by two spoiled cats.

Ashlyn loves to hear from readers! Visit ashlynchase .com to sign up for her newsletter. She's also on Facebook (AuthorAshlynChase), Twitter (@GoddessAsh), Yahoo groups (ashlynsnewbestfriends), and Instagram (ashlynlaughin).

Also by Ashlyn Chase